"Come over here and sit down and let me—"

"No," Rill interrupted, picking up his hat and room key off the table. "You're not the kind of woman I need tonight."

His meaning was clear, but what surprised Juliana was that she wanted to challenge his assumption. "What kind of woman would that be?"

He chuckled bitterly for a moment. "One who wears cheap perfume and can drink a pint of whiskey."

Her heartbeat hammered, warning her she was getting in over her head, but it didn't keep her from saying, "I don't want you to leave. I need comfort from you tonight, too."

"No." Rill backed away. "Not from me. Not tonight."

Juliana stepped forward and took the key and Stetson from his hands and replaced them on the table. "A saloon woman might satisfy you, but she won't understand you. I do. Stay with me."

A growling sound preceded his husky, "Don't tempt me, Juliana. Right now I'm angry as hell and I need a woman who'll let me—" Rill stopped.

Juliana knew what kind of woman Rill thought he needed. She intended to change his mind.

Praise for

RANSOM

"An action-packed, fast-paced adventure with a feisty heroine and macho hero. Western fans will love this tale of courage, justice, loyalty, and romance."

—*Romantic Times*

"*Ransom* is full of fun and adventure. Gloria Dale Skinner is at her best. This book screams, 'Keeper, keeper, keeper!' "
—Kevin A. Beard, Waldenbooks

"Emotionally charged . . . powerful . . . a love story that leaves one breathless even until the final page."
—Donna Harsell, Voyager Books

"An adventuresome, fast-paced romp through the West with a fascinating pair of sharpshooters. Loved it!"
—Suzanne Coleburn, Belles and Beaux of Romance

"Excellent. . . . Ms. Skinner proves once again that she can write and write well. 4 Bells!"
—Donita Lawrence, Bell, Book, & Candle

"What a good read! *Ransom* is a fast-paced book. I will hand-sell this one!"

—Nita Burns, Sunshine Books

"A rootin'-tootin', old-time romance that made me believe Cupid uses six-shooters, too!"

—Melinda Matuch, The Book Rack

"Kasey was a wonderfully spunky heroine and Grason was man enough to let her be one. I enjoyed it!"

—Cheri France, Books Connection

"Touching. . . . *Ransom* will capture the reader's heart and hold it for ransom."

—Sharon Walters, Paperback Place

"Strong characters [and a] great story line make *Ransom* a book you can't put down until you've read the last word. Great!"

—Margaret Stilson, Paperback Exchange

"Fast-paced, packed with action. A real page turner."

—Yvonne Zalinski, Paperback Outlet

"Nonstop action! Couldn't put it down. Kept me up all night!"

—Tami Sandlin, Books Galore 'N' More

"Fun and entertaining. . . . Kasey and Grason strike sparks off each other all the way through."

—Martha Ostadimitris, Old Book Barn Gazette

"I love this book. Good story, strong characters. I'll sell a lot of *Ransom*."

—Barbara Cumnock, Bell's Books

GLORIA DALE SKINNER

Juliana

POCKET BOOKS

New York London Toronto Sydney Tokyo Singapore

An *Original* Publication of POCKET BOOKS

 POCKET BOOKS, a division of Simon & Schuster Inc. 1230 Avenue of the Americas, New York, NY 10020

Copyright © 1997 by Gloria Dale Skinner

ISBN: 1-4165-0182-7

This Pocket Books paperback printing May 2004

10 9 8 7 6 5 4 3 2 1

POCKET and colophon are registered trademarks of Simon & Schuster Inc.

Front cover illustration by Matthew Rotunda

Printed in the U.S.A.

Dedicated to the memory of
Starla, Bryant, and Erin Hasty

Juliana

❧ *Prologue* ❧

Kansas City
1878

Juliana's eyes popped open.

She jerked upright in her bed and listened, not knowing what had startled her awake. She rested on her elbows and scanned the darkened corners of her room for signs of a prowler. Nothing appeared out of place.

Usually, she wasn't so jumpy. Tonight was different. This was the first time the servants had had the night off since she came to work for Ward Cabot. Juliana and her six-year-old charge, Cassandra Rakefield, were alone in the three-story, twenty-room mansion.

From the adjoining chamber came a noise that sounded like Cassandra tossing in her sleep. Thinking the little girl might be having a nightmare, Juliana crept from her bed, tiptoed across the wooden floor, and peeked through the door cracked open between the rooms.

Her eyes quickly adjusted to the child's moonlit

1

bedroom. The shadowy, indistinct figure of a man loomed over Cassandra.

Horrified, Juliana clamped a palm over her mouth to hold in her scream.

The man pressed Cassandra to the bed and held a pillow over her face. She made a muffled sound and tried to shove the pillow away with her small hands.

Fear and outrage bolted through Juliana like summer lightning.

She glanced back around her room. Moonlight flickered off the rim of a brass candlestick on the dressing table. She grabbed the heavy object, flung the door wide, and rushed into the room, her arm posed to strike.

The intruder spun around to confront her. It was Ward Cabot, Cassandra's stepfather! His face twisted into the expression of an angry beast. A low growl burst from him. His hand flew out to disarm her.

"No!" Juliana screamed. Her arm came down fast, hard, sure.

The weapon crashed against the side of his head with a dull thud. His eyes rolled upward, showing ghostly white eyeballs.

Ward grunted and crumpled to the floor.

Juliana dropped the candlestick. She fumbled with the box of matches on the bedside table and quickly lit the lamp. Cassandra huddled in the middle of her bed, staring down at her stepfather. Her face flushed, she gasped for each breath.

"Are you all right?" Juliana asked.

"I d—don't know. What h—happened to Papa Ward?"

Juliana stared at her charge and whispered, "Don't you know what he was doing?"

"No! I couldn't see anything. It was dark. I couldn't

breathe." Her faint pink lips quivered, and her teeth chattered.

Juliana's throat convulsed. Her heart felt as if it had lodged in her throat. Cassandra's doe-brown eyes glistened with unshed tears. She clutched the skirt of her nightgown in one small, white-knuckled fist and reached for her doll at the foot of the bed with the other.

Frantic, Juliana hugged her arms to her chest. Her gaze flitted from Cassandra to Mr. Cabot. Thick blackish-red blood trickled from the side of his head and stained his white shirt collar.

Gossip she'd heard from one of the servants about the possibility of Mr. Cabot planning to kill Cassandra for her money flashed across her mind. Now he had actually tried to murder her!

Juliana glanced at her employer's chest.

"Thank God, he's breathing," she mumbled to herself.

"Papa Ward needs help!" Cassandra cried. "He's bleeding. Is he dead?"

Groaning from fear, from shock, Juliana tore her gaze away from Ward Cabot and looked at the whimpering child. "It's all right, sweetie. Don't be frightened. Papa Ward's not badly hurt."

Juliana reached for Cassandra. The little girl came willingly into her embrace.

Cassandra wrapped her arms tightly around Juliana's neck and her legs around Juliana's waist. She felt the child's fright and confusion in her shaking body.

Juliana's heart beat wildly. What had she done? What was she going to do?

"Shh—don't cry, sweetheart," she said earnestly, and held Cassandra tighter. "I promise Papa Ward's going to be fine. He's just going to sleep for a little while."

Juliana prayed she spoke the truth.

Dear mercy! She'd knocked the man unconscious. She had to consider the consequences of her action. Mr. Cabot would be furious when he came to. He'd never admit he was trying to kill Cassandra.

Her head was spinning. Juliana had to calm herself and think rationally. She should go to the authorities. Yes! But would they believe her? Mr. Cabot knew them all. He was well-connected to most of the powerful men in the city. It would be her word against his.

Juliana glanced down at the bleeding man. She needed to think, but there wasn't time. Mr. Cabot could awaken at any moment and kill them both. She had to do something.

Holding Cassandra, she rushed past her employer and into her own room. She stood her charge down on the floor by the door between the two bedrooms and knelt in front of her.

Taking hold of Cassandra's small hands, Juliana said, "I want you to listen to me. Papa Ward was trying to hurt you. I had to stop him."

"Why would he hurt me?"

"I don't know, sweetheart," Juliana had to admit, although she had a pretty good idea it was because of the little girl's money. How could she explain Mr. Cabot's actions to Cassandra? She couldn't tell Cassandra that he had been trying to smother her. That would frighten her more.

"I couldn't see anything. It was too dark." Her lips started quivering again. Her gaze darted around the room as if looking for someone to come rescue her. "I want my mama."

Juliana's heart broke for Cassandra. "You know your

mother doesn't live here anymore," she said softly. "She's in heaven now with the angels, remember?"

Clear, sparkling tears spilled from Cassandra's rounded eyes and rolled down her chubby cheeks. "Is she hurt like Papa Ward?"

"Oh, no, sweetheart," Juliana managed to say in a comforting voice, knowing they needed to hurry, but not wanting to frighten Cassandra more than she already was. Juliana brushed Cassandra's tangled brown hair away from her face. "There's nothing wrong with your mother. The angels are taking very good care of her."

Juliana hated seeing the uncertainty in Cassandra's eyes. She was normally a strong-willed, bossy child who challenged Juliana every day.

"Grandpapa Rakefield said Mama wears big wings made of gold just like my real papa."

"I'm sure she does." The mention of Cassandra's only grandparent sparked an idea, and Juliana asked, "You like your grandfather, don't you?"

Cassandra nodded and sniffled.

"Good. I'm going to take you to see him. Would you like that?"

"He lives a long way from here," Cassandra said.

Juliana glanced back to Mr. Cabot. He was still out cold.

Anger over what had happened, suspicion about why, and bewilderment about what to do next and where to go warred inside Juliana. And there was no time to waste. She had to think clear and fast.

What would Auntie Vic do, Juliana asked herself? Victoria had been a governess for over thirty years and had taught Juliana everything she knew about taking care of children. Auntie Vic had known how to handle any kind of situation that could arise.

Juliana took a deep breath. In her mind's eye,

Victoria's stern, matronly face appeared before her. *Cassandra is your responsibility. Trust no one but yourself with her safety.*

Trying to quell the panic rising inside her, Juliana knew what she had to do.

"We must get away from here now, Cassandra. You are in danger."

Her eyes widened. "Papa Ward's going to hurt me?"

"Not if I can help it. Now listen to me. We have to dress quickly, pack a few clothes, and flee the house. Do you understand?"

She nodded and asked, "Are we going to Grandpapa Rakefield's house?"

"Yes."

"Who's going to help us get there?"

"No one. We have to do this by ourselves."

Juliana threw another glance toward Mr. Cabot through the open doorway and shivered. Later, she'd have to come to terms with what she'd done and learn to live with the decision she had made.

There wasn't time to dwell on that now. Mr. Cabot would be after them as soon as he awakened. If he caught them, he'd see to it that Juliana would rot in jail.

Once again she hesitated and thought about going to the authorities for help. Would the sheriff help her? Would he believe the word of an out-of-towner, a young woman who'd been Cassandra's governess little more than a month, over the word of the man who'd been her stepfather for three years?

No, she decided. Who in his right mind would believe that one of the most powerful men in Kansas City was trying to kill his stepdaughter, even if she was an heiress to a fortune in railroad stock?

❧ 1 ❧

"How long you known me, Rill?"

Rill Banks kept his back to his friend Cropper, as he uncinched the straps on his saddle. "Ten or twelve years, maybe. I've lost count. Why?"

"You ever known the hairs on the back of my neck to stand out when there weren't no Indians following us?"

Rill yanked the saddle off his horse, carried it over to the campfire, and plopped it down before glancing up at his companion again. He didn't know where this conversation was heading, but the old man's expression was grim.

"Never have," Rill finally said, his gaze skillfully sweeping the far-stretching landscape for signs of riders.

Cropper switched his wad of chew from one side of his mouth to the other. He rubbed a leathered palm over his beard and said, "Me neither, but I've had this ticklish feeling right here square between my shoulders all day like someone was watching me. You think

7

it's old age getting to me or someone's tailing us I ain't spotted yet?"

"Could be either, I guess."

Rill walked over to where his horse stood and pulled the saddle blanket off the stallion's back. Rill had enough confidence in the old drover to know it wasn't age getting to him. If Cropper said something was wrong, then something was wrong.

Rill slowly turned, searching the area more carefully. A brassy sun inched its way toward the blue horizon, streaking the sky with shards of color. An occasional scrub tree dotted the surrounding land that looked like a sea of grassland. Tall, colorful bluestem swayed in the late-afternoon breeze. Rill didn't see any other sign of movement across the prairie.

Twilight wasn't far away, but he had time to backtrack before darkness overtook the light to see if he could spot anyone or pick up a trail.

They'd made good time since leaving Kansas City before dawn. Rill had planned the journey well, wanting to move fast and steady so they could make it to the Wyoming Territory and the small ranch he'd purchased before winter set in.

They were traveling light, but Rill had packed enough food and supplies in the wagon so they wouldn't have to restock in any towns on the way to Cheyenne. He'd heard that winter came early, and he wanted to be settled in before the first snow.

The two men had decided to eat in the mornings what was left over from supper the night before and stop only long enough during the day to rest and water the animals before making camp for the night. If the weather held and the old Pony Express trail proved to be as easy to travel as Rill had been told, they should reach their destination in less than the usual six weeks.

Cropper took off his worn gray hat and scratched the back of his thick neck with fingers roughened from handling reins most of his life.

"You haven't seen any sign?" Rill asked after scanning the prairie again.

The big man grimaced, and deep wrinkles formed at the edges of his eyes and ran out toward his gray-streaked hair. "Nope. Been looking all day. Ain't seen a thing yet. Even peeked in the wagon a time or two. Nothing there. Can't figure it. Never been wrong before when I get this feeling in my bones."

Rill shrugged his shoulders. "Could be you're just anxious about leaving Kansas and going all the way to the Wyoming Territory. You don't have to go, you know. It's not too late to turn around."

Cropper spit a stream of brown juice onto the dirt, then wiped his mouth on his shirtsleeve. "Naw, it ain't that. You know me better."

Rill believed the old man, but his jittery feelings puzzled Rill. They were not far enough from Kansas City for Indians to be tailing them for their supplies. Besides, the military was doing a good job of keeping settlers heading farther west safe from renegade bands of Indians who still roamed the prairie looking for easy targets to raid.

"Maybe it's the new horses learning to work as a team that has you spooked. I couldn't help but notice they gave you trouble all day."

"Nope. I've worked with skittish horses like these before. They're mule-headed for sure, but it ain't that."

Again, Rill looked over at the wagon with water barrel, ax, shovel, and other tools tied to the outside. A thought flashed through his mind. He remembered the time, years ago, when he was only a greenhorn drover. A street kid had managed to find a place to hide in the front of their chuck wagon. The outfit was a week into the trail drive before they discovered the wily rascal.

Could be that it had happened again. That would certainly explain why Cropper had the feeling there was someone behind him.

"I'll take a look in the wagon," Rill said.

"Already have. Told you there ain't nothin' in there except our fixin's."

"It doesn't hurt to make sure," Rill said, knowing that a young boy could hide in a small spot.

He strode over to the Conestoga and untied the rope holding the two side flaps of canvas together at the bottom and opened them wide, tying the ends to pegs on each side. A rush of warmth blasted him in the face, startling him. The air held the scent of a sweet-smelling flower that reminded him of a woman's perfume. *Lilacs?* Rill shook his head. It wasn't like him to be fanciful.

The lowering sun hung at a right angle to pierce the inside of the wagon with sharp brightness. Rill peered in and saw bedrolls, ropes, an oxhide-covered trunk, a couple of lanterns, and Cropper's cooking utensils. The wagon held few personal possessions. Other than his weapons, the only things Rill had of value were the shaving mug and brush his father had given him fifteen years ago.

Stacked in the front of the wagon were sacks of flour, coffee, beans, bacon, sweet potatoes, and two smoked hams he and Cropper had loaded yesterday.

They had piled the supplies neatly when they put them inside. Now they were all askew. It was possible that jarring of the wagon over the rough ground had made them fall to the side.

Rill started to tell Cropper that everything was fine when he caught sight of a piece of dark blue material showing from between two of the bulging bags.

An uneasy feeling stole over him.

He looked at Cropper and put a gloved finger to his lips. Quietly, he unsnapped the safety strap on his holster and took out his Colt.

The muscles in his arms tensed. He stepped back and aimed inside the wagon. "You have till the count of three to come out or I start shooting. One, two, th—"

Sacks started tumbling.

Rill watched as feminine hands and arms poked from between the beans and potato bags, pushing the coffee and flour aside. As the supplies toppled, Rill's gaze whisked past a chubby-cheeked little girl with big brown eyes and lighted on the face of a blue-eyed young woman beautiful enough to be an angel.

"Don't shoot!" The lady's cry of alarm was soft and plaintive. "We're not armed." She scrambled on her hands and knees over to the girl and thrust her body in front of her.

"Damn," Rill breathed to himself.

"Tarnation!" Cropper exclaimed loudly.

The woman's quick and valiant effort to protect the child immediately touched something inside Rill. He hadn't meant to frighten them. He never would have pulled his gun if he'd known females were hiding in his wagon.

Rill let out a gusty breath and eased the hammer on his pistol back in place. He dropped the Colt into his single loop holster and resnapped the safety.

"Calm down. I'm not going to shoot," he said in an irritated voice.

Leaning in close to Rill's shoulder, Cropper whispered, "We've caught us a woman and a girl."

"I can see that," he told the old man without taking his gaze off the frightened pair staring at him.

"I knew when I had that worrisome feelin' someone was a-watchin' me, and I was right again."

Rill's eyes narrowed on the young woman, and his body relaxed. "What the hell are you two doing in there?"

The woman's lashes flew upward toward arched brows framed by loose strands of golden blond curls.

"Sir, please don't swear in front of the child."

Her reprimand rankled. Especially, since she looked to be at least ten years younger than he was, and she was stealing a ride on his wagon.

Rill settled his hat lower on his forehead and fixed the lady with an aggravated expression. "Since you've already taught her how to hitch a ride without asking for permission or paying a fare, I'll assume she's had opportunity to hear the word a time or two. If she hasn't, she won't know what it means anyway. Now, what in the *hell* are you doing in my supply wagon?"

A pink stain crept up her cheeks. Her blush was so unexpected it momentarily distracted him. He hadn't expected his language to embarrass either of the females.

The little girl squirmed and pushed out from behind the young woman and stood up on a coffee sack. "I've probably heard that word more times than Juliana has, and I know what it means, too. It's the place where bad people go when they die and what men say when they're angry."

The lady gasped and snapped her head around to glare at the girl. Long, dark brown hair lay in a mess of tangled curls about the child's shoulders. He guessed her to be about six or seven years old.

Cropper snickered.

Rill probably would have laughed, too, if he hadn't realized what a predicament they were in. The last thing he needed was to worry about two stowaways.

"Cassandra!" the young woman whispered in shock. "I'm ashamed you'd let such rubbish talk come out of your mouth. You know better."

"I didn't say the bad word. He did." The girl pointed at Rill.

"Nonetheless," Juliana said, brushing a strand of golden-colored hair from her face. "I'm afraid we need an apology from you and the gentleman."

"I won't say I'm sorry until he does. He started it." She folded her arms across her chest and set her bottom lip in a firm pout.

"This is not a good time to disobey me, Cassandra, nor will we forget our manners."

Juliana and Cassandra. At least now they had names. And judging from how headstrong both were he'd bet his last nickel they were sisters.

Juliana pulled a dark green bonnet from underneath a potato sack, and remaining on her knees, placed it on Cassandra's head.

The top of Juliana's head came just above Cassandra's shoulders as she knelt in front of the girl to tie the bonnet in place. Underneath folds and layers of a blue skirt and blouse, Juliana appeared to be a slightly built woman but not thin. His gaze swept down her shapely form, briefly stopping at the swell of her breasts and flare of her hips. Definitely not skinny.

Without conscious thought, Rill let his gaze travel to Juliana's hands. Her skin looked soft and free of the redness and calluses that came from hard work. Her fingers were long, but not bony. She had neatly trimmed nails with short and tapered tips.

Her hands deftly worked the satin ribbon of the

little girl's bonnet and fashioned a perfect bow underneath Cassandra's chin. It surprised him how still and quiet the outspoken girl remained while Juliana finished the task.

Realizing he was letting the young woman distract him again, Rill said, "You didn't answer me. Who are you? Why are you in my wagon?"

She turned and looked at him with eyes so clear and intelligent it startled him. "Mr.—"

His mouth tightened. "No mister. Just Rill. He's Cropper."

Rays from the sun glinted off the heart-shaped brooch pinned on a swatch of lace that nestled near the hollow of her throat. "Ah—well—we couldn't possibly address you by your given names."

Rill bristled. She was as pretty a woman as he'd ever seen, but who was she to act so damn proper out here with two strangers in the middle of nowhere?

"The name's Rill." His tone became less tolerant.

In a resigned voice she said, "In that case, I'm Juliana, and this is Cassandra."

Juliana, he said in his mind for the second time. It seemed to fit her. The name was soft-sounding, almost musical, and beautiful—like her. And, even though a few moments before he'd suspected the two were sisters, he now wondered if that was true.

Cropper elbowed up beside Rill and stared into the wagon. "What did you ladies do? Crawl in the wrong wagon?"

Juliana's gaze darted to the older man. "Not exactly." She took a deep breath and lifted her chin. Returning her attention to Rill, she said, "I know what we did wasn't right, but when we took refuge in here last night we had no idea you'd be pulling out of town before sunrise. When I awakened and realized this, I should have spoken up immediately and asked you to stop and let us out, but in truth, we needed to get out of town. It seemed prudent to remain quiet and let you help us accomplish that."

"And ride off with strangers? That was a reckless thing for you to do."

She blinked rapidly. "I—I— You're right. It was foolhardy. I could have been putting Cassandra in even more danger."

Rill tensed. What kind of danger could the two have been in? He rolled one shoulder and sighed. It didn't matter. They weren't his problem.

Growing impatient, he said, "What I want to know is what you plan to do now that you're here."

"We have money," Cassandra piped up in a very grown-up tone. "Juliana will pay you."

Cropper snickered again, then spit tobacco juice that landed with a dull splat.

Juliana gave the girl another stern look, but kept her voice soft and under control when she said, "Cassandra, please remain quiet and let me handle this." Juliana shifted on her knees to face him. "Of course, you mean for *hitching* a ride as you so aptly put it. I've apologized for that, and I'll be happy to pay you for your trouble."

No, that wasn't what he meant. His eyes twitched with frustration. He didn't want or need the bother of a pretty woman and a bratty little girl. They weren't in his traveling plans.

He didn't know much about women's clothes but he recognized expensive, well-tailored dresses when he saw them. Cassandra and Juliana were not common waifs stealing a ride. He didn't doubt she had money enough to pay him, but Rill wasn't interested. These two females spelled trouble with a big T.

"No, you didn't apologize."

Juliana's spine lifted in protest. She opened her mouth to speak but Rill didn't give her the opportunity.

"You merely told me you were wrong," he continued. "And you were. Now, I don't want your damn—" Rill stopped and quickly glanced over at the little girl.

Cassandra rolled her eyes heavenward. "I've heard that word, too."

Rill shifted the position of his hat on his head again. Years on the trail with a bunch of hands who didn't care how they talked hadn't given him much incentive to watch his language.

"I don't want your money. I want to know what you propose to do now that you're more than a day's ride from anywhere. It's a long walk back to town."

Her beautiful eyes searched his face and caused a quickening in his chest. He could see her pondering his words, but that didn't keep her appraisal of him from sending a rush of heat scouring through his insides like a hot branding iron.

To cover the unexpected feelings she'd stirred in him, Rill said, "You have no horse, no carriage or wagon. Walking is the only way you can get back to Kansas City unless I decide to backtrack and lose two days' traveling, which I don't intend to do for two stowaways."

"Oh, but I told you—"

"What's a stowaway?" Cassandra interrupted.

"An uninvited guest," Rill retorted.

Juliana stiffened again and softly cleared her throat. "More accurately, it's someone who obtains transportation by secrecy," Juliana returned promptly, then faced Rill again. "We wanted to leave town, and we don't intend to return to the city."

"Are you running away from someone?" Rill asked. "Maybe from your father?"

"Stepfather," Cassandra piped in and said before Juliana could open her mouth. "He was trying to—"

"Dear mercy, it's been a long day," Juliana said, interrupting Cassandra. The young woman reached over and grabbed Cassandra's hand and squeezed it as she helped the girl off the sack of coffee onto the floor of the wagon.

"Mr.—" She stopped. The corners of her mouth dimpled with a soft smile. "I'm sorry, Rill, we've been in this wagon a long time. If you'll give us a few minutes of privacy to attend to—necessary business, I'll be happy to continue this conversation."

Necessary business? Why didn't she just say nature was calling? He was tempted to respond to her delicate phrasing with a smile, but he didn't want to give her any reason to think he approved of what she'd done. And he'd bet a winning hand of poker that Juliana was going to have a sisterly talk with the little one and curb her loose tongue.

"All right." He looked at Cassandra and reached out his hands to her. "Come here, and I'll help you down."

"Wait, I have to get Miss Watkins."

"Danged it, Rill," Cropper remarked. "They got another woman hiding in there."

"Oh, no, we don't." Cassandra giggled, pulling a fancy-dressed doll from underneath a bean bag and holding it up for him to see. Her eyes brightened and a dancing smile softened her chubby cheeks. "This is Miss Watkins."

"We should have guessed," Rill said and held out his hands to her.

From underneath a lumpy sack, Juliana tugged a

garnet-colored velvet reticule. She slipped the corded drawstrings over her hand, leaving the purse to dangle from her wrist.

Cassandra almost leapt into Rill's waiting arms. He lifted her from the wagon and stood her beside Cropper, then he reached his hand up for Juliana.

Their eyes met. Held.

Juliana placed her hand in his. The pads of his fingers rubbed the soft skin on the underside of her palm before clasping tight. He felt her quickening pulse.

Her hand quivered.

He felt a distinct tightening in his loins.

Rill placed his other hand on the curve of Juliana's indented waist and lifted her. She was light but sturdy. As the air moved past him, he smelled the fresh flower scent that had caught his attention when he opened the wagon. *Definitely lilac.* For a wild, split second he had the urge to pull her to his chest and kiss her.

Her feet landed softly on the ground. She slid her hand out of his and quickly moved a respectable distance away from him.

"Thank you."

Rill felt as if his throat was clogged with dust. He couldn't take his eyes off her face. Juliana jarred all his senses. He couldn't remember a time he'd been so aware of a woman. Had he ever?

"Can we go now, Juliana?" Cassandra complained.

"Yes. You've been patient long enough."

Rill cleared his throat and said, "Don't go too far from the wagon."

"No, we won't," she answered, meeting his observant stare.

"I'm thirsty and hungry, too," Cassandra complained.

Rill looked down at her, thankful for the distraction of the girl. "I'll have Cropper start supper."

"Thank you," Juliana said again, then reached for Cassandra's hand. "Remember to shuffle your feet and make a noise so we'll let the bugs and animals know they should get out of our way," Juliana said to Cassandra.

"You mean so we can chase away the snakes, don't you?"

Cropper chuckled and shook his head as Juliana and Cassandra walked away. "That little one is a bundle and a half, ain't she?"

Rill nodded, but it wasn't the girl who was on his mind. It was Juliana. He watched her walk away. She held her back and shoulders so straight there was very little sway to her hips. Long strands of blond hair had pulled loose from her bun and hung down her back like flowing gold curls.

Everything about Juliana—her dress, her manners, her speech—indicated she was a lady and of the finest upbringing. And all he could think of was that he wanted to take her in his arms and kiss her.

As he continued to watch the two walk farther away, Rill thought about what Cassandra had said about them running away from their stepfather and what Juliana had said about putting Cassandra in more danger.

Anger knotted his gut. Men could be mean to women. He'd seen evidence of that on some of the whores he'd been with.

He wished Juliana hadn't felt so good to him when he'd helped her off the wagon. He didn't want to get mixed up with her troubles—but his hand still tingled from her warmth.

Rill removed his hat and knocked it a couple of times on his leg to shake off the dust. He had already spent more time thinking about Juliana than he had about any five other women put together.

What was the matter with him? He'd had enough of being responsible for other people to last him a lifetime. The only thing Juliana was to him was a nuisance.

"Did you hear me?"

Rill blinked and turned to Cropper. "No, what'd you say?"

"I'll start the beans and coffee while you rub down Doc. It don't look like you're going to have to start chasing after Indians."

"I'd rather take on Indians than women," Rill mumbled to the old man.

Cropper laughed. "Who would've thought two females would've climbed into our wagon? There must have been more'n a dozen or two in the stockyard. Darnest thing I've ever run across." He looked up at Rill. "What are we goin' to do?"

"Get rid of them." Rill stuffed his hat back on his head and headed toward the campfire.

2

Juliana didn't know if it was the sun searing her neck as she marched Cassandra away from the camp or the ruggedly handsome cowboy's gaze burning her skin.

He had made an obvious appraisal of her, letting his eyes linger on her face far too long, taking note of every detail about her.

She couldn't blame Rill for not being more cordial, like the large bearded man, Cropper. The accusing tone of Rill's voice, the suspicion in his eyes and the frown on his face left no doubt that she had picked the wrong wagon to crawl into. But, at the time, she had had no other choice. Her only thought had been hiding so that Ward Cabot and the sheriff couldn't find them.

Panic had flooded her when Rill had said he was going to shoot if they didn't come out. For a moment, she thought they had managed to escape Mr. Cabot and Kansas City only to be killed by a trigger-happy stranger.

It had been difficult for her to remain calm and not

show her fear while she tried to keep control of the situation. She quickly realized that trying to remain prim and proper as Auntie Vic had taught her to do was useless under their current circumstances.

"You're walking too fast," Cassandra complained, tugging on Juliana's arm.

Juliana mentally shook herself and relaxed a little. "Oh, I guess I still feel as though we're in a hurry to get away."

"Papa Ward can't find us here, can he? He won't hurt me now, will he?"

"No, of course not. You're safe here."

Even though Cassandra couldn't remember that Mr. Cabot had been holding a pillow over her face, she seemed to take Juliana's word for the fact that her stepfather was trying to harm her.

The dark-eyed cowboy had remained hard and unyielding, giving her no reason to think he was a reasonable man until he'd taken hold of her hand and helped her from the wagon. When he touched her, she felt warmth and gentleness in him even though none of those things had shown on his face. Juliana knew then they were not in imminent peril.

She liked the way the black felt hat rode low on his forehead, almost hiding his eyes. He was tall and filled out his clothes in a commendable fashion. His face was tanned, but not so sunburned and leathery as Cropper's skin.

With a will of their own, Juliana's fingers closed over her palm and she caressed the underside of her hand. An unexpected glow of pleasure filled her as she remembered the tender brush of Rill's fingertips lightly caressing her skin as she placed her hand in his.

The heel of his palm had molded to her waistline, and his fingers had outlined her ribs. She immediately felt strength in him—in his arms and inside him for the kind of man he was. Something about the way he'd touched her, the way he'd stared so easily into her eyes without blinking, let her know he wouldn't try to harm them, but could she trust him with the truth about why they were in his wagon?

The entire day she'd thought of nothing but the fact she'd kidnapped her charge. She was sure Ward Cabot and the authorities would be after her. She had to get Cassandra to her grandfather before Ward caught up with them.

Fear and doubt about what she'd done clawed at her insides. Had she been right in taking Cassandra away from Ward and her home? Would the authorities have believed her if she'd gone to them rather than escaped into the night with Cassandra?

Had Mr. Cabot awakened soon after they left the house? More than once she'd wondered if she might have hit him so hard he would die before the morning servants arrived and found help for him.

Juliana shivered at the thought. She hadn't wanted to harm her employer. Her only desire was to do her job and protect Cassandra.

No, she wouldn't think of him as dead. She had to deny those feelings and prepare for Ward Cabot being very much alive and desperate to find her and Cassandra.

Juliana gritted her teeth and squeezed her hand into a fierce fist. She couldn't doubt what she'd seen or what she had done. Cassandra had been in danger. Juliana had had no choice but to stop Ward.

After the sun had come up, Juliana had chanced a peek out of the wagon and realized they were heading west. She had no idea of Rill and Cropper's destination, but for now, they were going in the right direction. To Cheyenne.

"Is this far enough? I'm ready to go. I can't hold it any longer."

Juliana stopped and looked to see if they were a safe distance from the camp. Her gaze drifted over to Rill and Cropper, who were busy with their chores.

"Yes, this is a good place."

A couple of minutes later, Juliana stood up in the lush grass and glanced around them. Directly overhead, the sky was a dark shade of blue. Near the horizon, azure faded and flamed into deep shades of molten gold and the coppery blazing fires of sunset.

"I want to take my bonnet off. You don't have yours on."

Juliana's hand jerked up to the top of her head, her reticule dancing from her wrist. "Dear mercy." Rill had her so flustered she forgot about her own headpiece. "It must be under one of those sacks." Her fingers combed through her tresses. "And it feels like half of my hair is down around my face. I must be a dreadful sight."

Cassandra grinned. "You look like I do when I wake in the mornings."

"Heavens. Is it truly that bad?"

"Yes."

"I guess it is a little late in the day for this," she said, pulling at the ribbons under Cassandra's chin.

Cassandra laughed, a youthful, carefree sound that tinkled on the late-afternoon air and brought a smile to Juliana's face. She liked to see Cassandra's eyes sparkling with merriment, not tears of fright and confusion.

If only I had my aunt to talk to, Juliana thought as she tried, without much success, to rearrange her chignon. But Auntie Vic was gone, and it was past time for Juliana to make her own decisions. She couldn't help but wonder what her aunt would have done if she'd been in Juliana's position last night.

Faint memories invaded Juliana's thoughts. Her parents had died in a house fire when she was eleven. Auntie Vic had taken Juliana into her home and had taught her how to be the perfect governess so that she would be able to support herself when she was older. Victoria spent hours in the evenings teaching Juliana the correct way to approach any situation that could arise during her employment as a governess.

Auntie Vic wouldn't hear of Juliana considering any other lifestyle. Juliana had to be the best and make Victoria proud of her. She preached to Juliana that her own comfort, wishes, and desires no longer mattered. She was to forget about herself and learn how to be at the call of her employer with her brightest smile in place.

Juliana was taught to be strong, trust her instincts, and always be firm, yet polite, to the children in her keeping. Their care and safety was her only responsibility. Any dreams Juliana had of a home and children of her own had to be put aside. "You can't serve two masters," Auntie Vic said, referring to an employer and a husband.

Her job had to be her life, Victoria told her. She was to never forget that it was her duty to forsake her own happiness and do everything in her power to make sure her employer was happy with her service.

"What are we going to do, now that Rill and Cropper found us? Do we have to go back to Papa Ward?"

"No, of course not." Juliana returned her attention to Cassandra. She lifted her hand to the base of her throat and fingered the puffed gold heart pinned on her blouse. "I'm not taking you back there. It's not safe. I don't have all the answers yet, sweetie, but we're going to find a way to get to your grandfather's ranch. You trust me to take care of you, don't you?"

Cassandra nodded. Her big brown eyes were so unquestioning, so innocent, that Juliana knew she had to be strong for Cassandra. She couldn't let her down.

It pleased Juliana to know Cassandra trusted her, but it was also an awesome responsibility. That's why Juliana had to deny her fears and be courageous.

She placed her hands on Cassandra's shoulders. "I need to know something. Now that you've had the entire day to think it over, do you remember anything about what happened last night?"

"We went to sleep in the wagon with heavy sacks piled on top of us."

"Yes, but do you recollect why we left the house in such a hurry?"

"I woke up because I couldn't breathe. I opened my eyes and saw Papa Ward on the floor bleeding and you standing over him."

Juliana winced inside. She wouldn't have a chance of anyone believing her if the authorities found them and that's all Cassandra could recall. Juliana had hoped that Cassandra had seen Mr. Cabot walk into the room holding a pillow, or saw it coming down over her face.

"You don't remember what Papa Ward was doing before I hit him?"

Cassandra shook her head. "I don't like Papa Ward. I want to go to Grandpapa Rakefield. He was nice when he came to see me. He plays with me and reads to me."

Oh, dear! If Cassandra couldn't back up any of Juliana's story, would anyone, including Thomas Rakefield, ever believe her?

Juliana knew she was putting mountains of trust in a man she had never met, but because of Mr. Cabot's actions she had no choice. She had to believe that Mr. Rakefield would know what to do about Cassandra's guardian.

"Are we going to stay with Cropper and Rill?"

"I guess we are. For now, anyway. Rill said we're a long way from any town. And quite frankly that makes me feel more at ease."

She didn't know what she would do if Mr. Cabot or the authorities found her before she managed to get Cassandra to her grandfather, but she had a pretty good idea what they would do. Juliana's only hope was that Mr. Cabot wouldn't be able to hire enough men to follow and check every wagon that left Kansas City when he found no trace of them having traveled by train or stage.

Cassandra pulled on Juliana's arm. "Let's go. It's getting dark, and I'm hungry."

"How can you be hungry? You ate the whole loaf of sweet bread I took from the kitchen."

"My tummy's empty. That's why I'm hungry."

Juliana looked down at Cassandra. She was holding up well considering she was a spoiled girl when Juliana met her a month ago.

"All right, we'll get you something to eat, but I want you to be quiet when I talk to Rill and let me handle everything."

"Why can't I talk?"

"You're too young, and you say too much," Juliana answered as they stomped through the grass. "You have to keep in mind that it's best we don't tell Rill and Cropper anything about us. They have told us only their first names, and that's all we will tell them. Anything else will be our secret."

"That's not polite. You told me."

"I know, but I've done some reading about the West and cowboys like Rill and Cropper. Out here on the prairie, things are different from what we're used to. I have a feeling that most of the rules we've learned up to now won't apply, so we are going to have to adjust to the way they do things. Addressing these men by their first names is an example. It's something we'll both have to get used to."

"Not me. It's easy to say Rill and Cropper. I like it better than saying mister all the time."

Exasperated and tired, Juliana said, "If either of them questions you when I'm not around, you're not to say anything. We've said too much as it is, I'm sure. Our safety is at risk here. It's important that you not disobey me on this. Do you understand?"

Cassandra nodded again, then said, "I'm glad we met Rill and Cropper. I want to ride a horse like Rill."

"Well, I don't think we'll go that far with their customs. We'll settle for riding in the wagon for now."

"Good." She took Cassandra's hand as they walked back into camp.

Juliana brushed the hem of her skirt after they cleared the tall grass and took another swipe at repairing her hairdo. She finally gave up, knowing it was hopeless until she took the chignon down and started over again.

It was the first day of September, but the early evening air felt like a balmy summer evening in July, making her long-sleeved blouse of lightweight wool too warm to be comfortable.

She had filled one satchel with a change of clothing for each of them and grabbed their winter coats but little else. Not much for five or six weeks of traveling, but they'd have to make do.

Juliana marveled at the scene before her as they approached the camp. The vast windblown landscape was serene, unlike the turmoil going on inside her. Amid the flat plains, the dingy canvas-topped wagon was set against purple-ridged sky and barren Kansas rangeland that seemed to stretch forever.

The brief period between late afternoon and early evening had always been Juliana's favorite time of day. There was something special about that hour—when work was finished but the dinner hour hadn't begun—that always calmed her.

Cropper knelt in front of a blazing fire, stirring a kettle that hung from an iron spit. The four horses that pulled the Conestoga were tethered nearby. Dusk was settling around them.

The cowboy stood farther away from the campsite, rubbing down his stallion. Somehow, she knew that this never-ending land was his home. It struck her as fitting that he seemed to be a natural part of his surroundings. And knowing she had to confront him again caused a fluttering in her stomach.

She noticed that Rill's gun belt and holster rode low on his slim hips. The belt looked well-worn and serviceable with no fancy silver conchos, grips, or markings.

He had taken off the plain leather chaps that had covered his brown trousers and laid them aside. His dusty felt hat sat on top of them. He wore his thick hair combed away from his face. Dark and long, the strands waved an inch or so past his collar.

Juliana stopped near Cropper, but her gaze was on Rill. He turned and glanced at her but continued rubbing his horse.

As Juliana stood there watching him, her gaze was drawn once again to the way his hands and arms worked up and down the horse, stroking the reddish-brown animal with long, purposeful swipes. The horse's coat shone with health.

Rill glanced up and saw her watching him. It surprised Juliana that she felt no shame for staring at him.

He motioned with his finger for her to come to him. No man had ever asked her to come to him in such a commanding, yet intimate way. She didn't understand why he expected her to respond to the mere quirk of his finger.

She took a deep breath, willing her stomach to settle, hoping to convince this man to let her and Cassandra travel with them.

Juliana looked at Cropper and asked, "Do you mind if Cassandra sits here with you while I talk to your friend?"

His leathery face broke into a smile that wrinkled the skin around his eyes. A neatly trimmed gray-streaked beard covered his cheeks and chin. "Not a bit. It'll give us time to talk."

"Thank you."

Juliana listened to Cropper's and Cassandra's conversation as she passed them.

"What are you cooking?" Cassandra asked.

"Beans, ham, and biscuits."

"I don't like beans. Prepare something else," she ordered.

The old man harrumphed. "Well now, Cass, if you're a-willin', you can peel a sack of them potatoes over there, and I'll cook them for you. I don't have time to do all that tonight, but you go ahead."

"My name's Cassandra. You may call me Cassandra but no one is allowed to call me Cass."

"That name is bigger than you are. Cass fits you much better. It rhymes with sass."

"I don't like sass or Cass. And, I don't know how to peel potatoes, so you'll have to do it."

"Is that so? Well, if you don't know how to peel a

potato or cook a biscuit, I think it's a-gettin' time for you to learn how."

Juliana smiled to herself as she walked out of hearing range. Good for Cropper. He wasn't going to let Cassandra get the best of him.

Power showed in Rill's back and his upper arms as he made long firm strokes over his horse's back, down his flanks, and around his belly.

Rill turned toward her as she approached. His handsome face bore signs of long hours in the sun; darkly tan with a faint whiteness at the corners of his eyes. High cheekbones, square chin, and full lips finished his rugged appearance. A day's growth of beard darkened his cheeks, upper lip, and along his jawline.

His shirt, made from a faded red broadcloth, had two columns of nickel-colored buttons running down the front panel and forming a V at his leather belt. The kerchief tied around his neck was a muted plaid of green, red, and black. The sleeves of his shirt were rolled up past his elbow, showing firm, corded muscles in his forearms.

"You wanted to talk to me?" Her voice sounded breathless, and it bothered her that his arrogance had gotten to her.

"That should be obvious considering the trouble you're in."

Juliana flinched. Her heart started thudding crazily. Could he possibly know about what she had done? Of course not. It was guilt making her jumpy. She had to remain calm and not let him know she was worried.

"I'm not sure what you mean."

Rill took the reins and tied his horse to a low branch on the stunted cottonwood.

The width of Rill's shoulders and his broad chest

tapered into a slim waist and narrow hips. She marveled at the way the muscles in Rill's powerful-looking legs bulged and shifted with each movement he made.

Rill fixed his gaze on her face. "I don't plan on saying this but once. I don't care who you're running away from or why. And I don't want to listen to all your problems because I can't help you."

His curtness stung. She lifted her shoulders and stared into eyes that were big, round, that weren't gray or brown but a mixture of the two.

"I didn't offer to tell you my troubles."

"Good. We understand each other on that. Furthermore, I'm not going to backtrack all the way to Kansas City and lose two full days of travel just to take you home. It's a long way to the Wyoming Territory. I don't intend to be slowed down by two fe—"

"You're going to Wyoming?" she interrupted with a smile of happiness. She clasped her hands together as a rare feeling of giddiness assailed her. This was too good to be true. "So are we. How wonderful. We're going to a ranch near Cheyenne called the Triple R. Do you know of it?"

"No."

"Well, that doesn't matter. We'll find it when we get to Cheyenne."

"Just how are you planning on getting there?"

She continued to smile gleefully and took a step closer to him. This was working out better than she'd hoped. "Oh, just like you. By wagon."

"Where did you plan to get your wagon?" he asked, a hard, unyielding expression on his ruggedly handsome face.

Her gaze caught his, and she sobered a bit. She

hesitated before saying, "Naturally, I haven't had time to consider all our options, but my first thought was that we could travel with you on yours."

"Forget it."

Her smile faded almost as quickly as it had appeared. "Why?"

"I don't carry passengers."

"We can't go by rail or stage. We'd be discovered. I'm sure Mr. Cabot has telegraphed ahead by now, and his men will be looking everywhere for us."

Rill's eyes narrowed, and he moved a hand to rest on his hip. His heavy-lidded gaze wandered over her face and sent a rush of heat bolting through her.

"Who's Mr. Cabot?"

Too late, Juliana realized her mistake in giving her employer's name. She had forgotten her own warnings and had started babbling like Cassandra. She had to be more careful. With any luck, Rill wouldn't know Mr. Cabot.

She cleared her throat and carefully said, "The man we're running away from."

"You call your stepfather Mister?"

Juliana groaned inwardly. She didn't like evading the truth any more than she liked lies. But what was she to do? She'd never admitted to Rill that Ward Cabot was her stepfather. By staying quiet, she knew Rill assumed Mr. Cabot was her stepfather from what Cassandra had said.

If she were careful, maybe she could avoid untruths. "I sometimes think of him as Ward instead of Mr. Cabot," she answered, knowing she'd have to remember to think of Mr. Cabot as Ward from now on. "I'm sure he's already checking every train, stagecoach, and wagon out of Kansas City. I know there are several roads leading out of the city and probably more than one established trail that leads to the Wyoming Territory. That should make it doubly hard for him to find us. He couldn't possibly check every covered wagon between here and Cheyenne, could he?"

"You're the one telling me about this man."

Her mouth went dry. "Of course, you don't know anything about him." She couldn't figure out why this man was being so hard on them. She clutched her skirt in her hands. "Will you take us with you?"

"No."

She took a step forward. "I can pay you a handsome sum now and more after we reach the Triple R."

"No."

"We won't be any trouble."

Rill shifted his stance again. "You look like an educated woman to me. Let me spell it for you. N-O—No."

Juliana took another deep breath, exasperated at this man, angry at herself for not being able to talk him into her wishes. Her logic seemed lost on him.

"Won't you even take the time to think about it? This is very important to Cassandra, and I'm sure the money I can pay you will be an asset for whatever it is you plan to do in Wyoming."

"I'm not interested."

"How can you turn down something that will pay you money but not cause you one bit of trouble without at least considering your partner's wishes? He and Cassandra are as happy together as old friends," she said, stretching the truth again.

"I don't need any money. And Cropper isn't my partner; he's my helper."

"Oh." That meant she couldn't count on help from the older man.

But Juliana wasn't about to give up so easily. She'd

just have to ask the same question in a different manner. But how? Her knowledge of men was limited to knowing how to say and do the right things to keep her employer happy.

Her aunt had taught her everything she needed to survive in a household. She knew how to handle unruly children, fresh men, and groping servants. Juliana could administer medicines and diagnose most illnesses, but she knew nothing about how to make this man let her and Cassandra travel with him.

Now that she knew she and Rill and Cropper were heading in the same direction, it was the perfect way to get Cassandra to the Triple R without Ward finding them.

Juliana pondered. Would Rill change his mind and help her if she told him the truth? That Cassandra was heir to a fortune in railroad stock and that Juliana believed the child's stepfather had tried to kill her in order to inherit her money?

The idea was so shocking that Juliana wouldn't believe it herself if she'd hadn't seen Mr.— Ward trying to smother Cassandra. No, it was best she remain quiet for now. Rill could take her straight to the authorities. Juliana was sure Ward would have put up a reward for her capture.

Rill and Cropper appeared to be decent men, but good men could go bad when a lot of money was involved. Ward Cabot was a perfect example.

"Snap decisions aren't always the best. Would you please take time to reconsider?"

"I don't have to think about it. I'm not interested in taking care of you. I just quit a job where I was responsible for other people. I'm not going to get caught in that trap again for anyone."

Juliana knew by the faraway look in Rill's eyes that something troubled him, and it softened her. She immediately wanted to know what disturbed this man so deeply.

It wasn't any of her concern but she had to ask, "Who did you take care of?"

"Drovers."

She had been right when she thought of him as a cowboy, a man with a keen sense of honor. She didn't blink an eye at appealing to his integrity while at the same time trying to learn more about him. "You were the boss of a trail drive?" she asked, knowing only what she'd read in newspapers and books about the men who drove cattle from large ranches in Texas to the lucrative buying markets in Kansas and Missouri.

"That's right."

"From what I've read, I'm sure that was quite a responsibility."

"Can be," he said in a low voice and picked up his hat and smacked it against his leg a couple of times.

"What's the usual trail drive consist of? A dozen men and close to two thousand cattle?"

A glint formed in his eyes. "That sounds about right."

Pleased that her limited knowledge impressed him, Juliana lowered her voice and said, "If you can handle a group of men pushing longhorns for hundreds of miles in all kinds of weather, surely you can take care of one woman and one young girl on the way to the Wyoming Territory."

She watched him fight it, but despite his best efforts a smile eased across his lips as he stared at her in the fading light of day. His teeth were straight, even and white, giving him a handsome smile, softening the ruggedness of his face.

Denying his manly appeal, feeling victory within her tenuous grasp, Juliana went against what she'd been taught about proper behavior and pressed her small advantage. "You can take care of a woman, can't you, Rill?"

A trace of amusement flickered in his eyes, and he appeared pleased by her question. In that brief time, Juliana caught a glimpse of a man she'd like to get to know.

"You'll never find out."

That wasn't the answer she expected. "And why is that?"

He placed his hat on his head. "Because I'm leaving you and the girl in the next town we come to."

She tried to keep the disappointment off her face. "Most men would accept my challenge."

His smile remained in place, but his words were firm as he said, "Only a desperate man."

"And you're not." Her words sounded like an accusation to her own ears.

"Not even close."

Juliana's lack of experience with men showed in her inability to change Rill's mind.

Frustrated, she resorted to her original argument, knowing it wasn't getting her anywhere but unable to accept his answer, and said, "You won't have to do one thing for us. I can take care of myself and Cassandra. All we need is transportation. If you're going to the Wyoming Territory anyway, I can't see the harm in allowing us to ride in your wagon."

"You don't have to see the trouble. I do."

"Rill, I—"

"No."

She sighed heavily. His strength was undeniably impressive. "You're not being reasonable by not even taking time to consider my proposal."

"I don't have to be fair. It's my wagon. The answer is no for any reason you might come up with. I plan to take you to the next town and leave you there to find your own way to Wyoming or wherever you want to go. Now if you'll excuse me, I have more chores to do before Cropper calls supper."

Juliana watched the tall, broad-shouldered man walk away. She wondered what had happened to make him so hard.

Rill didn't know it yet, but she planned to find a way to convince him to take her and Cassandra with him on his journey to the Wyoming Territory.

3

Rill sneaked another glance at Juliana.

Smoke drifted up from the flames and lingered between them. Yellow light from the campfire glowed on her face, shone in her eyes, and shimmered off her hair like twinkling sparks of fire.

The air was balmy, heavy with the scent of burned wood and cooked food. Clouds darkened the sky and obscured the moon and stars with swift moving wisps of gray. They could be in for rain tomorrow, Rill thought, as he tried to keep his mind and his eyes off Juliana.

For thirteen years he'd been a drover, hunkering down around the campfire night after night, listening to complaints, jokes, and yarns about Indians, droughts, wild animals, and summer storms. But this was the first time he had a beautiful woman sitting opposite him, and it caused a wild sense of excitement to dance through his veins.

Of all the wagons in the Kansas City stockyard, why did Juliana have to pick his to crawl into?

He didn't like her filling his thoughts. He wanted to get rid of her so he and Cropper could continue their trip to his new ranch without delay. His plans were made, and he didn't intend for Juliana to upset them any more than she already had.

After talking with a pair of cowboys in Kansas City, he had decided against taking the well-traveled Oregon Trail west in favor of the less-traveled route the Pony Express riders had forged a few years back. Using an old map, he and Cropper had planned their journey well. They would spend most of their time in the northern section of Kansas but they'd eventually cover ground in Colorado before reaching Cheyenne. If their luck held and the weather stayed clear, they'd shave a week off traveling time.

Rill noticed that Cassandra hadn't touched the beans and ham Cropper had boiled, but she wouldn't starve. It hadn't taken her long to eat two of the biscuits he'd baked in the Dutch oven, after he'd cut them open for her and poured a generous amount of molasses between the halves.

Sitting around the campfire reminded him of the cattle drive he'd just finished. Rill tensed. He'd come to think of it as the trail drive from hell. Every damn thing had gone wrong after Lee Stedman—the bastard—had hired on.

Rill had known the drive was his last even before Stedman hit his outfit. With the way the railroad was expanding, long, expensive cattle drives would soon become a part of history anyway.

Rill had heard the Wyoming Territory was so big, a man could lose himself. That sounded like the kind of place he was looking for. Even his father had admitted that Texas rangeland wasn't what it used to be.

He glanced at Juliana again. He couldn't help it. He

was intensely aware of her presence. She was smiling affectionately at the girl.

Rill had told himself that he didn't want to hear about her troubles, but something about her intrigued him even though he was trying hard to ignore her. He wondered if Juliana was running away from more than a mean stepfather.

"All right, hold on to your horses, Cass, and I'll play a tune for you," Cropper said, taking his harmonica out of the inside pocket of his cowhide vest.

"Juliana was teaching me to play the piano. She knows every song by heart."

"Is that so?"

"Yes. Tell him, Juliana. She knows every piece of music that's been written."

"Well, let's see if she knows this one." Cropper cupped the instrument between his dry hands and put it to his lips.

A familiar tune that was slow and whiny like a lullaby eased from the harmonica. Rill smiled. Juliana wouldn't know that song. It was one Cropper had made up years ago to quiet restless cattle on stormy nights.

Rill's gaze strayed to Juliana again. He liked the way the firelight sparkled off her golden-colored hair. He liked listening to her gentle laughter. He wondered what it would be like sitting in a warm cozy room with a fire, candlelight, and Juliana playing the piano for him.

"What is it, Juliana?" Cass demanded. "Tell us what he's playing."

"I'm not sure yet. Shh—and let him finish."

Juliana had mettle. He had to give her that. And it didn't bother him that she spoke her mind. But now that he had time to see past the beautiful woman who had surprised him by popping out of his wagon, he saw that she was deeply troubled by something. Why else would she risk leaving town with strangers?

"There," Cropper said, palming the harmonica and looking at Juliana. "What's the name of that song?"

"It sounds like a lullaby but I can't place it. I don't believe I've ever heard that exact song before."

"That's because it's my tune, and it doesn't have a name. I made it up."

"You can't do that." Cassandra jumped up and folded her arms across her chest. "That's not fair. You cheated." She stuck her lips out in a forced pout.

"No, I didn't," Cropper defended. "I don't have to cheat to win. You said she knew every song, and I just proved to you she didn't."

"Juliana, he didn't win. He cheated," Cassandra complained.

"Now, sweetheart," Juliana said, "that's not a very nice thing to say."

Seeing the makings of an argument he didn't want to hear, Rill lit the wick on the lantern, then stood up. He looked down at Juliana and said, "I guess it's time to make a bed in the wagon for you and the girl."

"She has a name," Juliana said, looking up at him. There was a defensive crispness to her voice. "A very pretty name. And, I might add, so do I."

He stared down at her. "I don't want to get personal enough to remember either of your names. We won't be together that long."

Juliana rose and brushed her skirt. "That's not being personal. It's being polite."

"You're a funny one to keep spouting all these rules to me about what's proper behavior. Have you forgotten you stole a ride in my wagon?"

"How can I? You keep bringing it up."

"No need to feel guilty if you're not."

"I agree, and I don't. I've apologized and—"

He lifted his eyebrows.

"Are you two arguing?" Cassandra piped up.

Juliana sighed. "Of course not, sweetheart. You win, Rill. If I have to say it outright to make you happy, I will. I apologize for being so rude as to take shelter in your wagon without your permission."

"I apologize, too," Cassandra said in a sleepy voice. "Now I want Cropper to teach me how to play the harmonica."

"Well, then, Miss Cassafras," Cropper chimed in, "come over here and sit closer to me, and I'll show you how."

She huffed. "I told you my name is Cassandra. Why do you call me other names?"

"Because that name don't fit you. You're too bossy for it."

Juliana turned to her charge. "Cassandra, you can stay up only until I get the bed prepared."

"But I'm not sleepy."

"You will be soon."

"Go ahead," Cropper said to Juliana. "I'll keep her busy for you."

Rill reached down and picked up the lantern and turned up the flame. He started toward the wagon. Juliana walked beside him.

She should know when to quit, but something about Rill forced her to challenge him. "You didn't accept my apology."

"I didn't know I had to."

"That would be the nice thing to do."

"I don't recall ever being accused of being nice."

"I'd bet on it," she shot back quickly.

Rill chuckled.

"Look, I offered to pay you to let us travel with you.

If you don't want to take the money, fine. Just don't keep complaining."

She was right. He was making too much of her hiding in the wagon, but he had to do something to keep reminding himself not to get involved in her problems.

"Is that what I'm doing? Complaining?"

"Yes."

He hung the lantern on a peg outside the wagon and climbed inside. He turned and reached for her hand.

Their eyes met.

She hesitated.

Maybe she was remembering, like him, the last time they touched. Juliana put her hand in his and climbed up. Her hand was warm, soft, and a thrill tightened his stomach just as it had when he touched her before.

He threw his and Cropper's bedrolls out on the ground and went to work stacking the sacks of potatoes and beans in the front of the wagon, clearing a place big enough at the rear to spread a blanket for them to lie on.

Juliana helped by picking up the smaller sacks of coffee and flour and by rearranging some of the other items inside.

Rill had thrown extra blankets into the wagon in case they ran into freezing weather, and now he was glad he had. It was warm enough in the wagon that the extra blankets could be used to make a soft bed.

"It's not much room, but we weren't expecting company. I don't think it's going to get cool tonight, so you should be fine without cover."

"We have our winter coats and can use them if we need to. Are you sure you and Cropper don't need these blankets?"

He liked the fact that she thought about his and

Cropper's comfort. "No, you use them. Our bedrolls will be enough."

When Juliana remained quiet for a couple of minutes, Rill stopped working and looked over at her. She sat back on her heels in front of him, staring at him.

He quirked a brow. "What's wrong?" he asked.

"I just realized that I've been so concerned about getting to where we want to go that I never said thank you for not being angry with us about what we did."

The tone of her voice made her gratitude sound like a glowing compliment. He couldn't figure out why she was getting to him. Pale light coming in through the canvas opening shone clearly on her face. Sincerity was etched in every feature.

Rill watched her eyes and her lips as she spoke. His stomach did a flop. He was attracted to her. Hellfire! He'd just spent a week in town and had visited more than one upstairs room. Irritation at himself surged inside him. He instinctively knew that Juliana was no harpy for him to be getting ideas about, but he felt a distinct tightening in his loins.

He had to fight the pull she had on him.

"I am angry," he said tersely. "I thought it showed."

"No, you were upset, not angry. There's a difference. You could leave us here on our own or—"

"What?"

"Attempt to harm us."

His eyes held to hers. "I don't hurt women and children."

She gave him a sweet, easy smile. "Somehow I knew that, but does it mean you will hurt men?"

Rill hesitated before saying, "If I have to."

"I'm sure you would take proper care of anyone who caused you trouble."

Her expression was the gentlest he'd ever seen. He knew she was debating how much more she could ask before he cut her off. He wondered if she considered killing a man "proper care."

His effort faltered, and Rill gave in to her charm and responded with a smile. She was attempting to be friendly, and he might as well be nice, too. There was no reason why he couldn't enjoy being with her, looking at her, and talking to her—until he left her in town.

"That's right. I don't like trouble. By dusk tomorrow evening, I plan to be pulling into Leavenworth. It will take me a few miles out of the way, but it's a big enough town you should be able to find a marshal or whatever kind of help you need there."

"If it's out of your way, don't take us. We don't need to go to Leavenworth. Follow your original plan and make us both happy."

"Why are you so all fired up to get away? You'd think you were running from the law the way you're acting."

Her eyes blinked rapidly. Rill looked past Juliana's beauty and saw real fear. Not like when he first found her in the wagon, but a fear deeper and more disturbing. Something inside made him want to know what it was that frightened her and forced her to flee.

"You aren't, are you?" he asked.

"What?"

He noticed that she swallowed hard, and her voice sounded breathless. She started pressing the wrinkles out of the blanket with her hand. A funny feeling crawled up his back.

"Running from the law," he said.

"To the best of my knowledge, there are no authorities after us."

She avoided his eyes, and her answer was evasive,

but Rill decided not to push her for now. In a way he wanted to know everything about Juliana, but in another he knew the folly in becoming too attracted, too involved, and too attached to her.

Rill couldn't help but wonder if the stepfather had gotten out of line with them or if he was just a mean bastard. The thought of anyone putting their hands on Juliana or Cassandra angered him. Rill knew he didn't want anyone hurting either one of them.

Dismissing his fierce warning to himself, he asked, "Did Cassandra tell the truth? Are you two running from your stepfather?"

She winced in a brief spasm of guilt. How long could she allow him to think Mr. Cabot was her stepfather, too? "Yes, we're running from Ward Cabot."

"Where's your mother?"

"Dead." That wasn't a lie.

"Father?"

"Same." Again, it was easy to tell the truth. "Tell me why you won't let us travel with you when I've promised we won't be any trouble."

There wasn't a reason in the world why he should, but he liked her persistence. "And I'm supposed to take your word for that."

"Well, we haven't caused a problem so far."

"That's a matter of opinion."

"I think you owe me more of an explanation why you won't let us travel with you."

Rill bristled. "Owe you? Excuse me, did you say that I owe you?"

Her lashes flew up.

"Perhaps I said that wrong."

"Damn right, you did."

"I'm afraid I'm frustrated at the moment."

"So am I."

Dispiritedly, she sat back. "It wasn't my intention to make you angry. I'm only trying to understand and find a reason for you to allow us to travel with you. Surely there's something I can do for you. Wash and mend your clothes, cook or something."

"Cropper does all that. There's only one thing that I need from a woman."

"Wh—" Her eyes widened.

Rill smiled wryly. At last he had the upper hand, and it felt good. "What's the matter? Aren't you willing to keep my bed warm?"

Her shoulders lifted, and her chin rose an inch. "I most certainly am not. I couldn't possibly do such a thing as that."

"I understand, and that makes us even. I couldn't possibly do what you're asking."

All of a sudden, she reached out and placed her hand on top of his. A flood of warmth washed over him.

"Rill, I can't press upon you how desperately we need your assistance. Would you just please agree to think about it overnight? That's all I'm asking. Don't make a final decision right now. Sleep on it."

He looked down at her hand so warm and inviting against his. He almost relented and gave in to her wishes. But no, he didn't want to be responsible for their care and safety. The only reason Cropper was with him was because Rill knew the old man didn't need a keeper.

"So will you agree not to give me a decision until the morning?"

"I thought I had already given you a final answer," he said in a voice so low even he doubted its meaning.

"I'm certain you didn't."

His gaze traveled back up to her angelic face. She smiled at him, easily, effortlessly, and his heart tripped. Was he falling for her pretty face, her hard-luck story? That was so unlike him. Over the years of being a trail boss, he'd heard every story known to man when his drovers would come back to the herd late, drunk, or married. He never gave an inch. He couldn't afford to. But Juliana was making him re-think his hard line.

"All right," he conceded, wanting to please her in this small way. "But don't expect my answer to be any different in the morning."

She removed her hand, and Rill wanted to grab hold of her and not let go.

"The only thing I'm going to expect is a chance."

❧ 4 ❧

The next morning Juliana woke to sounds of Cropper hitching the team to the wagon.

Juliana tried to shake the wrinkles out of her skirt, but there was nothing to be done about the state of her attire. She'd just have to put up with the inconvenience of being unkempt until they reached the Triple R.

She twisted her hair into a loose chignon and pinned it at the back of her neck. By the time she'd donned her bonnet and climbed out of the wagon, Cropper was pouring coffee into a tin cup.

"Mornin'," he called, and motioned for her to join him by the campfire.

"Good morning, Cropper," she answered with a smile, but found herself searching for Rill.

It was a warm, late summer day. Bright, early morning sunshine found its way through gathering clouds and fell across her face. Light gray thunderclouds covered the sky in spotty patches.

Rill's horse was saddled and ready to ride, but she didn't see any sign of him.

"Cass still asleep?" Cropper asked.

"Yes. Yesterday was an—unusual day for all of us, I guess."

"Sure was. I told Rill, I ain't never found a woman in my wagon before."

Juliana rubbed her arms. "I hope to never do it again. We were taking a big risk."

"Told Rill that, too." He reached down and picked up another cup. "You got enough time to have a cup of coffee before we pull out. Rill's in a big rush to get on the road this mornin'. I've filled biscuits with the leftover beans and ham. They're wrapped in that cloth over there on the buckboard for when you're hungry. I poured molasses between some of them for Cass. No need to ask. Just help yourself."

"Thank you, Cropper. I'll have one a bit later in the morning."

Juliana couldn't explain it, but she felt safe with Rill and Cropper. Somehow, she knew these men would help her keep Cassandra safe, but would they want to if they knew what she'd done? She had to talk Rill into letting them join his journey. What did she have that she could offer a man like Rill? He had declined her offer of money.

The only thing she had of worth, other than the womanly service he'd expressed an interest in, was the brooch that had belonged to Auntie Vic. If he wouldn't take her money, he wouldn't want the small piece of gold.

She took a sobering breath as she remembered what he'd said last night. *The only thing I need a woman for is to warm my bed.* A wicked feeling of possibility seeped inside her and heated her cheeks. She quickly pushed the thought from her mind. Maybe she should offer him companionship and conversation. Yes, a woman was good at those things, too. She'd prove that to him if he'd give her the chance.

"Cropper, did Rill tell you that Cassandra and I would like to travel with the two of you to Cheyenne?"

His small eyes narrowed. "Didn't say a word to me. What'd he say to you?"

"So far, he hasn't agreed. Do you know why he'd be reluctant?"

"Yup, I can think of a reason or two."

"If I knew what they were, perhaps I could convince him otherwise."

"It ain't my business to say." He kicked dirt over the embers.

"You've known him a long time?"

"More'n a dozen years, I guess. Once he makes up his mind about something, he pretty well sticks to it. Don't much make him change direction."

"Well, I'm not going to give up on him yet. Rill said it would be late afternoon before we made it into Leavenworth."

"That's right."

"That gives me all day to talk him into letting us stay and ride in the wagon with you."

"Fancy dressed womenfolk like you and Cass don't need to be out on the trail with the likes of two old drovers. You can get to that place you want to go to easier and faster by taking the train as far as it goes and the stage the rest of the way."

"Yes, and it would also be easier for the man who's looking for us to find us."

His eyes narrowed, and his brow creased into a frown. "What man? Someone after you?"

Juliana had forgotten that Cropper didn't know

what she'd told Rill, and obviously Rill hadn't mentioned it to him. "There could be."

"Who is it?"

She liked Cropper's directness. "Cassandra's stepfather."

"He was a mean son of a—gun, was he?"

Juliana remembered seeing Ward Cabot's face just before she struck him with the candlestick, and a tremor of fear scampered up her spine.

"Yes," she whispered with a cold lump in her throat. Juliana sipped the warm coffee, trying to dispel the images filling her mind. "He's a deplorable man. I explained everything—well, most of the story—well, some of it—to Rill."

Cropper scratched his whiskery chin. "The days can get mighty long and lonesome out here. I wouldn't mind the extra company myself, but Rill's the boss. We'll have to do whatever he says."

"I have a feeling he's always been the boss, hasn't he?"

"I've had others, but he's the best. I'd trust him with anything I own, including my life."

She'd sensed that about Rill, too. That's exactly why she wanted to keep Cassandra with him. So far, Rill hadn't given her one word of encouragement, but she couldn't let that stop her.

"You ever been to his ranch?"

"No, and he ain't, neither. Just bought it off a feller there in Kansas City a week or so ago. Rill took most of his money out of the bank and gave it to him."

"He bought it sight unseen?"

"Yup, but he wired a bank up there in the Wyoming Territory and checked everything out to make sure there really was a Double Horseshoe Ranch before he handed over the money."

Cropper's words struck a cord in Juliana. "Sounds to me like our leader is running away from something, too."

"Could be. Not that you'd ever convince him to admit it."

"Well, if Rill still refuses to let us travel with you by the end of the day, I'm sure I can hire someone in Leavenworth to drive us to the ranch."

Cropper pulled a leather drawstring bag from his pocket and opened it. With his thumb and forefinger he reached inside and pinched a small amount of tobacco, and stuffed it to the side of his mouth.

"That don't sound safe to me. Womenfolk don't have no business trusting a stranger."

"Sometimes we don't have a choice, and sometimes we meet nice people like you."

Cropper rubbed his nose and looked embarrassed. "Well, it'll be close to dark before we come into town. So, go ahead and have some more coffee. It's gonna be a long day. We don't stop often, but if you or the little boss decides you need a nature call, just tell me. If Rill doesn't like it, we'll tell him to keep a-ridin'. We'll catch up with him later."

Juliana laughed at his reference to Cassandra as the little boss. "Thanks, Cropper. We'll try not to be too much trouble to you or Rill."

"Naw, you ain't no bother to me."

Movement caught Juliana's attention, and from the corner of her eye she saw Rill partially hidden behind a tree. Her first thought was that he was hiding from her, but she knew that couldn't be true about a man as bold as Rill. She sipped her coffee again, then walked over to him.

As she rounded the stunted tree, she saw Rill was shirtless, wiping the last of shaving soap from his face with a small brown cloth. She stared in stunned

54

wonderment at the way his firm muscles moved beneath the skin of his wide chest.

Juliana's eyes darted up to his. Her heart quickened when she saw how handsome he looked without the beard growth. His cheeks were damp, and his skin looked smooth and touchable.

She wanted to reach up and press her palm to his cheek, but instead she said, "Oh, I'm sorry."

"Are you looking for something?"

Her gaze fell to his manly shoulders, then skimmed down his broad chest to his narrow hips where his trousers were loosely fastened. The heat of a blush stained her face and neck.

She lifted her lashes and looked into his eyes. "No. I mean yes. I was looking for you, but I didn't mean to intrude on your—private time. I had no idea you were—busy."

"It didn't dawn on you that, if I was behind a tree, I might need privacy?"

She swallowed hard as her gaze drifted over his masculine chest once again. Why did she have this strange urge to be cradled in his arms?

"I'll be more careful next time."

"Next time?"

He was deliberately trying to make her uncomfortable. "I guess I'm interrupting you."

"I don't mind you looking me over, if you don't," he said with a hint of amusement in his eyes.

Victoria's training returned to Juliana. *If you happen upon a man in any stage of undress, you are to act and conduct yourself as if he's fully clothed and carry on with your duties.*

Juliana swallowed the lump in her throat. She couldn't help but wonder if Auntie Vic had ever seen a man as appealing to the senses as Rill. Somehow, she didn't think so.

"I didn't mean to stare, but you're a handsome man," she said, as if forgetting everything her aunt had taught her.

Rill ignored her compliment and pulled his shirt off a low branch and shoved his arms into it. "I've been thinking. If your stepfather is mean enough for you and Cass to run away from him, why didn't you go to the sheriff and ask him to help you?"

She watched his nimble fingers button his clean brown shirt. "That wouldn't help us. Mr. Cabot—Ward—is a very powerful and respected man. No one would believe my word against his."

Juliana reached up and touched the gold heart that rested at the base of her throat. Again, she considered telling Rill the truth. Maybe that would make him change his mind about not taking them with him. Her only worry was that the truth might make him decide to turn her over to the authorities.

She looked into Rill's eyes. Could she trust him with the truth? She didn't really know him. She just had this feeling she could count on him to keep Cassandra safe, but if he wasn't willing to help, she had no choice but to make other arrangements.

"If you decide not to let us travel with you, I'll find someone in Leavenworth who can take us on to Cheyenne. Even though you don't want or need the money, I'm sure I'll find someone who does."

"That's a damn fool thing for you to do. Ask a stranger to take you on a long trip like that. Do yourself and Cass a favor, and keep to public transportation."

"Juliana!" Cassandra screamed. "Juliana!"

In an instant, Juliana picked up her skirt, turned and bolted toward the wagon, running as fast as she could. Rill ran beside her. Cropper joined them at the back of the wagon. Juliana jumped up on the backboard and Rill helped her inside. She fell on her knees beside Cassandra.

Cassandra rushed into Juliana's arms, tears streaming down her cheeks. Her whole body shook with spasms.

"Shh— It's all right. Everything's fine," Juliana soothed her. "Were you having a bad dream?"

"I—I couldn't breathe. It was dark. I th—thought you'd l—left me." Cassandra sniffed and cried softly.

"Oh, no, sweetheart," Juliana whispered, holding her tightly as she kissed the top of her head. "You know I wouldn't do that."

"Don't leave me, Juliana. I don't want to be alone any more."

"Of course I won't. Don't be afraid. I promise I'm not going to leave you."

Cassandra sniffed and cut her eyes around to Rill. "You and Cropper will help keep us safe, won't you?"

Rill glanced up at Juliana, a hard expression on his face.

"As long as you're with me, you'll be safe. I won't let anything happen to you."

"Don't you worry your pretty head about anything," Cropper said. "Nobody'll bother you while we're around."

She sniffed again. "Thank you," she said in her little girl voice.

Rill's eyes zeroed in on Juliana's face. "You have five minutes, then we're pulling out."

Juliana didn't like the expression on Rill's face when he turned away. Did he think she'd staged this scene with Cassandra? He'd never agree to help them if he thought she was that manipulative. Should she follow him and explain that Cassandra's fears were real? No. It was best to let it go for now and let him cool down. When they arrived in town, she'd tell him the truth. She'd do anything to keep Cassandra away from Ward.

Later that afternoon, Cassandra was taking a nap when Juliana looked out the back of the wagon and saw riders coming their way. Her heart thudded in her chest. Could Ward's men have already found them? How was that possible? It had only been two days.

Maybe she was just plain jumpy. No, she couldn't take any chances. Juliana scampered toward the front and climbed out on the backboard seat beside Cropper. Rill rode ahead of them a short distance away.

"Cropper, catch up with Rill. I need to talk to him. Hurry!"

"We're on our way." He slapped the reins against the horses' rumps, and they took off.

"Rill!" she called to him when they drew near.

He turned around, and she motioned for him to come to them. He directed his horse closer to her.

"What's the matter?"

Her throat was so dry she could hardly speak. She felt her arms quivering from fear. "Riders. We have riders behind us."

"I knew my shoulders were a-itchin' for some reason. Where?" Cropper asked, his eyes immediately scanning the area on each side of the wagon.

"Behind us," she answered Cropper, but kept her sight on Rill.

A curious expression wrinkled his brow. "People travel this trail every day. We shouldn't be in any danger if they ain't Indians."

She moistened her lips and said, "These men might be looking for me and Cassandra."

"Did you recognize them?" Rill asked.

She shook her head. "They're too far away." Fear of being caught clamped around her heart like a vise.

She couldn't fail Cassandra. Her gaze shot from Rill to Cropper. "If they're looking for us, please don't say anything. I beg you. Help us to get away."

Rill cut his eyes to the horizon behind the wagon. Her heart sank. She knew what he was thinking. This could be his chance to get rid of them. He didn't want them along, anyway.

She didn't have time to explain to him that Ward had tried to kill Cassandra. Dear mercy, she should have told him earlier. It could have made a difference.

He remained quiet for so long she thought her heart would beat out of her chest. "I know there's not a reason in the world you should help us. I know we've been a burden and a problem to you, but I'm—"

"Stay in the wagon and keep Cass quiet and out of sight," he interrupted.

Her breath caught in her throat. She tried to tell him with her expression how much she appreciated what he was doing. "She's asleep. You won't hear a peep from her. Thank you," she said earnestly.

"Don't thank me yet. Now get inside, and be quick about it."

Juliana didn't know what else to say, so she crawled back into the wagon. She gently scooted Cassandra over to the side and covered them as best she could with the blankets and Rill's and Cropper's bedrolls.

She sat rigid, hardly breathing while she waited for the men to approach. It seemed to take forever before she heard Cropper yell "Whoa!" and stop the wagon. She sat motionless and listened, wishing she could see what the two men looked like.

"You got reason for stopping us?" Rill asked.

"Sure do," a man said. "Where you two men from?"

She didn't recognize the voice. That gave her hope.

"Here and there," Rill answered.

"We're drovers mostly," Cropper added. "Traveled over most of these here parts at one time or another I reckon. Why?"

"We're looking for a young woman and a young girl. They were last seen in Kansas City night before last. Seen anything of them?"

Juliana could hardly hold in her moan of agony. She squeezed her eyes shut and trembled. What had made her think she could outrun Ward Cabot? He had money and power to hire as many men as he needed to find them.

What was she going to do? Cassandra couldn't remember that her stepfather had tried to kill her—to back up Juliana's story. No one would believe her.

Fear and panic clawed at her chest and threatened to rob her of breath.

Ward was going to win.

What would happen to Cassandra? Ward would make another attempt to kill her. Who would save Cassandra next time?

Juliana's hands closed into fists. The sheriff would charge her with kidnapping, of that she was certain.

But would he put her in jail for the rest of her life, or would they hang her?

5

Then why are you way out here?" Cropper asked. "Seems to me Kansas City is where you need to be a-searchin'. Not out here on the prairie."

Rill took an instant dislike to the barrel-chested man with the tin star pinned to his black preacher's jacket. His partner, who was also sporting a deputy's badge, had bushy eyebrows that framed his small, deep-set eyes. His gaze continuously shifted from Rill to Cropper.

"There's men searching everywhere, including the town. The posse divided. We're checking all the trails leading out of Kansas City. I thought maybe you might have seen them," he answered with sarcasm. "We have reason to believe they've left the city."

"That so."

"The woman could have talked a family or some people into letting them ride in their wagon, or they could be traveling alone."

"Who's asking?"

The man turned to Rill. "Name's Baxter. My partner here is Nolen. Mr. Ward Cabot is the man looking for the woman and child. He's offered a reward for their return."

A muscle in Rill's cheek twitched. So far, everything Juliana had told him checked out.

"What kind of reward?" Cropper asked.

"Five thousand dollars."

"Whew!" Cropper coughed, choking on his tobacco wad. He spat it out and said, "Jumpin' jackrabbits. Who pays that kind of money for a woman?"

Rill knew. *A desperate man.*

"The woman's wanted by the U.S. Marshal," Baxter replied in an irritated tone. "Cassandra Rakefield is an heiress and worth a whole lot more money than that. Juliana Townsend, the girl's governess, hit Cassandra's stepfather over the head and almost killed him, then she kidnapped the little girl. 'Course no one expects Juliana will travel under her own name. We consider her armed and dangerous."

At first, Rill was too stunned to think about what the man had said, then it hit him. *Armed and dangerous? Juliana? A kidnapper?* A fierce sense of betrayal struck him in the gut. He'd been taken in by her innocent expression, by her tender pleadings for him to take them along.

She had lied to him!

But almost as quickly as those thoughts came to him, Rill knew something wasn't right. Common sense told him a kidnapper would have a better plan for escape than climbing into a wagon that was going God knows where. And Baxter was right. Kidnappers didn't use their own names.

Rill wasn't sure he believed Juliana was completely innocent, but he wasn't buying this man's story, either. He couldn't bring himself to turn her in, not yet. Not until he'd had the opportunity to have a few words with her and hear what she had to say.

Rill didn't chance a look at Cropper. He didn't want to do anything to make the men think they were sending signals to each other, so he said, "We haven't seen them."

"No, we ain't," Cropper answered right behind Rill. "But you can bet your last drink of water, we'll take them in to the nearest sheriff for you if we run across them. No sir, won't no woman get away from us with that kind of money on her head."

The man with the small eyes said, "Mind if we search your wagon?"

Cropper's gaze darted to Rill, and their eyes met for a half second. Rill knew what Cropper was doing, and he approved.

Returning his attention to the man who'd spoken, Cropper answered, "Naw, go ahead. We ain't got nothing but supplies in there."

The men started to move in closer, but Rill nudged his stallion between the wagon and the men. The other mounts snorted and Doc stamped his front hooves in complaint of the other animals coming so close. The team jerked the wagon forward.

"What the hell?" Nolen muttered as his horse almost unseated him.

"He might not mind, but I do," Rill said.

"The old codger said we could look," Baxter complained.

"It's not his wagon. It's mine."

"What does it matter if you're not hiding anything?" Nolen asked.

"I don't want to be bothered. We can't help you. Now you're holding us up."

"You in a mighty hurry?" Nolen asked, his eyes not leaving Rill's face.

"Sure are," Cropper answered for Rill. "We aim to make the Wyoming Territory before winter sets in. We've heard about late starters who got stranded in the snow and ended up food for the wolves."

Damn! Rill wished Cropper hadn't told the men where they were heading. That could be a big mistake. Rill rested the palm of his hand on his pistol. With a flip of his middle finger he lifted the safety snap on his holster.

Baxter and his partner stared at Rill for a long time, as if they were deciding whether to take him to task over his refusal to let them look in the wagon. Rill wondered just how far the man would push that badge he was wearing.

Finally Baxter asked, "You seen any other travelers out this way?"

Rill shook his head once.

Baxter touched the brim of his hat with two fingers and nodded. "Much obliged."

The two men turned their horses around and rode away.

Rill motioned with his hand for Cropper to get the horses going, and the old drover nodded, then took off.

There was something in the way the man with the small squinty eyes stared at the wagon that bothered Rill. He wondered if the man had somehow caught sight of Juliana or Cassandra. Or if he was just edgy.

As Rill watched the riders get farther away, he knew why he'd decided not to turn Juliana in to the men. What he couldn't understand was why hearing her side of the story was important to him.

In the short time Rill had been with them, he'd seen that Cassandra was fond of Juliana. And Juliana took too much time and care with Cassandra to want to harm her. He remembered the way Juliana had comforted the child when she had awakened and found herself alone in the wagon.

But hell, everything the men told him fit right in with what Juliana had said except for the fact that Juliana had led him to believe they were sisters. She'd lied. But why? The only thing he could think of was that she must have had a damn good reason for taking the girl.

What had he gotten into? He hadn't wanted to get mixed up with Juliana, Cass, or any of their problems.

He should have turned her in, he thought, as he turned his horse around and rode to catch up with the wagon. What Juliana had or hadn't done was none of his business. He didn't care, and he wasn't a judge. The authorities were the ones to decide her fate, not him—and not some two-bit deputy with reward money on his mind.

Juliana would be someone else's problem as soon as they reached Leavenworth. Not his.

He tried to convince himself that he didn't want to know her side of the story, that he didn't care, but it was futile. The hell of it was he did care, and he knew he couldn't take her to any town until he'd heard what she had to say in defense of her actions.

As he rode up beside the wagon, Juliana stuck her head out of the front opening. "Rill," she called.

Scowling, he glanced her way and said sharply, "Get back inside and stay there before someone sees you."

She blinked rapidly. He didn't like seeing the hurt that skittered across her pretty face, but he wasn't about to apologize.

"I wanted to thank you for not handing us over to those men."

"Don't thank me yet. I haven't decided what I'm going to do with you."

"How about giving me a chance to explain? You can't make a—"

"Get in the wagon and stay there," he said harshly. "Those men could be following us, just waiting for you to do something stupid like poke your head out."

"Oh, of course, you're right. We'll—talk later. After we know for sure they're gone."

"Don't come out until Cropper tells you it's safe."

Juliana ducked back inside the wagon.

Rill wanted, needed, to talk to her, but he'd wait until later tonight, after Cass had been put to bed. Juliana had a lot of explaining to do, and he didn't have time to listen to it right now.

"Cropper," Rill said, "don't let them out when you stop to make camp. Wait until dark."

The old man smiled. "I take it we're not stopping in Leavenworth tonight."

"That's right. Follow our original course."

"Good decision."

"That is, just until I hear what Juliana has to say about the kidnapping."

"I understand." He patted the rifle that lay on the floor by his feet. "Don't you worry, I'll take care of Cass and Julie."

Julie? Now Juliana had Cropper calling her a pet name, too.

"Do you think we fooled them deputies when I told 'em they could search the wagon if they wanted to?"

"Hard to tell. I didn't like the looks of them. When you make camp, I'll double back and check our trail. Won't hurt to know if they're following us."

Cropper nodded and picked up the horses' pace.

A strange emotion twisted inside Rill. He wanted to be rid of Juliana, yet he didn't.

He could have turned the two of them over right then and there. Been rid of them. He shouldn't have held back. He should be done with them right now, but he wasn't, and it was all because of Juliana.

She might be considered a kidnapper by the authorities, but he'd bet his brand-new ranch that what Juliana had done wasn't criminal.

Juliana's stomach was in so many knots she could hardly swallow. The thought of having almost been caught by Ward Cabot's men did crazy things to her insides and filled her head once again with doubts about what she was doing.

When dusk fell and they hadn't reached Leavenworth, she quizzed Cropper, and he told her Rill had decided against taking them to town tonight, but he didn't know what would happen tomorrow. Juliana felt a sense of relief, knowing that she'd have the opportunity to explain to Rill why she'd kidnapped Cassandra. She couldn't bear the thought of him thinking she'd intended to harm Cassandra or make money off her.

It had been a long afternoon, and they'd traveled until dark before Cropper stopped to make camp. Juliana hadn't let Cassandra peek out of the wagon for even a moment, so in order to keep the child busy, Juliana had opened a sack and showed Cassandra how to peel potatoes.

Cropper was delighted to have them ready to cook for dinner when the fire was made. Cassandra was too, declaring that red beans and ham were not proper food for a growing child to eat.

When Rill hadn't returned by the time they were ready to eat, Juliana worried, thinking Rill might have run into the men who were looking for her.

Cropper and Cassandra kept the conversation light as they ate their supper. Juliana had expected the old man to question her at length about the things the men had told him and Rill about her kidnapping Cassandra, but Cropper didn't say a word about what he'd heard.

She was grateful that he remained tactful. Explaining once to Rill would be more than enough.

There was no way Rill would take her and Cassandra along with him to Cheyenne now. She was sure of that. He wouldn't want anything to do with a kidnapper. But what bothered her the most was what he must be thinking about her. She had a feeling that to him no reason would be good enough to escape with a child. What she had to concentrate on now was talking him out of turning her over to the authorities. Somehow, she had to convince him.

She'd checked her reticule. She had her first month's salary with her. At the time she received the money, it had seemed like a lot. Now, she wondered if she had enough to pay someone to take them to the Wyoming Territory. If not, she'd hire a wagon and drive Cassandra there herself.

Auntie Vic had told her the only time it was appropriate to stretch the truth was when you were trying to make someone feel better, look better, or act better, and what she had been doing didn't fit into any of those categories. It seemed the harder she tried to do things the way her aunt had taught her, the more difficult it became.

While they were cleaning their plates, Rill came riding into camp. He dismounted and walked over to the fire and sat on the blanket beside Cropper. He didn't look at Juliana when she greeted him. A sharp pang of disappointment stabbed through her.

She didn't expect him to ask her anything in front of Cassandra, but it wouldn't have killed him to respond politely to her hello.

"You almost missed supper, Rill. Where have you been?" Cassandra asked.

Cropper picked up a tin plate and dipped into the boiled potatoes.

"Scouting the area," Rill said, and took the plate from Cropper.

"Did you see anything?"

"'Course he did," Cropper cut in. "There's prairie dogs and rabbits all over this land. And if you're quick enough, sometimes you can see a fox or a coyote. How about it, Rill? Did you see any two-legged foxes?"

"No."

"A fox doesn't have two legs," Cassandra stated.

"Some do," Cropper insisted. "I've seen them."

"Where? I want to see the fox," Cassandra said. "Show me one."

"Well." Cropper scratched his neck. "Next time I see one, I'll call you over to have a look at it. Should see plenty of them on this trail."

For the first time, Juliana didn't try to keep Cassandra from talking. Her charge kept her from having to look at Rill, but nothing could keep Juliana from thinking about him.

Cassandra turned to Rill and asked, "Did you know I peeled the potatoes? Juliana taught me how."

Juliana felt Rill's eyes on her, and she glanced at him. His expression was cold and unyielding. She could feel the anger pumping in his veins.

"Don't you think she's a little young to be handling a knife?"

"We were careful."

"I'll bet."

His spicy answer stung, and she shot back, "What's that supposed to mean?"

69

"Exactly what I said. She's too young to use a knife. She could get hurt."

Anger at Rill curled inside Juliana for the first time. She leaned forward, her eyes hard and unforgiving. "Nothing is more important to me than Cassandra's safety."

"I'm almost seven years old," Cassandra cut in. "Juliana taught me how to cut with the blade away from my body so I wouldn't hurt myself. Would you take me scouting with you tomorrow so I can see the two-legged fox?"

"Cassandra, it's not polite to invite yourself to accompany anyone," Juliana reprimanded, as she rose from her blanket. She needed to get away from Rill for a few minutes before she lost her temper and said something she'd regret.

"You told me the rules were different out here." Cassandra poked out her bottom lip.

"Some rules never change, and this is one of them. Now, say good night, and I'll put you to bed."

"But I'm not sleepy. I had a long nap this afternoon, remember."

"Nonetheless, it's bedtime for you, and off we go."

Rill rose and softly said, "I want to talk to you."

She looked into his eyes and swallowed hard at the dangerous undertone in his voice. "I'll return as soon as she falls asleep."

"Are you going to stay with me?" Cassandra asked.

"Of course." Juliana cupped the girl's chin in her palm and smiled at her. "I've promised I'm not going to leave you, and I won't. Have no fear about that. Now, do you remember where you put Miss Watkins?"

Nodding, Cassandra gave Juliana a trusting smile, then turned to the driver of the wagon. "Good night, Cropper. Thank you for the food." She turned to Rill.

"Thank you for not turning us in to those bad men who were asking about us. I knew you'd keep us safe from Papa Ward."

"Bad men?" Rill threw Juliana a glance.

She felt her heart sink. Why did Cassandra have to repeat everything Juliana said? Naturally, Rill would wonder why Cassandra thought those men were bad when he considered *her* the kidnapper.

She turned away from Rill without answering. "All right, off we go." Juliana took Cassandra's hand, and they walked toward the rear of the wagon.

"You didn't see any sign of them?" Cropper asked as soon as Juliana and Cassandra were inside the wagon.

Rill shook his head, then bit into a potato. They were soft, warm, and delicious. The soup was thick and filling, but for some reason, he felt empty inside. "It appears they're headed back to Kansas City."

"Get along, little doggie!" Cropper slapped his open palm on his leg. "We fooled 'em all right."

"Don't celebrate yet. Could be when they meet up with the others who are out looking, and no one has found Cass and Juliana, that they come back looking for us since I kept them out of the wagon."

"We'll be three or four days farther down the trail by then. We're making good time."

Cropper pulled his small leather pouch out of his pocket and dipped two fingers into it, pulling out a pinch of tobacco. He pressed the moist leaves together, then popped the wad into his mouth.

"Do you think the little boss is an heiress like those men said? You really think she has all that money?"

Rill cupped the tin coffee mug and thought of how warm, soft, and smooth Juliana's hand had felt in his. "Got no reason to doubt them. Everything else they said matched what Juliana has told us. Right down to the man's name she's running from."

Cropper shifted his chew in his mouth. "Naw, that jawing about kidnapping can't be true. Look at the way Julie takes care of Cass."

Rill had noticed, but he didn't answer Cropper. His gut feeling told him it was true. He just didn't know why Juliana had done it.

"Not that I believe any of it for a minute, you understand," Cropper said as he rubbed his chin, "but what if what them men say about kidnapping is true? Why do you think Julie hit the man and took Cass? You supposin' he was messin' around with her?"

Rill shook his head. "Could be. I don't know, but I intend to find out."

"Well, I'll clean up the camp and call it a day, so you and Julie can have privacy to talk. No use in me gettin' in on this. Ain't none of my business."

That was the problem. It wasn't any of Rill's business either, and it bothered him worse than poison ivy itched that he didn't want to take Juliana into town and turn her over to the sheriff.

Cropper rose and pulled his gun belt up farther on his hips. He paused and said, "Except—you ain't plannin' on doin' anything crazy like turnin' them in to the marshal, are you?"

Rill looked up at his friend. "I'm thinking about a lot of things."

"Julie told me she wants to ride with us to Cheyenne. You thinkin' about that?"

"Already have. I told her no."

"Yup. I figured as much, but dad-gone-it-all, Rill, those two females make this godforsaken prairie come to life. I'd miss them worse'n my sidearm."

"You know why I'm not interested in being responsible for anyone's safety."

Cropper nodded. "And I also know what happened wasn't your fault. It's time you stopped blamin' yourself."

Rill bristled. "Those men were my responsibility."

"Sure they were. But you couldn't have stopped Stedman if you'd been there."

"You don't know that."

"He would have just killed you, too. As it happened, you were lucky enough to live and avenge their deaths. Just be thankful for that."

Rill stared at his friend, but didn't comment, so Cropper turned and walked away.

The cup in Rill's hand shook as he remembered the rage that had gripped him a few weeks ago. He'd tried not to think about his men or Stedman. It wasn't like Cropper to bring that up. He knew how Rill felt about what had happened, about what he had been forced to do.

Taking something that didn't belong to you was ugly business. It didn't matter if it was a child or fifteen hundred head of cattle.

❧ 6 ❧

The hearty meal and warm night had Cassandra asleep long before Juliana had the courage to step out of the wagon to face Rill. She had lingered inside—repairing her hairdo, shaking the wrinkles from her skirt, and washing the dust from her face with water she'd drained into a pan from the barrel tied to the side of the wagon.

Her feet felt as though they were weighted with cannonballs as she climbed out of the wagon. Faint moonlight prevailed in the black sky. The prairie wind was tepid with the last days of summer.

She didn't see Cropper as she returned to the fire. Rill sat on the blanket. Waiting for her. She couldn't blame him for being angry. She had hidden a very important part of the truth from him. Her reasons were valid. She wasn't sure she trusted him not to turn her in to the authorities, but would he understand that?

Juliana sat down beside him. "Pleasant night, isn't it?" she said, trying to mask her feelings and get this

74

unavoidable conversation off to a good start even though tension knotted her throat.

"You tell me."

"All right. It is. With the gray skies, I thought we'd get rain today. I'm happy we didn't."

Rill didn't answer. Juliana thought back to what Auntie Vic had taught her about unpleasant conversations, and she knew she had to remain calm, keep her tone even.

"I hope I didn't keep you waiting too long."

"We're not in a drawing room, so you can stop with the formal talk."

"My, we are in a temper," she said, trying hard to stay in control. Anger would only make this more difficult. She didn't want that. "Anyway, I assume my tardiness gave you time to finish your dinner and take care of your horse."

"If you're waiting for me to thank you, I'm not going to."

"Why doesn't that surprise me?" she said tartly, forgetting about remaining calm. Obviously, her aunt had never met a man like Rill.

"You seem to be the only one with surprises."

Juliana wished Cropper would return. He was definitely more agreeable than this stone-faced man sitting next to her. "Where's Cropper?"

"He made his bedroll over on the other side of the wagon. He wanted to be close to Cass in case she awakened while we were talking."

"Is that what you think you're doing? I'm talking, you're arguing."

An exasperated sound escaped his lips, and he ran a hand through his hair. "You have a lot to tell, Juliana. Start talking."

Startled, her gaze swept up and down his moonlit

face. It was the first time he'd said her name. It rolled off his tongue like a summer breeze across the river.

"Did you kidnap Cass?"

She shifted. "Not exactly."

"What the hell does that mean?"

"Well, I did take her without her guardian's permission, but—"

"Are you crazy?" he interrupted, a fierce expression on his face.

"Of course not," she promptly replied.

"You can go to jail for that."

She flinched even though she'd already come to that conclusion. It didn't help that he agreed with her. "I had a good reason for taking her."

He sighed. "That's what I want to know about. You might as well start at the beginning."

She took a deep breath and said, "I was born twenty-one years ago to parents who were the hired help for a wealthy family in Chicago. My mother and father didn't marry until late in life, and I was a big surprise to—"

"Juliana, am I going to have to get the truth from Cass?"

He'd spoken softly, gently, firmly, leaving no doubt he wanted to bypass her history and get straight to the present. She saw the reflection of the flames dancing in his eyes, and she wondered if his anger at her was as hot as the fire that burned between them.

"No, of course not," she said in a resigned tone. "It's just that it's not a story I relish telling. I wish none of it had happened."

His expression and his voice softened. "We've all got things we wish hadn't happened. Putting it off isn't going to make it any easier."

Juliana responded to the change in him even as she wondered what had happened in his life that he wished hadn't. All of a sudden, she realized she wanted him to know everything. It no longer mattered whether or not he would believe her. The truth had to be told.

"I came to work for Ward Cabot a month ago. Prior to that, I was a governess to the same family in Chicago for five years. The child I was taking care of was enrolled in a girl's boarding school in Boston, and I was no longer needed. The agency I hired to help me find new employment had me apply for a post in Kansas City."

"Looking after Cassandra?"

"Yes. Since the last of my relatives had died more than a year before, I decided to apply, and was actually quite surprised when I was chosen. I was prepared for Mr. Cabot to select someone from Kansas City. But I accepted, and I considered this job opportunity as a challenge and an adventure."

"Why did you let me believe you and Cass were sisters and that Cabot was your stepfather, too?"

"You assumed a lot and letting you was easier than explaining."

"What happened to your family?"

"As I said, my parents were both employed by the same household and didn't marry until my mother was past forty. Unfortunately, they were killed in a house fire where they were employed when I was eleven."

"I'm sorry."

"Thank you," she said, pleased to know he had some soft feelings about him. "I then went to live with my mother's maiden sister, Victoria Schuster. She taught me everything she knew about being a governess." Juliana's hand automatically went to the gold brooch at the base of her throat, and her voice softened considerably. "She was an intelligent, resourceful woman. She had such respect for the job of a governess and great loyalty to the profession. She took ill a year ago and died."

"That left you alone?"

Juliana nodded. She still missed Victoria.

"What happened to Cass's parents?"

"I can tell you what I've been told and what I've heard the servants say, but I can't swear any of it's true. It all happened before I came to the house."

"What have you heard?"

"Cassandra's father was killed in a carriage accident when she was just a year old. Her mother married Ward—Mr. Cabot—three years later. Six months ago, her mother was killed—strangled while she slept." Juliana closed her eyes for a moment when she thought of how close Cassandra had come to her mother's fate.

"Did they find out who did it?"

Juliana opened her eyes and sighed. "One of the servants was convicted of the crime and hung within a couple of months after her death."

"And you think they sentenced the wrong man?"

Rill was astute. "I do believe that now. A couple of months ago, Ward decided Cassandra needed a governess so he fired the nanny who'd taken care of her since her birth."

"And you were hired."

"Yes. I should have known at the time that it was strange he wanted someone from another city, but I was too eager to leave Chicago."

"Why did you want to leave Chicago?"

She glanced up at him and saw his questioning expression. "It's not what you think. I wasn't in any kind of trouble. I had no family, no friends to speak of because my work had been my life. I wanted this job. I was happy to have such a wonderful opportunity. I knew Auntie Vic would have been proud of my securing employment with such a wealthy and well-known family."

"All right, so why did you kidnap Cass?"

Juliana sucked in her breath. He made her sound so guilty. She was glad she was sitting beside Rill and not in front of him where she'd be forced to watch his face all the time. She didn't want to see his repulsion when she made her admission.

"That sounds so harsh. It's not what you think. I didn't really kidnap her."

"Juliana, you have Cass, and you admit you took her without her legal guardian's permission. What else would you call it? I've had enough lies, evading, and half-truths. Tell me why you took her."

His voice was so low it was almost seductive. She snapped her head around to face him.

"You're deliberately being cruel. I didn't lie. I simply omitted some of the truth."

"Same thing from where I'm sitting."

"Not in any way are they similar." Her voice rose. Her eyes became moist. "I was merely being cautious when we met. Rill, you have to believe that I did what I had to for Cassandra's safety, and I'd do it again under the same circumstances."

"Tell me what happened, Juliana."

With a gusty breath, she lowered her voice and said, "Cassandra and I were in the house alone. The servants get one night a month away from the house. Ward was supposed to be out of town, too. Something awakened me in the middle of the night. I heard a strange noise coming from Cassandra's room so I got up and peeped through the doorway between our rooms." She folded her arms across her chest and winced as she remembered.

"What did you see?"

Her voice softened again, and she stared into the fire. "It was dark. I didn't know what was going on at first, then I realized someone was standing over Cassandra—holding a pillow over her face. She was thrashing, her arms flailing and trying to push the pillow away. I had to stop him."

"What did you do?"

"I hit him over the head with a brass candlestick."

"Is that when you realized it was Cabot?"

"Just before. He heard me rush into the room. He turned and growled like a raging beast caught in a trap and grabbed for me. It was horrible. I only meant to stop him, not harm him."

"The blow knocked him out?"

"Yes. I know he was trying to kill Cassandra. That's why I have to keep her from him." She was breathless by the time she'd finished. It was too real for her not to tremble at the thought of what Ward had done to Cassandra.

"If what you say is true, you had every reason to go to the sheriff. Why didn't you?"

"If?" She shot him a questioning look. "Does that mean you don't believe me?"

He hesitated. "It means I'm being cautious."

She shook her head. "You don't understand. I considered going to the authorities, but Mr. Cabot has friends all over town. He knows all the judges, the lawyers, the political leaders, the cattle barons. Everyone who's anyone is his friend. Who would believe he was trying to kill a helpless six-year-old girl? It's hard for *me* to believe, and I saw it with my own eyes."

"Why would he want to kill her if he already controls her money?"

"I don't know. The only thing I can figure out is that if she were dead, he'd inherit her estate and not be subject to her grandfather or anyone else questioning how he handled her money."

"She has a grandfather? Why didn't you go to him for help?"

"We are. He's the one who owns the ranch in Cheyenne. There are no other relatives that I'm aware of. That's why I'm desperate to get her there before Ward finds us. I have to believe Thomas Rakefield will help me keep her safe and away from Ward."

"But you haven't spoken with him, so you're not sure about his feelings. As far as you know, he could just want her money, too."

"Yes. I'm afraid that's a possibility. Cassandra's wealth came from her mother's family, and there's no one left."

"Damn, what a situation for a young girl to be in."

Rill's eyes and his voice conveyed the message that he was softening, and Juliana responded by relaxing, too.

"I agree. I know her grandfather tried to get custody of Cassandra when her mother died. Ward had all the power of his friends in the courts of Kansas City behind him and control of all Cassandra's money to back him. Mr. Rakefield didn't have a chance."

"Does Ward have any money of his own?"

"Not much, from what I've heard. What he had going for him when he came to Kansas City a few years ago was his distant relationship to the Peabodys of Massachusetts. That family is considered one of the most respected in the East."

Juliana scooted closer to him, placed her hand on Rill's arm, and leaned toward him. His muscle twitched beneath her palm. She felt strength and sensed honor inside him, and she wanted to draw those things from him.

"I realize I was wrong to try to involve you and Cropper in this. I've broken the law. I'm a wanted woman, but I didn't know what else to do. I couldn't leave Cassandra with her stepfather."

"You've never met her grandfather?"

"No. Everything I've told you about Ward, I've heard from the servants. I can't swear to anything except what happened the night we fled the house."

"And we don't know how reliable their information is."

"No, but I know what I saw Ward Cabot do. My job is to take care of Cassandra and to see that she is safe at all times, and I take that seriously. I have no other responsibility. Ward was trying to kill her. I can't let her go back to that man, to that house."

"You're certain of this?"

"Yes. I'm convinced she'll never see her next birthday if she does! Ward will find a way to kill her. An accident or—"

"Go on."

"I might as well tell you everything. I believe it was Ward who killed Cassandra's mother and blamed it on the servant. I also believe he was going to kill Cassandra and blame it on me. That's why he wanted a governess from out of town."

Rill nodded. "And convenient for him that you would have no family to ask for help when you went to trial."

"Exactly. I'm certain he planned to blame Cassandra's murder on me."

"And they would have believed him because he's from a well-respected family in the East."

"Yes," she answered, beginning to feel that he might actually believe her.

Juliana swallowed hard and moistened her lips. She realized she continued to grip the firm muscles of his

82

arm in her hand but she didn't want to let go of him. Even though he'd not given her any reason to, she felt safe when she was with him.

"What does Cassandra think about all this?"

"That's part of my problem. She doesn't remember anything about what happened. All she can remember is that it was dark and she couldn't breathe. She doesn't know the reason was that her stepfather was holding a pillow over her face. I only told her he was trying to harm her so we had to get away fast."

"And she believed you without reservation?"

"Cassandra knows she can trust me."

"Does that mean she doesn't trust Cabot?"

"He's never tried to develop a rapport with her. Look, I know none of this helps me. Mr. Cabot could say he came into Cassandra's room and saw me trying to kill her and I hit him when he tried to stop me."

She saw a shadow of doubt cross Rill's face. Juliana winced. If a stranger wouldn't believe her story, how could she expect someone who thought of Ward as a perfect gentleman believe he tried to kill Cassandra?

"I'm telling the truth," she said earnestly, pleading for his faith in her to become real.

"If you are, you're in one hell of a mess."

"I know. Believe me, I've had doubts that I did the right thing in not going to the authorities, but I don't have doubts about what I saw. If you won't turn us in to the sheriff, I'll find someone else to help get us to the Triple R Ranch and get out of your life. I don't care if I have to buy a map and a wagon and take Cassandra to Cheyenne by myself. I'll do it."

"Don't be stupid."

"I'm not. I'm being careful with Cassandra's life. I'm begging you not to turn us in to the authorities, Rill, and to help me keep her safe."

He looked down at her hand on his arm and said, "I

don't know that I believe everything you've said, but I don't like the thought of those men on your tail, either."

"Where does that leave us?"

Rill looked away from the fire, out into the darkness. "I'll let you know in the morning."

After spending most of the night wrestling with her thoughts and all the stern warnings she'd received from Auntie Vic, Juliana woke with a plan that left her feeling stronger, calmer, and more sure of herself. If she was to be half the governess that her aunt had been, Juliana had to take matters into her own hands.

She believed Rill to be an honorable man and, because of that, he might decide the right thing to do would be to turn her in to the authorities and let them decide who should take care of Cassandra. If she waited for Rill's answer, it might be too late to escape.

She and Cassandra changed into their fresh dresses, combed their hair, and put on their bonnets even though the sun wasn't shining. If things went as smoothly as they'd gone yesterday morning, Rill's horse would be saddled and ready to ride.

Juliana planned to steal it.

She hated the thought of being so treacherous to a man who had been kind to them, but stealing was no worse than what she'd already done. Besides, she didn't have a choice, and she didn't plan on getting caught.

Juliana slipped her reticule over her wrist, knelt in front of Cassandra, and took hold of her hands. "You trust me not to let anything happen to you, don't you?"

Cassandra nodded as she bit down on her bottom lip.

"I want you to listen to me. We have to get on Rill's

horse when he isn't looking and ride as fast as we can to get away from here."

"Why? What's wrong? I like Rill and Cropper."

"So do I, but Cassandra, I'm afraid they'll turn us in to the sheriff before we can get to Grandpapa Rakefield. I can't let that happen. We have to make a run for it."

"The sheriff's supposed to help people."

"That's true, most of the time. But—well, you see I'm afraid the sheriff will take Papa Ward's side in this, and I'm sure that is not the best thing for you." Cassandra's eyes remained blank. "I know all of this is difficult for you to understand. You must trust me. Everything I'm doing is for your safety."

Cassandra pursed her lips, then asked, "Have you ever ridden a horse, Juliana?"

"No, but I've watched other people ride. It can't be too difficult, can it? You just hop up on the saddle, put your feet in the stirrups, and kick the horse in his sides with your heels, and he takes off. That's all you do." Now that she had explained it to Cassandra, it sounded easy.

Cassandra shrugged and held tightly to the foot of Miss Watkins.

"Don't worry. We'll be fine, sweetheart. We can do this."

"Taking Rill's horse isn't right. Isn't that stealing, Juliana?"

Cassandra knew exactly how to make Juliana feel worse than she already did. It bothered her that she'd been forced to resort to knocking Ward out, stealing a ride, and now a horse. After she had delivered Cassandra safely to her grandfather, she'd have to accept whatever punishment the law required of her.

Not wanting to lie to her charge, she said, "Yes, sweetheart, that's exactly what it is. It's not a nice thing or the proper thing to do, but right now it's what we must do. Would you feel better if we left Rill some money here in the wagon to pay for the horse?"

She nodded.

"Good. I think that's the right thing to do." Juliana opened her purse and took out several coins and laid them on the floor. She hated leaving their winter coats and the extra clothing but there was no way she could smuggle it onto the horse without arousing suspicion.

"I want you to listen carefully to me. We have to work together on this plan."

A few minutes later, Juliana climbed out of the wagon and helped Cassandra down. She was light-headed with relief when she saw that Rill's horse was saddled and ready to ride. She didn't see Rill anywhere, for which she was thankful. Something about him made her feel that, at times, he could read her mind.

Cropper stood near the fire. "Come on over," he said and motioned with his hand for them to join him. "Coffee's hot, and I have a special treat for the little boss."

"Good morning," Juliana said as they approached him. "Dear mercy, it does look like we are in for a beautiful day, doesn't it?"

Cropper breathed in deeply and said, "Yup. We should make good time today."

"What do you have for me, Cropper?" Cassandra asked.

"Here's a biscuit. I got up extra early this morning and fried some bacon just for you."

A smile lit her face. "You did?" She took the biscuit and bacon, then turned to Juliana, and her joyful expression turned to a frown.

Juliana knew what caused Cassandra's immediate

change. She was thinking, how can we be leaving two men who are so nice to us?

"I see you have Miss Watkins with you. Does she want one?"

"Of course not, silly. She's a doll. She can't eat."

Juliana heard a noise behind her and looked to see Rill walking into camp.

"Good morning," he said.

The first thing she noticed about him was that he'd shaved again. His face appeared softer, not as rugged, and much more handsome than he had last night. She wanted to reach out to him for comfort and understanding, but she knew that was impossible. Something about him drew her to him, and she knew what it was. Even with all that was between them, she was attracted to him.

She didn't want to take Rill's horse. He and Cropper had been so good to feed them, shelter them, and offer safety. Juliana took a deep breath and swallowed those feelings. Her only thoughts, her only loyalty had to be to Cassandra. She *must* do this for her.

Auntie Vic had told Juliana it would happen. That some day a man would touch her heart, and she would want to respond to him. But she knew she had to deny those feelings when she remembered hearing Victoria say, "You must not let a handsome young man turn your head. You are to be married to your job as I have been."

"Can't you speak this morning?"

"Oh, I'm sorry. I—I was just thinking how lucky we've been not to have any rain." She turned away. She didn't want him to read in her eyes that she was going to betray him.

Juliana looked over at Cassandra. She was eating her biscuit and wandering close to Rill's horse just like Juliana had told her to do. She was a smart girl. The next step was Juliana's.

"Here's a cup of coffee."

"Thank you, Cropper." She took the hot brew while keeping an eye on Cassandra and ignoring Rill. She didn't want to hear him tell her he had to turn them over to the proper authorities.

"Are we ready to roll?"

"Will be as soon as I put away the coffeepot."

Juliana had to move quickly. Rill was ready to go. She looked at Cassandra. She was in place. Juliana turned and walked toward the wagon.

All of a sudden, she dropped her cup and screamed, "Snake! Rill, Cropper, come quick! There's a snake by the wagon."

Juliana backed away as Cropper and Rill ran up to her.

"Where?" Rill asked, pulling his Colt.

"There, by the wheel," she said.

As soon as their backs were turned to her, she picked up her skirts and ran toward Cassandra. Juliana grabbed the child under the arms and strained to lift her onto the saddle. The horse was taller, bigger, more powerful than Juliana had realized. She struggled to get Cassandra high enough to seat her.

Doc snorted and sidestepped with the strange weight on his back. Juliana's trembling fingers fumbled with the stiff leather reins as she jerked them free of the tree limb and held them tight.

Quickly, she pulled up her dress and grabbed the saddle horn. She stuck a foot in the stirrup. The stallion whinnied and snorted again, pawing the earth. He tried to move away from her, but she followed him by hopping on her tiptoes alongside him.

"Hey! What're you doin'?" she heard Cropper call.

She glanced toward the men and saw Cropper coming toward her and Rill crawling out from underneath the wagon.

"Get away from the horse!" Rill yelled. "He'll throw you."

Juliana jumped, but didn't make it high enough to throw her leg over the saddle. Doc shied away from her again. She took a deep breath and tried again. This time, she managed to swing herself into the saddle behind Cassandra. Her dress came up, showing her black stocking-clad legs all the way up to her thighs.

Cropper was closing in on them with Rill right behind him.

"Hold on to Doc's mane, and don't let go," she told Cassandra.

Juliana kicked the horse in the sides with her heels.

Doc reared up, almost unseating her.

Cassandra screamed.

Juliana gasped and pulled the reins shorter. She nudged Doc again, softer this time, and he took off at a gallop just before Cropper reached them.

She heard both men calling her name. She glanced back and saw fury in Rill's face as the horse gathered speed.

Her heart leapt with relief.

They were going to make it.

Rill and Cropper would never catch up with them now.

❧ 7 ❧

Doc kicked up dust in Rill's face. He coughed.

Juliana and Cassandra bounced in the saddle like limp rag dolls. Rill expected the horse to stop and throw them any second.

"That stallion's gonna kill them both," Cropper thundered. "Do something!"

Rill put his two middle fingers to his lips and whistled loudly. Doc pulled to an abrupt halt. Juliana and Cassandra pitched forward over the horse's neck, but somehow managed to hang on to the stallion. The well-trained horse whinnied and yanked at the reins with his head as he turned and started trotting back toward Rill.

"I never would have believed it," Cropper said, fanning dust away from his face with his hand. "It don't make sense to me, them tryin' to steal your horse. What do you reckon got into Julie?"

"I suspected she might do something, but not climb on the back of the stallion. Doesn't she know how dangerous that is?"

"What'd you say to her to make her want to run away?"

That's what Rill wanted to know. It bothered him that she didn't trust him to do the right thing for Cassandra.

"No! Stop! Turn around!" Juliana pleaded, jerking on the reins, trying to force the huge animal to follow her instructions.

Rill wasn't worried. Doc wouldn't disobey his master's command.

As the horse came closer, Rill strode out to meet them. He grabbed hold of the reins. Juliana tried to strip the leather from his hands.

"Let go, you big brute!" She dug her heels into Doc's belly again. The stallion stomped and shuddered but made no move to take off.

"Settle down, Juliana. You're not going anywhere."

Rill patted Doc's neck, and the horse snorted his approval.

"Let us go, Rill!" Cass pleaded in a demanding voice. "We have to get away."

"Not today, Cass," he answered, but kept his eyes on Juliana. "You're staying with us."

As if sensing that her struggle was useless, Juliana let out a deep sigh. Her hands dropped into her lap.

"That's better," Rill said calmly.

Juliana looked down at him with eyes that seemed to burn into his soul. He saw strength, determination, and frustration in her features. She was courageous. He had to give her that. And, from the expression on her face, she wouldn't let anything keep her from her goal. She might not have succeeded this time, but that didn't mean she wouldn't try again if he was unwilling to help her.

Rill reached up and grabbed Cassandra underneath

her arms, lifted her from the horse, then set her down on her feet. "Go with Cropper."

"No, I don't want to leave Juliana," Cass cried, holding Miss Watkins tightly to her chest.

"Juliana's not going anywhere you can't see her. I want you to ride on the wagon with Cropper." Rill took hold of Juliana's ankle, pulled her foot from the stirrup, and inserted his own foot. He swung himself up on the saddle behind Juliana. Reaching around her, Rill held the reins together in front of Juliana. He looked down at Cassandra. "Juliana is riding with me."

"Come on, Cass," Cropper said.

"I want to ride the horse, too," Cass complained, refusing to take the hand Cropper offered. "Why does Juliana get to ride the horse and I don't?"

"'Cause she's bigger than you are and, besides, Rill said so," Cropper said and took Cass's hand.

"That's not fair." She pulled free of Cropper, threw Miss Watkins into the dirt, and stomped her foot. "You're never fair to me! I don't want to go with you, I want to go with Rill. Tell him, Juliana."

"Cassandra, I—"

"Now, if that ain't the meanest face I've ever seen," Cropper said, not allowing Juliana to talk. "Your lips are pursed so tight you won't be able to breathe if you don't straighten them up right now."

"I don't want to!"

"Go with Cropper, Cassandra," Juliana said softly. "I won't be far away, I promise."

"No!" Cass screamed and cried harder.

"Now listen here, Miss Cassafras," Cropper said firmly, picking up her doll and brushing the dust off her skirt. "You're not riding on the horse, and that's the end of that. The way I see it, you got two choices.

You can walk or you can ride on the wagon with me. Which is it going to be?"

She sniffed loudly and asked, "Will you let me help you with the reins?"

Cropper rubbed his bearded chin and considered her request. "Yup, I can, but I'm gonna tell you right now, it'll hurt those soft hands of yours. Rill bought these mares young, so I'm a-havin' to teach them everything. These horses are still gettin' used to working together, and they're a handful."

"It won't hurt me. I'll show you." Cassandra grabbed the doll from his hands and took off, marching toward the wagon.

Cropper looked up at Rill and Juliana. "She's all right now. Don't worry about her. I won't let her hurt her hands with the reins. Go ahead. We'll catch up to you before you know it."

Rill knew Juliana wasn't happy he'd spoiled her plan to get away. She kept her head high, her back straight, and her mouth shut as Doc took off at a slow walk.

In a rush of awareness, the heat from Juliana's body enveloped him. There was something soothing and intimate about her being so near him that their bodies brushed with each step the horse took. Rill had the urge to snuggle against her warm back and kiss her beautiful nape where wispy curls framed her neck.

"What happened?" Rill asked when it was clear she wasn't going to speak first, let alone attempt an apology for trying to steal his horse and run out on him. "Did you decide you didn't like our company?"

Juliana sighed audibly. "I just keep thinking that we almost got away," she said in a resigned tone.

"You weren't even close. Besides, it's not smart to try to steal a man's horse, Juliana. Some men consider it a hanging offense."

She turned her head and cut her eyes around to him. "Do you?"

He had to smile. "No."

"Good, because you'd have to stand in line behind Ward Cabot. I'm sure he thinks I deserve hanging, too."

Rill didn't like the thought of anyone hurting Juliana. "Why did you try to run away?"

"I figured I had nothing to lose. If Mr. Cabot catches me, I'm going to jail anyway."

Rill's stomach knotted. He supposed he should take some responsibility for what she had done. He had left it up in the air last night whether he'd help her. She couldn't have known that he'd decided to go against his vow never to accept responsibility for another person again. She couldn't have known he'd decided not to turn her in—not yet.

"I had no idea you'd trained this animal so well, or I might not have tried to get away."

"You're not giving yourself enough credit. I don't think anything would have stopped you from trying. You're damn lucky Doc let you mount him. That's never happened before. He's not usually so gentle with unfamiliar weight."

"You call this stallion gentle? Twice, he almost threw us to the ground. I don't know how we managed to hang on."

Rill chuckled lightly. "I don't know, either. Sheer willpower, I guess."

Her hands squeezed into tight fists. "I know we could have managed to get away with a different horse. Doc minds you too well."

"Too bad you don't," Rill quipped.

"I'm not an animal. I don't have to obey your every whistle."

Her quick retort pleased Rill, and he smiled. "I

don't want you to obey my every command, Juliana, just the important ones."

"I was under the impression that you thought everything you said was important."

"Well then, let's not change that belief."

"Oh, you're an impossible man to understand. I believe you are an honorable man, yet you don't want to help a woman in jeopardy."

Her words hung between them for a few moments. He wasn't about to go spilling his guts to her, so he moved the conversation back to a safe subject. "You haven't had much experience riding, have you?"

"No, I've never ridden a horse."

Her admission stunned him. She was one gutsy lady. "Never? Climbing on Doc was a damn foolish thing to do. You could have broken your neck or Cass's."

"We could have, but we didn't," Juliana shot back defensively. "I'd say we did all right for first-time riders."

"Don't try it again. Any horse can be dangerous, but especially a stallion, if you don't know a few basic rules. I don't want anything happening to you or Cass while you're in my care."

As Rill stewed about her foolhardy behavior, his gaze traveled down to Juliana's shapely legs. Her dress rode high on her thighs, showing just enough of the garter that held the stockings she wore to make him want to see the rest of what lay underneath her blue skirt. The muscles in his stomach tightened at the thought.

Juliana must have sensed where his gaze had wandered because she tried to lower her skirt. He liked the fact that she did. Not only was Juliana circumspect, she was intelligent, strong, and personable. He admired all those things about her, but it was the vulnerable side of her that drove him to distraction.

He leaned forward so that his lips were near her ear and asked, "Why didn't you wait for my answer before you tried to run away?"

Juliana brushed a strand of golden-colored hair away from her face. "I couldn't take a chance on you turning us in to the sheriff. You might not believe Cassandra's life is in danger, but I know it is."

"Who said I didn't believe you?"

She snapped her head around and looked at him. "You don't, do you?"

In her eyes, he saw that she needed him to believe her and that made him feel closer to her.

"You believe me?" she asked before he had time to answer.

He nodded once. Relief washed down her face like water over falls.

"Oh, Rill!" She twisted in the saddle and threw her arms around his neck and pressed close to him. She turned her face into the crook of his neck. Her excited breath fanned and tickled his skin. His muscles tightened. He loved the feel of her embracing him.

Rill drew her up against him. He breathed in deeply her intoxicating, womanly scent. He knew at that moment that he would do anything Juliana wanted him to do. He couldn't turn away from her desperate plea. It didn't matter who was after her or why.

"You should have trusted me, Juliana," he whispered, as his lips grazed the top of her ear. He wanted to bury the side of his face in her hair and rub the softness against his cheek. He wanted to forget they were riding in front of Cropper and Cass and kiss her.

"I wanted to. I needed to, but you didn't give me much hope."

When she looked into his eyes, his heart melted, and a shiver of excitement raced through him. He moved his face closer to hers. Her lips were full, tempting. He wanted to kiss her then, more than he'd wanted anything else in his life.

"I'm agreeing to keep the two of you with us, for now, because it's the right thing to do," he answered, and realized his voice sounded breathless.

Her shoulders dropped. "Not because you want to."

"That's right."

Juliana lowered her arms and faced front again. Rill started to pull her against him once more, but he heard the wagon coming up behind them. Instead, he moved his arms inward so that they grazed her sides as the horse continued at a slow walk.

"You told me last night that you weren't sure you believed everything I said."

"That's true. I know that Cass is a wealthy young miss who is nowhere near the age of managing her own affairs. I know that you have her, and Cabot and his men want her. But look at this from where I am. How do I know you didn't kidnap Cass for her grandfather, and that he's paying you a lot of money to take Cass to him?"

"What?" She turned around to look at him again. "That's a horrible thing to say! I wouldn't put Cassandra in harm's way for any amount of money."

He smiled. "Don't get so upset, Juliana. I'm just giving you an example of the kind of situation that could be going on here. What if Cass's grandfather turns out to be like her stepfather, and he only wants her for her money? The hell of it is that I'm not sure Cass is safe with anyone."

"Including me." A troubled expression settled into

Juliana's features. "I see what you mean. In truth, Rill, I'm not sure taking her to Thomas Rakefield is the right thing to do, either. I only know that leaving her with Ward Cabot is the wrong thing to do."

"How much of all this is Cass aware of?"

"Only that her stepfather wanted to hurt her, and that's why we're going to her grandfather's where she'll be safe."

"Has Cabot ever tried to hurt her before that you know about?"

"Not as far as I know. From what I observed the month I was in the house, he seldom sees her. He's out of the house most evenings until after she's in bed, and he doesn't like her downstairs in the mornings until after he leaves for his office. He wants complete silence in the house while he reads the paper and eats breakfast."

"Cass just took you at your word that Ward tried to harm her?"

"She trusts me. The first two weeks we were together were difficult, to say the least. She was used to a nanny who indulged her every whim. She finally decided we could get along together when Mr. Cabot told her I wasn't leaving. That's when I agreed she could address me as Juliana without saying Miss, and we'd be friends."

"I wouldn't have mistaken you two for sisters if she'd called you Miss Juliana. Why did you agree to that?"

Her eyes softened still more. "Cassandra never had a friend to play with. Her mother didn't want her to be hurt or influenced by other children's behavior, so she never invited anyone with children over. From what the servants say, she was always worried Cassandra might be kidnapped and held for ransom, so she seldom allowed Cassandra out of the house. I wanted her to accept me as a friend who taught her how to read and write, how to stitch, and how to set a table."

"That must have worked."

Juliana nodded, then asked, "Do you think Ward will send men ahead to the Triple R to wait for us?"

"I'd bet on it, if I were you."

"That's what I was thinking. I hope Mr. Rakefield will send Ward's men back where they came from. From what I hear, there's no love lost between the two men."

"After what you've told me, you should be planning on Cabot being at the ranch when you get there."

"Yes," she said tightly. "He will probably be waiting there with his arms wide open for Cassandra."

"Keep in mind, too, that if Cabot killed her mother, as you think he has, would he hesitate to kill Rakefield so you would have no one to turn to?"

She stiffened. "I guess I have to consider that possibility, too. What will I do if that happens? How can I keep Cassandra safe?"

"That's a good question."

The wagon pulled up beside them.

"You want me to take the lead?" Cropper asked.

"I'll do it," Rill said. "Hold up, so Juliana can get on with you."

He enjoyed Juliana riding with him, but knew it was best to put her back on the wagon. He'd talk to her again tonight after Cass had gone to sleep.

"We need to get moving and put as much distance as we can between us and those men. They won't stop looking," he told Cropper.

"I think you're right."

Juliana stared into Rill's eyes. "Rill, I know you're not happy about being a part of this, but I do thank you for doing this for Cassandra."

He stopped the horse and helped her down. He watched as she strolled over to the wagon and climbed on board. She titillated him, aroused him with her innocence. Juliana was poised, self-assured, and unwavering. He had no business thinking the kind of thoughts about her that were going through his head.

Rill was of the mind that the sooner he delivered Juliana and Cassandra to the Triple R, the sooner he could get Juliana off his mind and concentrate on getting settled on his new ranch. He was becoming too attached, too comfortable, and too hungry to possess Juliana's sweet mouth. He'd never been in love, but he recognized the warning signals.

Damn, he wished Cropper hadn't told Ward's men they were heading to the Wyoming Territory. It wouldn't take a smart man long to put two and two together. When Cass and Juliana didn't show up from any of the other searches, those men would remember that they never saw inside Rill's wagon.

Well into the afternoon of the next day the sun shone bright as on a midsummer day, without a cloud in sight. Clear skies covered flat land that seemed to stretch forever. Most of the day, the sky was so clear and blue that Juliana was sure she could see all the way to heaven.

A balmy breeze like Juliana had seldom felt in Chicago blew across the near-barren Kansas plains and left the air heavy with tepid heat that dampened the skin. She'd gotten used to wide open spaces. Occasionally, they passed a stunted willow or cotton-wood trees that always seemed to grow on small patches of land where grass was spotty.

The rumbling of the iron-covered wheels was all that she heard for most of the day. She continually searched the flat landscape but saw no sign of their being followed.

Not far ahead of the wagon, Rill sat tall, erect, and at ease in the saddle. She watched as he constantly turned his head from side to side searching the area with watchful eyes. About midday, he'd stopped by long enough for Cropper to hand him a cold biscuit, then he rode back in front, leading the way. She'd noticed that he seldom rode out of sight of the wagon.

Cropper pulled the team to a halt and set the brake. "I'm going to take a nature stop. It'll be the last one before supper. Anybody else want to go?"

Juliana looked down at Cassandra, who was talking to her doll. The wide brim of her bonnet shielded her face from the bright sun.

"Would you like to take a break and stretch your legs?"

"Yep," she said, in a voice that sounded very much as though she was trying to mimic Cropper.

"You two go that way." He pointed toward a sparse cluster of short, spindly-looking trees. "I'll go this way."

A few minutes later, Juliana and Cassandra returned to the wagon and climbed back onto the driver's seat.

The short walk had felt good. Sitting on the wagon seat most of the day made her stiff and sore. She'd read about women and children walking alongside wagons bound for Oregon, but Cropper and Rill kept the horses moving too fast for anyone walking to keep up.

She lifted her face to the cloudless sky and wondered if she looked at it long enough whether she would get freckles across her nose and cheeks.

Cassandra moved over into Cropper's seat and picked up the reins. She pretended to be driving the team. She made the same giddap, clucking, and whoa sounds Cropper made. Juliana smiled at Cassandra's playing. She enjoyed seeing the little girl happy and carefree.

When she saw Cassandra take hold of the brake handle and pull on it, Juliana said, "Don't touch that, Cassandra."

"You're not my mama."

"No, but right now I am your guardian. You have to listen to me."

"Why?"

"Because I said so."

"I'm not going to hurt the handle."

"Just the same, see that you don't touch it."

"What does it do?"

"It blocks the wheels and keeps the horses from pulling the wagon."

Out of the corner of her eye, Juliana caught sight of Rill, and her attention turned to him.

She didn't think he'd noticed that they'd stopped because he kept going. She wondered if he was in deep thought, as she'd been since her ride with him on his horse yesterday morning.

Juliana closed her eyes, shutting out the wide expanse of prairie before her. The late-summer breeze felt good against her face. She remembered how hard and warm Rill's body had felt next to hers. His breath had fanned her face, and his arms had tightened around her when she'd hugged him. Juliana breathed in deeply. Even now, she could recall the scent of leather, horse, and shaving soap when she'd pressed her face to his neck.

She also thought about how much she'd wanted him to kiss her at that moment, a purely feminine reaction she was sure. She liked the way he'd looked so understandingly into her eyes.

It didn't bother her that he was being cautious

about believing her story. She was cautious, too. And she was grateful he'd decided to help them, even if he had made it clear he wasn't committing to taking them all the way to the Triple R.

Closing her eyes, she remembered the feel of his arms around her, the pressure of his hand at the small of her back, and the huskiness of his voice when he'd whispered that she should have trusted him.

She'd felt a stirring power over him when she'd heard his intake of breath as she'd wrapped her arms around his neck and hugged him.

She'd wanted him to kiss her. The only time she'd been kissed was when Ward Cabot had caught her coming out of her bedroom the second day of her employment. At first, she'd been too stunned to do anything, but when she'd finally wrenched away from his brutish behavior, she knew exactly what to do. Following Auntie Vic's instructions about amorous employers, she'd told him she'd have to quit her post immediately should he ever do that again. Ward had never tried again. And now she knew why. He had other plans for her. The wagon jerked, and Juliana's eyes flew open.

A gunshot rang out and split the quiet. Cassandra screamed. The wagon jerked again. The horses bolted.

Juliana spun and watched in horror as the reins flew from Cassandra's hands and she toppled backward into the wagon.

Juliana lunged for Cassandra. The wagon lurched as the horses took off. Juliana tried to recover her balance, but it was too late. She tumbled from the wagon and landed on her shoulder with a hard, crushing blow.

A stabbing pain shot through her arm.

For a moment, Juliana lay motionless, the wind

knocked out of her. The clanging and clacking of the wagon speeding over bumpy terrain spurred her into action.

She tried to push herself to her feet with her hand, but cried out as a fierce pain took her breath away again. She had no time to think about herself. She rose on her knees and looked around.

The horses were running wild with Cassandra in the wagon.

8

Above the pounding of the horses' hooves on the hard-packed ground and the rattle and clanking of the wagon speeding over the rough trail, Cassandra's high-pitched scream filled the air.

Fear for Cassandra forced Juliana to deny her pain and stand up. She lifted her skirt and started running after the wagon.

"Rill!" she yelled as she ran, searching the landscape, hoping to spot him somewhere in the distance. He was Cassandra's only hope. If the wagon hit a hole or ran over a large rock, it could wreck the Conestoga and kill her.

A cloud of dust kicked up by the wild horses flew in Juliana's face and mouth, clogging her throat and burning her lungs bruised from her fall.

She coughed and struggled for breath but ran as fast as she could with her petticoats and skirt tangling about her legs.

Fear and guilt filled her. This was her fault for

daydreaming about Rill and not watching what Cassandra was doing.

The wagon was getting farther ahead. Desperate, she tried to run faster, but her legs and feet wouldn't cooperate over the rocky ground.

From the corner of her eye, she saw Cropper catching up to her, laboring heavily for breath as he ran up beside her.

"What in tarnation happened?" he yelled.

"Gunfire—frightened the horses. They took off—threw me from the wagon." She was so winded she could hardly breathe. Her left side felt as though it were splitting and her shoulder burned.

"Damn skittish greenhorn horses," Cropper muttered angrily, matching each stride she made. "Those shots shouldn't have scared the devil out of them."

"What can we do?"

"Nothin' right now. Look, there's Rill hightailin' it after them. He'll stop the wagon."

Juliana veered from behind the wagon, so she could see what was happening. Rill on Doc raced toward the horses at an angle.

Auntie Vic's stern face flashed before Juliana's eyes, and her aunt's voice sounded in Juliana's ears as her feet pounded the dry earth. *Your charge is your responsibility and no one else's. You will be her mother, her father, her teacher, and her protector.*

"Protector," she mumbled to herself, forcing down tears of frustration. She was failing miserably in all areas. How could she have ever thought she would be as good a governess as her aunt?

Juliana watched as Rill threw his rope into the air and twirled it round and round. She felt as if she could hear it whipping through the air. He let the lariat fly, and it caught around the lead mare's neck.

Fear for Rill's safety flooded her. If he fell, would he be trampled by the horses?

"Be careful!" she yelled, knowing Rill couldn't possibly hear her.

Rill rose in his stirrups, putting all his weight there while tugging back on the rope. The animal fought the constricting bind of the lasso. Rill kept the rope tight until the mare slowed enough for him to reach out and grab the harness. He yanked on the leather straps until the horses gave up and stopped.

Juliana's legs went weak with relief. She fought the tears of joy that rushed to her eyes. From her side, her lungs, and the back of her shoulder arrows of pain shot through her body, but she didn't slow down.

"I knew Rill'd—stop them. You can slow down—now," Cropper panted.

Her strength had drained, but Juliana kept running. "Can't," she managed to say. "I have—to get to—Cassandra." She had to know that the little girl hadn't been harmed from being thrown around in the speeding wagon.

When Juliana made it to the wagon, she fell against the backboard, letting the wood support her weight a few moments while she regained enough strength to continue. She allowed herself three deep breaths, then she took off toward the front calling, "Rill! Cassandra!"

Rill sat on the driver's seat, holding a whimpering Cassandra on his lap. Juliana was at once touched by the possessive expression on his face and how he held and comforted Cassandra with soft words.

"How is she? Is she hurt?" Juliana asked as she leaned against the shaft, forcing herself to remain upright.

"She's fine, just frightened."

"Thank God."

"What the hell happened?"

Tension knotted in her throat as Rill's dark gaze bore down on her. "I—I'm not sure exactly," she admitted. "Shots scared the horses."

"Not only could Cass have been killed, we could have lost the wagon and all our supplies."

"I know."

His condemning look chilled Juliana, but she couldn't blame him. She'd already admonished herself and taken full responsibility for the near disaster.

"It's my fault," she managed to say as Cropper came loping up beside her.

"Is Cass—all right?"

"Yeah," Rill replied. "Was that you who fired?"

"A rabbit came hopping right in front of me when I was walking back to the wagon. Gunfire wouldn't have spooked trained horses. This is the dangest team of green broncs I've ever seen. I'm beginning to wonder if we'll ever get them wagon-broke."

"Did you set the brake?"

"You know me better than—" Cropper stopped abruptly and scratched his neck. "Well, maybe I forgot this time."

Cringing, Juliana glanced at the kind man trying to protect her and Cassandra. It didn't make her look any better for Cropper to take the blame for something everyone knew he didn't do.

Juliana tried to lift her shoulder, but a sharp pain stabbed her. She managed to hide the agony that tore through her body.

Rill glared at Juliana. "You should have been watching her."

Any other time, his accusing expression would have made her angry, but right now she was too weak from fear, from relief, from the truth of his words to challenge him.

"Weren't no one's fault, Rill," Cropper said. "Cass must have accidentally moved the brake lever. When the horses heard the shots, they took off, and Juliana tumbled backward out of the wagon."

Rill's expression immediately changed to one of concern as he looked at Juliana. "You fell out of the wagon? Are you all right? You're pale."

Suddenly, her legs trembled so badly she could hardly stand. The piercing pain continued to plague her left shoulder, making her light-headed. She blinked rapidly, trying to clear her fuzzy head.

"I'm fine. Really. The important thing is that Cassandra's not harmed. I'm grateful to you for that."

Cassandra pushed away from Rill. Her nose was red from crying, and her face was streaked with tears. From somewhere she'd managed to find Miss Watkins, and she held onto the doll's arm.

"I didn't mean to make the horses run away, Juliana. I was just playing with the reins like Cropper showed me. It wasn't my fault," she whined.

Juliana leaned in close and patted Cassandra's knee. "We'll talk about that later, sweetie. Right now, I'm just glad you're not hurt."

"She might not be, but you are," Cropper said, peering behind Juliana. "Your shoulder's—"

"Giving me a bit of trouble," Juliana said, cutting off his words. In a whispered breath, she explained, "I don't want Cassandra to know I'm hurt. I don't want to frighten her any more than she already has been today. Don't say anything else about it."

Cropper looked grim. He kept his voice low and said, "That shoulder needs seein' to right now. I didn't notice before, but you have blood on your back. I'll take care of the little boss until you get fixed up."

"Thank you. I'd appreciate that."

"Cass, come on down here and go with me to pick up the rabbit I killed, before the buzzards think I shot him for their supper instead of ours."

A big tear rolled down her chubby cheek as she looked at Juliana for permission.

"It's all right." Juliana tried to smile but wasn't sure she had. In Kansas City, she would have never agreed for Cassandra to see a dead rabbit. "You can go with Cropper. He needs your help."

"I sure do. Come on, let's walk back to where I shot the rabbit. It might be hard to find him in that tall grass. Your eyes are better than mine."

She sniffed and rubbed her eyes with the back of her hand. "Are you sure he's dead?"

"Well, I believe he is, but no, I'm not sure. Let's you and me go find out." Cropper reached for her.

Cassandra looked at Rill and threw her small arms around his neck and said, "Thank you for stopping those mean horses, Rill." Then she turned away from him and fell into Cropper's waiting arms.

Juliana leaned against the wagon as they walked away. She was beginning to wonder if she would manage to remain standing until Cropper could get Cassandra out of sight. Juliana felt as if her legs were turning to water, and the sun suddenly felt unbearably hot.

"What was Cropper talking about? Where are you hurt?" Rill asked as he jumped down from the wagon and stood before her. His gaze flew up and down her body.

Her vision blurred. Suddenly, there were two Rills in front of her. She moistened her lips with her tongue and tried to swallow past a dry throat. The concern she saw in Rill's features made her feel better.

"The back of my shoulder. I think I must have hit something when I fell." She turned for him to see.

"Damn! Juliana, your shoulder is covered in blood. Why didn't you say something?"

"I didn't want Cassandra to know I was hurt. It would upset her even more than she already was."

"How do you think she would have felt if you'd fainted in front of her?"

Rill placed one arm gently around her shoulder and hooked his other arm behind her knees and lifted her into his arms.

"Rill, please," she protested, pushing at his strong, firm arms. "I'm not injured that badly. I can walk."

"Not right now, you can't. You look like you're ready to drop."

Juliana accepted his take-charge attitude and allowed herself to sink into his warm, comforting embrace as he carried her to the back of the wagon. With one hand, he untied the flaps of the canvas cover and helped her inside before climbing into the wagon behind her. He gently helped her to sit down on the wagon bed, then he settled on his knees behind her.

She immediately missed his strength. "How bad does it look?"

"I can't tell yet. Your blouse's torn, and the material has soaked up the blood. The wound might not be as bad as it looks. I don't think you're still bleeding. What in the hell happened?"

Letting her forehead drop into her palm, Juliana answered, "When the horses took off, the wagon jerked. I was standing up. I couldn't get my balance, so I fell. I think I hit something hard."

"And something sharp and jagged. No wonder you're so pale. You're going to have to take your blouse off so I can clean the wound."

She snapped her head around and looked into his eyes. "I—can't do that."

"Have you ever been to a doctor?" he asked, reaching inside the ox-hide trunk and pulling out a small wooden box and sliding it beside him.

"No. I've never been sick—or hurt."

"Well, now you are, so just pretend I'm a doctor. Unbutton your blouse."

A blush crept up Juliana's neck and flamed in her cheeks. "I can't just disrobe in front of you."

"Do you have undergarments on under your blouse?"

Juliana's throat felt like it was coated in trail dust. Her mouth was so dry she could hardly speak. "Of course, not that it's any of your business."

"Right now, keeping you and Cass safe is my business, remember. You made it so when you crawled into this wagon and hitched a ride."

"How could I not remember when you remind me so often?" she huffed. "You don't have to see to my arm. I can do it myself."

"No, you can't. Now, help me do my job. You're hurt. This isn't the time to argue or to be modest."

She saw in his eyes that he meant what he said and that relieved some of her fears. Juliana took a deep breath and relaxed, even though pain stabbed through her shoulder.

"That's better," he said. "I've patched up wounded drovers for years. I know what I'm doing."

"Does that mean you'll pretend I'm a man?"

His gaze caught hers, and he must have realized she was trying to make the best of a situation she didn't want to be in. He gave her a comforting smile. "No. That's pushing my doctoring abilities too far."

Rill reached into the trunk again and pulled out a

bottle of liquor. He popped the cork out and poured a generous amount into a tin cup. As she watched him, Juliana tried to unfasten the gold brooch at her throat, but couldn't. Her fingers were too cold, too trembly, and too uncertain of what was to come, to manage the task.

Still on his knees, Rill scooted around to face her. "Here, drink this. I'll unhook that thing for you."

She took the cup from him and peeked inside. The pungent smell almost took her breath away, and she pushed the cup from her. It was more than half full. Juliana raised her lashes and looked at him.

"It's the best whiskey made in Kentucky. Don't worry. It won't hurt you."

"What will it do to me?"

"If we're lucky, it'll help relax you so I can see how badly you're hurt."

Rill fiddled with the catch on the brooch. The knuckles of his fingers tickled the soft skin of her neck and under her chin, sending tremors of warmth flooding through her, warning her he was too close. Within a few seconds, he had the gold heart and square of lace off her blouse and he laid them aside.

"Drink," he ordered huskily.

Juliana put the cup to her lips. She had never sipped spirits before and wasn't sure what to expect. Auntie Vic had told her no employer would take kindly to a governess who indulged. The strong scent had her wrinkling her nose long before the amber liquid touched her lips. The liquor burned her tongue, flowed like liquid flames down her throat, and settled like hot coals in the pit of her stomach. She coughed and tears sprang to her eyes.

"Dear mercy, that's like drinking fire. It makes my throat and stomach burn worse than my shoulder."

"That's a natural reaction," he said, taking some clean white linen and two brown bottles out of the wooden medicine case.

Not sure she could speak if she wanted to, Juliana followed Rill's instructions and took another swallow. The whiskey burned as bad as the first time. Heat covered her body like a blanket, suddenly making it too warm inside the wagon.

She held the cup in one hand and sipped from it while with the other she tried unbuttoning the front of her blouse.

"Here, let me help you with that. You'll never get it off working those tiny buttons with one hand."

Rill pushed her hand aside and took over the task.

"I'm not going to hurt you," he said. "There's no reason to be nervous."

"I'm not," she lied, knowing a thrill of desire shooting through her as his deft fingers worked down her chest. Her abdomen constricted when the underside of Rill's wrists and the heels of his hands grazed the tips of her breasts as he passed over them. Juliana held her breath, wanting to prolong that wonderful feeling.

"Then why are you trembling, Juliana?" Rill asked as he cupped her chin with the tips of his fingers.

His voice lowered to a seductive pitch, and she knew she didn't need the liquor to make her forget the pain. Rill was all she needed.

Goose bumps peppered her skin. "I've never had a man ask me to undress before."

A devilish grin lifted one corner of his mouth. "As pretty as you are? I'm sure you've had your share of men wanting to take off your clothes whether or not they actually ever asked."

His words were provocative and intimate, but she felt no fear or embarrassment. Where were the alarm bells that should be going off, telling her that Rill was too close, too tempting, too compelling?

"I haven't been around many men. I've worked with children since I was seventeen."

"No gentlemen callers before then?"

"Auntie Vic forbade it."

"Nice woman," he said, his eyes conveying the message that he believed just the opposite to be true.

"Oh, you don't understand." Juliana hurried to defend Victoria's rule. "Auntie Vic was right not to allow beaus. I couldn't possibly do my job properly if I had someone other than my charge occupying my time or my thoughts."

He quirked a brow. "Is that what she told you?"

"Yes."

"And you wouldn't want me to argue with what she had to say, would you?"

"No."

"Because?"

"You'd be wrong."

His eyes locked with hers. For a moment, she thought she saw compassion in his eyes. Juliana didn't know how to make him understand how good it was of Auntie Vic to leave a job she dearly loved and make a home for Juliana so Victoria could train her to be a governess. Everyone respected her aunt's opinion and called upon her for advice long after she had retired. Juliana had seen many letters of recommendation that held her aunt in the highest regard.

When Rill reached the last button below her waist her blouse fell open, revealing the wide strap of her white corset cover.

Rill placed his hand over hers and slowly pushed the cup to her lips. She felt strength in his touch.

"Drink."

His command was so gentle that she obeyed without question, sipping the fiery liquid again. The warmth, the pressure of his hand against hers sent a feeling of contentment spiraling through her, making her forgive his disapproval of Victoria, making her forget there was a jabbing pain in her shoulder.

"That's better."

A buzzing sound filled her head. Juliana felt as if the wagon was moving, even though she knew they were standing still. Suddenly, all she wanted to do was close her eyes, lie back, and rest.

Juliana forced her eyes to stay open, and she watched Rill dig into his ox-hide chest again and pull out a buckled leather bag. He dumped the contents onto a clean white cloth. Scissors, ointments, salves, and small dark brown bottles fell out, along with a needle and a spool of black thread.

Juliana cringed, then stiffened.

"Here, take the cup in the other hand, and let me help you with this sleeve."

She hesitated.

"I know. Auntie Vic told you to never show a man your underclothes, right?"

He was very perceptive. She nodded.

"I think we've found something that your aunt and I agree on, but I can't help you if you don't take this off. Now, hold your arm down straight like this."

Realizing she had no choice, Juliana stretched out her limb. Rill pushed the blouse off her shoulder, down her arm, and peeled the garment away from her back.

"Damn," he whispered with a gusty breath for the second time.

"Is it bad?"

Rill scooted farther behind her. "It's not good." Without bothering to ask permission, he finished taking off her blouse and threw the soiled garment aside.

"What is it?" Juliana snapped her head around and threw her shoulder forward, trying to see her wound. "Mercy!" she cried out as pain sliced through her back.

"Careful," Rill said, laying an open palm on her naked arm to steady her. "You'll spread the wound open and make it start bleeding again. Don't make any sudden moves for the next couple of days."

"I don't think I'll have any trouble remembering that," she murmured.

"Looks like a rock caused a deep gash about three inches long across your shoulder blade." His eyes met hers. "I'm going to have to clean it—then sew it."

She blinked rapidly. Already, she was feeling the effects of the liquor. "Are you sure you have to stitch it?"

"I might take the chance it would heal properly, if you were a man. But your skin is too pretty to let the cut close without trying to even up the line."

"Will it hurt?"

"Like hell."

She took a deep breath and rubbed her forehead with a shaky hand. "Dear mercy. What am I going to do? I don't want Cassandra to see that I've been hurt. I'm afraid it will frighten her."

"If we're careful, she won't have to know anything about this. I'll wash your blouse and have Cropper mend it before we give it back to you."

"Oh, I couldn't possibly ask that of you. I can take care of it."

"You're not asking. I'm offering. Besides, you can't clean this without Cass seeing that it has a blood stain on it. We'll take care of it for you."

Her gaze went no farther than his arresting gray-brown eyes. "You and Cropper would do that for me?" It astonished her that he was willing to do such a menial task for her, and her heart went out to him.

"Between the two of us, there isn't much we haven't done."

Rill gave her a comforting smile that sent her heartbeat racing against her breathing. How could she have been so lucky as to crawl into this man's wagon? She knew *he* wasn't happy about it, but she was thrilled.

Juliana trembled slightly. She'd never been in such an intimate situation with a man before. She should feel uncomfortable and self-conscious sitting in front of Rill half-dressed, but she didn't. Surely, it wasn't natural for a lady to be so at ease in these circumstances.

If anyone had told her a week ago she would allow any man this kind of freedom, she would have sworn on Auntie Vic's grave that it couldn't happen. It must be the liquor making her feel relaxed. But there were other feelings inside her she knew she couldn't blame on the drink. Rill stirred her. She couldn't deny that she'd been drawn to him from the first time she saw him.

He picked up one of Cropper's tin buckets. "I'm going to get some water. I want that drink finished by the time I get back."

Juliana watched Rill crawl out of the wagon, then she let her shoulders droop. If only she'd been paying attention to Cassandra, none of this would have happened. She had spent too much time thinking about Rill and the way he was affecting her and not enough time seeing to Cass's needs.

She knew the rules. Auntie Vic had drilled them into her. Juliana had to deny these romantic feelings that Rill aroused in her and think only of keeping Cassandra safe. She couldn't help but wonder if her aunt had ever felt some of the feelings that were stirring inside her right now. And if Victoria had, how did she fight them?

Feeling too tired to think about Victoria, Juliana put the tin cup to her lips, then held her nose closed with the thumb and forefinger of her other hand and finished off the liquor without taking a breath. When she took the cup away, she let it fall to the floor of the wagon. She coughed and heaved as fumes of liquid heat escaped her lips.

An attractive chuckle of amusement came from the back of the wagon.

Juliana turned to see Rill standing in front of the opening, staring at her.

She wanted to snap at him that her shoulder was killing her. A buzzing sound filled her ears, and she felt like she had downed a whole cup of liquid fire, but all she could think of was how well laughter suited Rill's face, making a quiver of longing shudder through her.

9

Rill shoved the water bucket into the wagon and climbed inside. "I thought I'd seen liquor downed any way a man could do it," he said, "but I've never seen anyone hold his nose and gulp it like bad-tasting medicine."

Juliana blew out her breath. "It's not that it tastes bad, it's that it burns like a roaring fire, and I thought it might help if I didn't breathe in the scent." She pressed her hand to her chest and coughed.

"Did it?"

"No."

He knelt down beside her. "How is your shoulder feeling?" Rill took off his hat and laid it beside him on the wagon bed. He pulled a lantern from a wooden crate in the corner and lit it.

"I don't even feel it right now because my ears ring, my eyelids are heavy, and my stomach burns. Other than that, I'm in fine shape."

"Good. That means the liquor is working."

"I think it means if my wound doesn't kill me, the liquor will."

Rill chuckled again. "I'm glad you feel good enough to tease. That'll make my job a lot easier."

"Surely, you don't think I was teasing?"

Juliana gave him a bit of a smile, and it couldn't have affected him more if she'd thrown her arms around him and kissed him. Desire, hot and demanding, shot through him. Rill had to get hold of himself quick. For some reason, he was courting feelings toward Juliana. That would never do. He knew at that moment that he had to stop denying that he wanted Juliana and figure out a way to keep his hands off her.

He moved around her. His boots scrubbed and his spurs clinked on the wooden floor as he moved around to her back.

"No," he finally said and dipped a strip of cloth into the water. He touched the wet material to her wound. Juliana jerked and gasped. He wished he could take the pain for her as he gently washed the dried blood away from the wound.

"Keep your shoulder relaxed. I have to wipe away the dried blood so I can see what I'm doing."

"I know. I'll try."

Rill moved the lantern to where he could see the cut better. As the blood washed away he saw several scratches that should heal in a day or two without any problems. The jagged gash would take a week or more. Bruising and swelling had already started settling into the tender skin around the abrasion.

"The bleeding's stopped, but I still think we need to sew it up. The gash will heal faster and won't leave as bad a scar, but it's your decision."

"If stitching will make it get better faster, do it. And it might help keep down an infection."

"All right, we'll get started."

"I can't remember if I thanked you for saving Cassandra."

"You did."

"I don't know how I would have lived with myself if anything had happened to her."

It didn't surprise him to hear that even though Juliana had fallen off the wagon, she had run like the devil because her real concern was for Cass. Juliana probably wouldn't have let anyone know she was hurt if blood hadn't soaked through her blouse.

"I know I promised you we wouldn't be any trouble," she continued. "You have every right to be angry with me. I'll—"

"Don't, Juliana," Rill interrupted her. "You don't have to apologize. What happened was an accident."

"But, I—"

"But, nothing," he cut in. "If you want to lay blame, throw it on the horses. They're young, and the gunshot scared them, that's all."

Relief swept down her lovely face and relaxed her features. She looked as if she were about to thank him again so he quickly said, "And don't give me any more gratitude. I'm filled to here with it." He pointed to the air above his head.

"I wasn't going to. I only wanted to say that I intend to find a way to repay you for all that you're doing for Cassandra."

"We've already talked about payment, too. I don't want any, so don't mention that again, either."

He grunted as he shifted from his knees to sit on his rump, then crossed his legs in front of him. "You forget how small a wagon is until you start crawling around in one."

"You're not a small man."

Rill's skin tingled at her words. He remembered

when she'd told him he was a handsome man. It pleased him that she thought so.

He took hold of the wide strap of her undergarment and slipped it off her shoulder and down her arm. He was used to seeing women dressed in red and purple satin trimmed with black, scratchy lace. Juliana's white cotton camisole had no lace, bows, or satin trim, but on her it looked sexy as hell.

The yellow glow from the lantern made her skin glow. She had a lovely back, free of blemish or marks and perfectly feminine in shape. He loved the look of her slender neck, softly rounded shoulders, and indented waist. This was going to be harder than he had thought.

"I'm going to rub a decoction around the wound."

"What is it?"

"A powder that's made from the purple coneflower. Indian shamans used to crush the root, rub it all over their hands, then stick them in boiling water to impress their tribesmen."

"I guess that means it works?"

"It will numb the outside skin, but nothing's going to keep you from feeling the needle go in."

"I promise not to scream, if you're worried that I might."

Her voice reflected the fact that the liquor was taking effect. "I'm not worried, and you don't need to be, either," he said calmly. "I've been sewing up drovers for ten years. I'll make this as painless as possible."

She turned her head again and looked over her shoulder into his eyes. "I trust you."

Those three words sent Rill's confidence soaring, yet left him feeling queer and out of sorts with himself. He'd never wanted to get involved with a woman—until Juliana.

Where were all these notions of hearth, home, and family coming from? Even when he had decided to buy the ranch and settle down, he'd resisted the natural instinct of thinking about a wife to take care of his home and keep him satisfied at night. He didn't want those kinds of entanglements. He'd always told his brothers he wasn't ever going to settle down. And he used to mean it. Juliana was making him rethink too many things.

Rill remained quiet with his thoughts as he rubbed the compound onto her soft, scratched skin, then quickly threaded the needle.

Juliana gasped at the pricking pain, and her hands curled into tight fists. He was being careful, but he knew pulling and tugging the edges of the wound together hurt like the devil.

"Would it help if I gave you something to bite on?"

"No," she whispered. "Just do it as fast as you can. I want this over with so I can redress. Cassandra could return at any minute now."

"Don't worry about her. Cropper will keep her busy until he knows we're through."

Juliana's muscles tightened and she flinched every time he pulled the skin together. Wishing he could take the pain for her didn't make him feel any better. Like her, he just wanted it over with.

It was warm inside the wagon but not hot. Cropper's and Cassandra's voices had drifted out of earshot some time ago, leaving only the sounds of the wind blowing across the quiet prairie, snorts from the horses, and an occasional muffled gasp from Juliana.

"Tell me about your family," she said from between clenched teeth. "Maybe it will help keep my mind off what you're doing if we talk."

"Not much to tell," he said. "I grew up on a good-sized spread in the middle of Texas. The youngest of three boys."

"Where are your brothers? Still in Texas?"

"Parents, too. Older brother Web lives at the ranch and brother Clay has his own spread a few miles away."

"How do they feel about you buying a ranch in a place as far away as the Wyoming Territory?"

"They're all right about it."

"Even your mother? I'd think she'd miss you terribly."

"She understands I've always done things differently from my brothers. Besides, Web and Clay are close by."

"How often do you see your family?"

"Usually after every trail drive."

"But not this year."

She was perceptive. "That's right."

"Why didn't you want to buy land near your family in Texas?"

Rill's hands stilled for a second or two as he remembered the argument he'd had with his oldest brother the last time he'd been home. "Sometimes it's better not to live at your family's back door."

"You get along with them, don't you?"

"Most of the time, except for my oldest brother, Web," he answered truthfully.

"And why is that?"

Rill chuckled lightly. "If I didn't know better, I'd think you got hurt just so you could find out anything you wanted to about me. How's the pain?"

"Bearable."

"It should start feeling better when I finish. Tugging and stretching the skin is what makes it hurt."

"Why don't you get along with Web?"

"I thought we'd left that subject."

"You did. I didn't."

"Mmm—well, then I must have had a reason, don't you think?"

"Probably a good one. What was it?"

He chuckled at her insistence, and there was something about her that made him want to talk to her. "Big brother has a bad habit of treating me like I'm still seventeen and leaving home to go on my first cattle drive."

"Sounds to me like he loves you."

"Yeah, well, it feels like control."

"I take it he wanted you to stay on the ranch with him."

"And marry the woman he picked out for me."

"But you couldn't do that."

"No. I saw how he manipulated Clay, and I refused to let that happen to me."

"Is Web the reason you stayed away from home and on the trail so long?"

"No. I actually liked the challenge of the drive." He paused. "That is, until this last one."

"What happened to make it different?"

"Nothing I want to talk about."

"Why's that?"

Because it's too painful. "Some things are best left unsaid."

"Doesn't change what happened not to talk about it, does it?"

"No, but talking makes it harder to forget. There, that's the last stitch," he said, tying a knot in the black thread.

She let out a deep breath. "Thank God. I was beginning to wonder if I was going to make it."

"Me, too," he said, realizing if they had kept talking how easy it would have been for him to spill his guts to her about Stedman killing his men and stealing his herd.

Juliana slowly moved her arm back and forth. "It feels tight—like a dull ache."

"It will for a few days," he answered, thankful she'd let her questions about the cattle drive drop.

Rill opened a small brown bottle and shook a pinch of dried brown powder into the palm of his hand. He moistened it with a drop of water from his fingertip and mixed the compound, then rubbed it onto her wound.

"What is that?" she asked.

"Crushed root of an unidentified herb. This should help take the soreness out and keep down infection. I should check the wound again in a couple of days to make sure it's healing. We'll take the stitches out in a week or so, depending on how it heals."

"All right."

Juliana looked over her shoulder at him. Their eyes met, and Rill felt a stirring deep within him. He picked up a cloth and wiped his hands.

She scooted around on her buttocks so that she faced him.

"It's going to be difficult to bandage the wound because of where it is on your shoulder. It's too high to wrap the cloth under your arm."

"I have—an undergarment I can wear that will cover the stitches to keep my clothes from rubbing it."

"That'll work," he said, unable to stop staring at her.

One strap hung off her shoulder, the slight swell of her breasts rose out of the confines of her white undergarments. The prim, square neckline accented her innocence. The camisole she wore buttoned up the front the same way her blouse had.

Rill suddenly had such a desperate urge to unfasten her cover and look at her.

He swallowed hard. Over the years, he'd seen women in all stages of undress, but he couldn't ever remember being as awestruck as he was with Juliana's beauty and poise. Did she know how beautiful she was even with smudges of dirt on her cheek and blades of grass tangled in her hair?

But Rill wasn't fooling himself. It wasn't just her loveliness that drew him. He was also attracted to her determination, her strength, and her protectiveness of the child in her possession. Cassandra's welfare was always her first concern.

Looking at Juliana now, he realized that her innocence made him want to protect her from himself. Fear that he could hurt her made him wonder if she knew what a dangerous situation they were in. How could she know that he wasn't used to denying himself any woman he wanted?

And Rill wanted Juliana.

"Is something wrong? You're staring at me."

He pulled on the knot of his kerchief. It was too damn hot in the wagon. "I was just thinking you're the most beautiful woman I've ever seen."

Her eyes didn't waver from his. "That's kind of you to say, but surely in Kansas City you saw women more comely to look at than I am."

Rill's gaze lingered on Juliana's face before sweeping farther down her neck. "No. What I said is the truth. Your eyes sparkle like the bluest sky in the heart of summer. You have nice skin. White. Soft. Perfectly rounded shoulders."

Her long, velvet lashes fluttered like butterfly wings in flight.

All of a sudden, Juliana reached up and kissed him

on the cheek, letting her pink lips linger against his skin. Her liquor-flavored breath fanned his face, enticing him. The fragrance of this woman filled him and made his blood sing with an urgency to mate with her. His lower body instantly responded to her innocent advance.

Rill was stunned. The brevity, the chasteness of that one unsolicited kiss hit him so hard his trousers pinched. He couldn't remember a woman ever kissing his cheek in such a casual, intimate way.

Slowly, she moved away.

"What was that for?" He realized his voice sounded more husky, more seductive, more hungry than he intended, but Juliana had him reeling.

"For taking care of me and Cassandra. For all you've done for us. You won't let me say thank you, so I'll have to show my appreciation."

"Is that all the kiss was? Gratitude?" He was baiting her but he couldn't stop himself.

"No." Her voice was whispery soft.

"What else?" He wanted to hear her say it.

"I wanted to kiss you."

Rill tensed at her admission. She moistened her lips, and Rill thought he'd go crazy with wanting to touch her, but still he hesitated.

Juliana was under his care. She was hurt. She'd just finished four ounces of eighty-proof whiskey. He knew the liquor could be motivating her initiative. He should leave her alone. He knew all this—but—Rill couldn't deny himself this chance alone with her to see where that first unprovoked kiss might take them.

Following her lead, Rill reached over and kissed her lightly on the soft skin of her neck just under her jawline, where he could feel the frantic beat of her pulse against his lips. He heard her intake of breath. He strained to hold himself in check. Instinct told him she was receptive to him, and that aroused him more.

There were no sounds to disturb what was happening between them. There were only the two of them in the wagon, on the vast Kansas prairie.

Rill lifted his head and stared into her eyes. She smiled, reached out her hand, and cupped the side of his face. Her touch was gentle, warm, tempting him as no other woman ever had.

Keeping with her slow manner, he covered her hand with his and turned his nose into her palm and breathed in deeply, filling himself with her essence. He planted a wet kiss in the center of her hand. As she gently slid her fingers through his, Rill stuck out his tongue and laved the soft skin.

Her choppy gasp thrilled him, excited him.

"Do I need to shave?" he asked. He knew it was a stupid, inane thing to say, but Juliana had him feeling as limber as a tall blade of Turkey Red wheat.

"No. I like the way you feel."

Not allowing his gaze to leave hers, Rill placed an open palm on the front of her naked chest where his fingertips caressed the hollow of her throat, and the heel of his palm rested on the crest of her breasts.

Damn, he wanted her. Now.

Rill gently clasped her upper arms and pulled her up against him. She was too close, too receptive, for him not to take advantage of the opportunity to kiss her. He lowered his head and captured her lips with his, pressing softly.

Within a second, he realized she didn't know how to kiss. The thought that no other lips had touched hers sent a rush of pride spiraling through him like lightning through a dead tree. He was so hot and ready for her he ached. He wanted to lay her down on the pallet and love her. Making her his for the night was dangerous, crazy, but how could he deny himself or her when they were so attuned to each other?

He'd never been with a virgin. Wasn't it time he made love to a woman as sweet and innocent as Juliana?

His lower body responded quickly to his thoughts, urging him to take the lead and teach her everything he knew about loving.

He raised his head only a little and stared into eyes bright with wonder. "Have you ever been kissed?"

"Once, but it wasn't a real kiss."

"Do you want to learn how?"

She nodded.

"Is your shoulder hurting?"

She shook her head.

"Open your mouth like this, and follow what I do."

He sought her sweet mouth with his and moaned softly with pleasure at the faint taste of liquor. He coached her with his lips and his tongue, teaching her to give and accept the intimate caressing of a passionate kiss.

She learned quickly and moved her lips seductively against his.

Rill grew harder. His breathing became gusty breaths of passion.

His hands slowly skimmed down each side of her neck, glided across the top of her shoulders and drifted over her arms, steering clear of her injured back. Her flesh pebbled with goose bumps, letting him know that she felt the same way he did. Her skin was warm and heavenly soft to his callused touch.

Juliana leaned into the kiss and laid her arm against his chest. His muscles tightened beneath her touch. Her breasts pressed against him. The fires of desire soared through him like flames through parched grass.

He deepened their kiss and she responded, matching him desire for desire, heat for heat, and passion for passion.

He wanted Juliana.

She responded with such fervor Rill thought he was going to lose the tight control he had on his body.

He couldn't taste her enough, he couldn't touch her enough, he couldn't love her enough. His mind and his body were demanding that he do what came naturally and bury himself deep within her without delay.

"Oh God, you're the most beautiful woman I've ever touched," he mumbled into the depth of her sweet mouth.

"I've never felt this way before," she answered, not allowing her lips to leave his.

"Me, either."

"I hope it doesn't go away."

"Hell, no," he whispered. "I won't let it."

"Is kissing always this wonderful?"

"No, Juliana," he murmured, "it's never been this good."

The purely masculine sensations she created inside him had never been so alive, so compelling. He had never been so caught up by desire for a woman that he couldn't think of anything but loving her.

Heat covered him like a soothing blanket. He slipped his hand down to her breast but was barred access to her softness by the crisp cotton of her camisole and the firm stays of her corset.

The barrier sobered Rill. He wanted Juliana, but not this way. Not when she'd been hurt and not when she had just enough liquor in her to lose her inhibitions. When he made love to her, he wanted her to know exactly what she was doing and exactly what he was doing to her.

Slowly, Rill raised his head and looked into her eyes.

She smiled.

He smiled. "I'd like to continue what we're doing, but I'm not going to."

Her lips relaxed and her lashes fluttered. She pushed her damp hair away from her forehead.

Rill took hold of her hand and said, "Juliana. Don't be embarrassed by our kiss."

She searched his face. "I'm not. I agree, it's best that we stopped when we did."

He nodded. *For you. Not for me.*

"Do you want me to help you dress?"

"No. I can do it. I'd feel better if you checked on Cassandra and Cropper."

"All right. Take your time. I want you to lie down and rest until we make camp."

"Oh, I can't do that. I need to spend some time with Cassandra."

"She's fine. You're not." He pointed a finger at her and said, "No arguments. If I see you come out of here before Cropper calls supper, I'll pick you up and put you back inside. Besides, you'll get over the side effects of the liquor quicker if you sleep for a couple of hours."

She sighed. "All right. Maybe I can get rid of this fuzziness in my head if I lie down for a while."

He gave her a cocky smile. "I like a woman who sees things my way." Rill picked up her blouse. "I'll take care of this and get it back to you."

He pushed the canvas flap aside and eased down the step, his lower body throbbing with each movement, from not finishing what they had started. He leaned against the side of the wagon to let his ache subside.

Rill had made love to every kind of woman—

except a woman like Juliana. He'd been with women who hated sex, women who loved it, and those who could care less about it as long as they were paid. He'd been with women who had ridden him all night and still wanted more. He'd been with those who wanted to please him and those who wanted him to please them. But, he'd never been with a woman he hadn't paid, and he'd never been with a woman who hadn't lain with a dozen or more men before him.

Juliana. He sang her name in his mind. Everything about her was different, from the way she dressed, talked, and acted to the way she smelled of lilacs.

He'd wanted to take his time undressing her. He'd wanted to gaze at her beautiful body. He'd wanted to touch her breasts and kiss the hollow of her stomach. He'd wanted to take his time and savor her.

Rill almost laughed out loud. What was he doing thinking about a word like savor? And what did he know about the scent of lilacs? He was thirty years old and had been on the trail for thirteen years. What was happening to him? Was he going soft? That was how Juliana affected him. She had him thinking about courting, which was something else he had never done.

It wasn't like him to be so attracted to a woman. He'd gotten over wanting to bed every tempting woman he saw, years ago. Now when he went into town, he was a bit choosier than he used to be. He still had all the deep desires for a woman but he tempered them now.

He never took the time to get to know any woman that he'd bedded, wanting only sexual relief. There was no reason to ask more than a name. Maybe one day he would have shown an interest in one of the eligible young ladies in his hometown, if Web hadn't ordered him to leave the trail, find a wife, and settle down.

Rill wanted to court Juliana. He wanted to bring her flowers, tease her, laugh with her. He wanted to sit by the fire with her, hold her hand, and stare into her eyes. He wanted to protect her and have her for his own. For the first time in his life, he wanted more than a quick poke from a woman. He knew at that moment he had to stop denying that he wanted Juliana and figure out a way to keep his hands off her.

I am going soft!

For the first time in his life, he was thinking about caring for a woman. And, not just any woman would do, as had always been the case before. Rill wanted Juliana.

Only Juliana.

A feeling that had hitherto been foreign to Rill welled up inside him as he headed for Doc. He recognized it, and the thought of that elusive, dangerous emotion scared the hell out of him. *Love.*

Could he be falling in love with Juliana?

❧ 10 ❧

Sounds of talking and laughter awakened Juliana and she smiled, thinking how nice it was to hear Cassandra's youthful glee, Cropper's amusing laugh, and Rill's throaty chuckle wafting on the air the first thing in the morning.

Juliana rolled, stretched her arms over her head, and winced. There was a deep throbbing ache in the back of her shoulder. Her eyes popped open. The soft hues of late-afternoon sunshine spilled through the canvas of the wagon, not the white light of early morning sun. Juliana raised on her elbow and saw the medicine box at her feet.

She sat upright as she remembered what had happened to cause the pain in her shoulder and what had happened between her and Rill in the wagon. Her face flushed with heat. Her first thought was that the passionate embrace she'd shared with Rill should have never taken place, and she had to see that it wouldn't happen again. But it was her second thought that caught her attention.

I want it to happen again!

Her eyes closed. A flood of remembrance washed over Juliana. She placed her fingertips to her lips and pressed gently. She slipped the palm of her hand up to her nose and breathed in, remembering Rill's manly scent. She inhaled deeply, then kissed the palm of her hand as all the sensations that Rill had created in her surfaced in her mind. How could Rill's touch have stirred such a tidal wave of desire rushing inside her?

What were these new feelings she was having all about?

Cassandra's shrill laughter startled Juliana, and her lashes popped up. She shook her head to clear her thoughts from Rill. The last thing she remembered was that Rill insisted she rest while they rode to where they would make camp for the night. Obviously, she'd slept through the entire ride.

Juliana rose and dressed in her only other change of clothes. She hurriedly repaired her hairdo and straightened the things in the wagon. She had caught herself thinking about Rill too many times, but wondered how she could stop when his kisses had opened up a brand-new world for her.

When Juliana stepped down from the wagon she saw Rill, Cropper, and Cassandra sitting by the campfire. A round silvery moon hung in the dark blue sky in the distance behind them as twilight ebbed out the last rays of the sunset. Clouds stayed at bay, and only the brightest stars in the heavens had appeared. The early evening air was pleasant and as warm as a midsummer breeze.

"There you are! We've been waiting for you," Cassandra exclaimed, running over to Juliana and throwing her small arms around Juliana's waist. "I didn't think you were going to ever wake up."

"That's your fault, sweetheart," Juliana said, hugging Cassandra to her, loving the comfort the little girl gave her. "Why didn't you wake me?"

She looked up at Juliana and pouted prettily. "Rill wouldn't let me. He said you were tired from running after the wagon, and I should let you sleep."

Juliana glanced over at Rill. His gaze caressed her face with a light sweeping glance. A tremor shook her. God help her, she wanted Rill to kiss her again and again. She had no doubt she and Cassandra were safe with Rill, but now she worried that her heart would not come out of this journey unscathed.

"Come on," Cassandra said, taking her hand and leading her over to the campfire. "We've already eaten. Cropper has your dinner waiting, and I helped him cook it."

"Did you? What do we have?" She forced her gaze off Rill and gave her attention to Cass.

"Rabbit stew and it's delicious, even with beans in it."

"In that case, I must have some."

Juliana looked at Cropper as she sat down on the blanket opposite him and Rill. She was careful not to use her injured arm for support. So far, Cassandra had no idea Juliana had been hurt, and she wanted to keep it that way.

She continued to look at Cropper. "Someone really should have awakened me."

"No need to," Cropper said and dipped a ladle into the cast-iron pot sitting on a bed of coals. "We didn't need you to do anything."

"I'm sure you took care of everything, but I slept so long, I'll probably have trouble sleeping tonight."

"Just let me know if you do, and I'll play my harmonica for you," Cropper said. "I know a tune that puts the cattle to sleep in no time at all. I bet it will work for you, too."

She smiled. "Thank you. I'll keep that in mind."

Cropper handed her a tin plate, and over his shoulder she caught a glimpse of Rill watching her. Their eyes met, and wicked pleasure shot through her. He smiled at her. Heat flooded her cheeks. She wondered if he noticed that her hands shook. She wondered if his smile meant that he remembered, like her, every detail of their passionate embrace.

Of course not, a soft voice from inside her head admonished her. *No doubt Rill has kissed many women, and you have kissed only one man.*

"Are you feeling better?" Cassandra asked.

"Oh, yes, I'm quite fine," Juliana answered before tasting the delicious hot meal.

"You're not angry with me for playing with the brake handle after you told me not to, are you?"

Juliana wrinkled her brow and pretended to think about the question before saying, "We talked about how you need to obey me, didn't we?"

Cassandra nodded slowly.

"Do you think you've learned your lesson and now understand how dangerous it can be when you don't mind what I say?"

"I won't disobey you again."

She gave Cassandra a serious look. "All right, but should you forget, there will have to be a punishment next time."

"I won't forget," she answered solemnly, then quickly said in a brighter voice, "Did you know I helped Cropper skin the rabbit?"

Juliana sat straighter on the blanket and glanced at Cropper, knowing that Cassandra shouldn't have even seen the dead rabbit, let alone be anywhere near when he was preparing the rabbit for dinner.

Cropper shrugged his shoulders innocently, then looked away.

"No, of course I didn't know. I was asleep, remember." She took another bite of the stew.

"I bet you didn't know that the first cut with the knife is made across the back of the neck like this so most of the blood will run out." Cassandra made a slicing motion with her hand.

Juliana's stomach quaked. She held her breath for a moment. Suddenly, the juicy hunks of rabbit in the thick red bean stew didn't have the same appeal as when she had taken her first bite. She wiped the corners of her mouth with her fingertips. Her eyes drifted over to Rill. She could see he was holding back laughter.

"You're right, I didn't know that," Juliana managed to say after a couple of deep breaths.

"The next place Cropper cut was down the center of the rabbit's belly, and all the guts and—"

"Cassandra!" Juliana interrupted sharply. "Hearing how an animal is prepared is not something we want to know about while we are eating."

Cassandra stared up at Juliana with expressive, innocent brown eyes. "Why?"

"Because it takes away the appetite." She cut her eyes around to Cropper. "And you're much too young to have participated. After we reach your grandfather's house, you're not likely to ever have to prepare your own food and certainly not to such an extent."

Cropper started whistling. Apparently he didn't want to be lectured to.

Rill cleared his throat and rose. "I'm going down to the stream. I'll be back later."

Cassandra jumped up and ran over to Rill, taking hold of his hand. "I want to go with you."

"Can you swim?" Rill asked.

She looked at Juliana, frowned, then turned back to Rill. "I can learn fast. Tell him I can, Juliana."

Rill chuckled, and Juliana was struck again at how well laughter suited his face, how attractive and how approachable it made him seem.

"Not on this trip," Rill spoke before Juliana had the chance. "Some other time."

Cassandra stomped her foot. "But I want to go. You have to take me."

"Is that so? Why?"

"Because I'm young, and I'm supposed to get whatever I want."

"Does Juliana always let you have your way?"

Cassandra glanced at Juliana. "No, but she's different."

"So am I. If you can't swim, you can't go near the water, young lady," he said firmly.

"He's right, Cassandra," Juliana agreed, her gaze fixed on Rill's face. "It's too dangerous."

Rill cupped her chin. "Now be good for Juliana, and I'll take you for a ride on Doc tomorrow."

"Do you promise?" Cassandra's eyes shone like sunshine on water.

"You bet." Rill looked at Juliana again before turning away.

Juliana's heart thudded like the well-oiled machinery of a lumber mill. All Rill had to do was look her way, and she felt light-headed. The kiss had changed everything. She was more aware of him than ever. She wanted to ride with him on Doc again, too. She wanted to be caught up in those strong arms again and held close. She had to do something to hide what she was feeling before Rill recognized the fact that he was winning her heart.

Cassandra folded her arms across her chest and

stood before Juliana like a soldier staring at a weak opponent. "Show me how to swim so I can go with Rill next time."

It amazed Juliana at how quickly Cassandra's moods could change. One moment she was a sweet, dear child, and the next she was ordering Juliana around as if she were a common servant.

"I can't because I don't know how. Besides, I'm sure it's not something that you can learn quickly. Isn't that right, Cropper?"

"It'd take more than a time or two of jumping in the water for a young one like you, I'd expect."

"You teach me," said Cassandra, turning to the old man.

He scratched the back of his neck and shook his head. "I don't think that'd be the proper thing to do."

"And I agree," Juliana said. "But it's something we can surely talk to your grandfather about when we see him. You do need to learn how to swim."

Cassandra huffed and flopped down beside Juliana again. "I don't know if Grandpapa Rakefield will like me any better than Papa Ward. He might send me to my room all the time, too."

Juliana set the bowl aside. "Of course he will like you. He is your father's father. He will love you and spend a great deal of time with you like Cropper does." She looked up at the older man and asked for confirmation with her eyes.

"You bet he will," Cropper agreed. "And if he don't, you tell me, and I'll have a talk with him and explain everything to him."

"Do you promise?" she asked.

"'Course I will. Now come over here, Cass," Cropper said, pulling his harmonica out of his pocket. "It's time for your music lesson."

Cassandra's eyes brightened again. She jumped up and hurried over to him.

Juliana took one look at the child and the man huddled together and wished with all her heart that Thomas Rakefield would make Cassandra a good grandfather. Too many bad things had happened in her life.

"Listen to this," Cassandra said.

Juliana rose. Twilight had fallen on the camp. She had to admit she felt better now that she had rested for a couple of hours and had eaten. There was a constant ache in her shoulder but it was bearable.

"I think I'll take a walk and stretch my legs," she announced.

"Didn't you like the stew?" Cassandra asked. "You didn't finish it."

"Oh, yes, it was very good. When I come back, I'll expect you to play a song for me. All right?"

"I will."

"Good."

Juliana swore to herself that it wasn't intentional that she walked toward the stream, but she didn't turn the other way when she saw Rill, shirtless, sitting on the short grass in front of the water taking off his boots.

Several stunted willows lined banks that were surrounded by plum bushes and sloughgrass. Darkness continued to edge out twilight, and a scattering of bright stars appeared in the deep purple sky.

Rill turned around as she approached. He rose and walked to meet her. His bare feet made no sound on the ground.

"I had a feeling it was you coming up behind me."

A shiver of pleasure momentarily distracted her. "Did you hear me?" she asked.

He stopped in front of her and peered down into her eyes. "No. I felt your presence. How's the shoulder?"

The muscles in Rill's upper arms and chest bulged with the firmness of a ripe apple. His wide shoulders tapered to a slim waist and slender hips that were barely hidden by dark brown trousers.

"Sore, but I'm sure it will be better by morning." She tried to force her eyes away from him but she couldn't. The sight of his body gave her too much pleasure to deny herself the looking at him.

A burnished fire glowed in his eyes. "Did you come down here for a particular reason?"

His question took her by surprise. "I—I wanted to get away from—I mean Cassandra does better with her music lesson if I'm not around."

Rill chuckled. "I think she's too young to learn to play that thing but Cropper won't give up. Anyway, I'm glad you decided to follow me."

"While we have a moment alone, I should tell you that I—well—I don't plan to repeat what happened this afternoon."

"Look, it wasn't your fault. It was an accident. It's not like you left Cass alone in the wagon. And I don't want to hear about it again."

Her lashes slowly blinked. Juliana cleared her dry throat and wondered if she should continue. Yes, to get this over with. "I'm not talking about the accident. I'm talking about the kiss. Between you and me."

Humor lit in his eyes, and he nodded as he continued to stare down into her eyes. "Oh, *that* kiss."

She ignored his teasing, realizing this was a serious matter. "It's my fault. I realize I started the—the whole thing when I kissed you on the cheek. I shouldn't have done that."

"I didn't know what happened was something we had to assess blame to."

"No, of course not."

"I rather liked it."

Should she admit she enjoyed the kiss, too? She took a deep breath and tried to glance past him into the surrounding darkness, but how could she not look at him when she was so acutely aware of him? "I also wanted you to know I don't make a habit of going around kissing men."

"You told me that already."

He took a step closer to her, putting his wide expanse of chest in front of her face. Even though he didn't touch her, she felt his power.

"Oh—well—it must have been the liquor I drank. I can't think of anything else that would have made me behave in such a loose manner."

"That right?" he asked.

He moved still closer, his gaze sweeping up and down her face, causing her heart to flutter crazily. The wind blew his brown hair away from his forehead, and all she could think of was that she wanted him to kiss her again.

Her breathing became erratic. He did crazy things to her senses. "Yes. You believe it too, don't you? That's the only possible answer to why I kissed you."

"And why you enjoyed it?"

"Yes."

"No."

Juliana was startled. She hadn't expected him to disagree with her. "Why?"

"I wasn't drinking, and I kissed you." He paused. "And I enjoyed it very much."

"Yes, but you are a man."

"What does that have to do with it?"

She moistened her lips. She shouldn't have allowed

herself to start this conversation but she hadn't been able to stop herself. The truth was that she wanted to spend time with him no matter what they talked about.

"Auntie Vic told me that men have certain—urges and needs that ladies don't have."

One corner of his mouth lifted in a slight grin. "Your aunt told you that, did she?"

"Yes."

"The one that knew everything, right?"

"Yes."

"And properly brought-up young ladies like you aren't supposed to feel the way you felt when I kissed you today, so it must have been the liquor I gave you, which your aunt told you not to drink."

She sighed. Thank God he understood. Now she felt better about the whole incident. She relaxed. "Yes, that's right."

"So what all this means is that you enjoyed the kiss even though you weren't supposed to."

"Oh, very much—I mean—" Her lashes fluttered, and she cleared her throat again and lifted her chin. "It was a pleasant experience."

"And the liquor caused it all?"

"Oh, indeed," she answered, feeling vindicated.

Rill rubbed his chin thoughtfully. "Let's see." Suddenly, he gently grabbed Juliana around the waist and swung her up to his bare chest, lifting her onto her toes. He swooped his head down to hers and captured her lips with his.

Stunned, Juliana closed her hands around the firm muscles of Rill's upper arms and pushed, trying to squirm away from his forceful hold. But the gentle pressure of Rill's lips and the heat of his body fused with hers, tempted her, weakened her insignificant struggle. The feel of his bare skin beneath her hands stopped her. Instead of pushing him away, her hands slid up his bare, muscular chest, over his broad shoulders, and ran down the corded muscles of his back. Her fingers caressed and kneaded his firm skin.

Desire built and flared inside her without warning. Juliana melted into Rill's embrace. Her hands touched, stroked, planed over the angle of his shoulders and the ridges of his spine with a freedom she'd never experienced before.

"Am I hurting your shoulder?" he asked without letting his lips leave hers.

"Not when you touch me like this."

She opened her mouth to accept his tongue and to give her own. Her lips matched his, movement for movement. She felt as if her feet had left the ground and she floated on air. She closed her eyes and pressed and molded the length of her body to his. She moaned from the sheer pleasure of Rill—being in his arms, kissing him.

All of a sudden, Rill turned her loose and stepped back. Bereft, she reached for him, but touched only air. Her lashes flew up, and she looked into his pleasing face.

He gave her a knowing smile. "Now tell me the truth, Juliana? Did the liquor cause your response to my kisses this afternoon?"

"I thought so."

"If that's true, what made you respond to me just now? It's been at least four hours since you drank the whiskey."

She stood there, caught up in her frustration, then let out an audible breath. His touch lingered on her skin. She'd never felt such wanting. *Mercy!* He was right. The strong drink hadn't drugged her. Rill's kisses had, and she no longer wanted to deny it.

"I'm afraid that I'm attracted to you."

"And you think that's bad?"

Juliana nodded.

"Why?"

"Auntie Vic—"

"Didn't know everything," he cut in.

"I have to disagree with that."

"Tell me, was she ever married?"

"No."

"Then don't trust anything she ever had to say about men."

Juliana stiffened. "Victoria was the most respected governess in Chicago. She never had one blemish on her character. Many people sought her opinion about proper behavior."

"Maybe about children, and keeping house, but I doubt very many women asked an old maid about men."

Juliana clutched her skirt with tight fists. How dare he? She'd never heard anyone say anything disrespectful about her aunt. "You—you don't know anything about her, so I suggest you not try to advise me about her."

His eyes softened, his voice lowered. "You're right about that, but I'm beginning to know you. I admire your loyalty to your aunt, even though I think she was wrong on some things. She obviously taught you a lot of good things you needed to know. But trust your own feelings when it comes to men, Juliana. Live your own life. Not Victoria's."

Not trust what Auntie Vic said? Rill was crazy to suggest such a thing. How could she forsake the teachings of the woman who gave up her job to take care of an orphan girl with a meager inheritance?

Juliana shook with the need to prove him wrong and banish his words from her mind. "You are the one who is wrong. You are trying to make me forget all that I've been taught."

"No. I'm trying to make you see that you're as good a governess as your aunt and that there's nothing wrong with enjoying my kisses."

She gasped, outraged by his suggestion that she was equal to Auntie Vic in any way. She wasn't. She'd failed miserably. And how could Rill think her aunt had been wrong about men? Victoria had never been wrong.

"Juliana, where are you?" Cassandra called.

"Excuse me." Trembling, Juliana pivoted away in frustration and fled to camp, feeling as if, for the first time, her armor had been pierced.

What kind of woman was she? She couldn't deny that she felt like a different person when she was in Rill's embrace, but she couldn't ignore her aunt's teachings, either.

A lump formed in Juliana's throat. She was angry with herself. Deep inside a hidden part of her heart, she desperately wanted Rill's words to be true and not Victoria's.

❧ 11 ❧

Stars were fading, and the first pink streaks of early morning broke across a dark sky that seemed to stretch forever as Rill held a long match to dry kindling. Once the sun came up, daybreak would spread quickly over the prairie with no hills or mountains to block the light.

They were more than halfway into the second week of their journey across Kansas. He'd pushed hard for Cropper and the wagon team to cover ground. They started early each morning, stopping only twice, and traveled until late in the day. At the rate they were covering ground, Rill thought they just might make his goal of shaving off a week of traveling time.

Occasionally during the day, they'd pass near a soddy with a few head of cattle grazing nearby and a patch of corn or wheat on either side of the small windowless house. The old Pony Express route sometimes took them by abandoned relay stations, but for most of the day, all Rill saw was dry, endless land covered in short clumpy grasses and skies such a bright shade of blue it hurt his eyes to look at them.

One of the things Rill disliked about Kansas was the lack of trees. The land was so flat and barren that there were few places a man could find privacy. One of the things he liked about the state was that there was always a breeze. The wind blew incessantly, keeping him cool during the day when the sun heated his skin and lulling him to sleep at night with a low moan as it swept across the plains.

Flames caught the wood, and a twist of blue-white smoke spiraled upward into the semidarkness.

He breathed in deeply the scent of burned wood. This was their first cool morning. During the night, a chill had moved in and settled into the area, leaving behind a light frost on the ground. Rill pulled the front panels of his deerskin jacket together, then warmed his hands over the low burning fire. The flickering flames licked at the air and struggled to stay bright as the wind whipped them.

Rill pondered as he stared into the depths of the fire. Since their passionate embrace in the wagon several days ago, Rill had stayed away from Juliana, and she'd been unnecessarily polite toward him. He knew she was upset with him.

When he'd taken the stitches out of Juliana's shoulder last night, he'd been tempted to apologize for what he'd said about her Auntie Vic, but he couldn't bring himself to do it—because he was right.

For some reason, Juliana wanted to stay sheltered in the shadow of her aunt.

Over the last week they'd traveled, he'd been bothered by the fatherly emotions he'd developed for Cass, and by the loving desire he had for Juliana. They were working their way into his life. He'd tried to deny it. Now he realized he'd move heaven and earth to keep them safe.

Love. It still scared him to think about settling down with one woman and taking care of her for the rest of his life, but Juliana had him thinking that way. For the first time in his life, he was thinking about falling in love and taking a wife, but how did Juliana feel about him?

He had to put what had happened on his last trail behind him, and not let it control the rest of his life. Thinking he could run away from what had happened to his trail hands and his herd had been foolish. Stedman was dead. Now it was time for Rill to bury the past and get on with his life.

After they delivered Cass to her grandfather, then he would make Juliana see that her aunt was wrong. Juliana was meant to be a wife taking care of her own family, not a governess looking after someone else's children.

Cropper eased from the shadows of darkness, yawning loudly. He shuffled noisily over to where Rill knelt in front of the fire, pulling his suspenders up and over his shoulders. Rill didn't miss the fact that the old drover's six-shooter was already strapped to his hip. Cropper sensed something was wrong. That bothered Rill.

He scanned the prairie, but it was too dark to see anything more than the shadowed outline of a tree or two far away in the distance.

"Dad-dang-it-all," Cropper whined, scratching the back of his neck with one hand and dragging his worn sheepskin coat along in the other as he walked toward Rill.

"What's your problem?" Rill asked.

Cropper rubbed sleep from his eyes and sniffed. "I feel like I just laid these old bones of mine down on my bedroll and closed my eyes. Here you are, already making the mornin' fire."

"You're not that old."

"Seen more'n my share of sunrises, some would say I reckon, but I don't like to complain. Did you sleep at all?"

"Enough," Rill answered.

Cropper knelt down beside him and drew an open hand down his beard to smooth it. "You ain't seen or heard nothin', have you? Woke up with an itch right square between my shoulders this mornin'. Can't get rid of this ticklish feelin'."

"Not a thing," Rill said, but took Cropper's feeling to heart. Those men who were after Juliana had had just about enough time to discover they might have been duped and might be closing in on them.

Rill looked down at the smoke drifting up from the burning twigs of scrub plants. "You thinking maybe we shouldn't have a fire this morning?"

"Yup. Might not be a good idea."

The two of them quickly scuffed dirt over the campfire, and within seconds it was out.

"We been pushin' the horses mighty hard. Do you think they're gettin' enough grazin' time?"

"They'll be all right. The farther we get from Kansas City, the better I feel."

"I know what you mean," said Cropper. "I'll feel a whole lot better once it gets daylight, so I can see what's in front of me and what's behind me. One thing good about this godforsaken land. You can see right into Nebraska."

Rill rose. "Let's not wait for light. I'll get the horses ready, and we'll head out."

"I'm with you on that. I got to find myself a spot and get my mornin' business taken care of, then I'll be back to give you a hand."

Cropper tramped away, and Rill stood in the open for a moment, searching the land. He heard the crackling of a twig behind him. His hand flew to the handle of his Colt and he spun. Juliana walked toward him. He took a deep breath and relaxed.

"Damn, Juliana," he swore lightly. "Don't sneak up on me this early in the morning."

She stopped in front of him. "I didn't mean to startle you. I've been up for a while. I couldn't sleep, so I went for a walk."

A wild feeling of protectiveness stabbed through him. "You left camp without telling anyone?"

"Yes, but I didn't go far."

He pointed a firm finger at her. "Don't do it again. Understand?"

"Well, I—"

"No excuses," he said harshly. "It's too dangerous. Don't do it."

"I understand," she said tightly. "And a very good morning to you, too."

"Juliana, I can't protect you if you go wandering off and I don't know where you are. Not to mention the fact that it's damn risky walking back into camp. I could have shot you."

He realized that her wandering around was probably what had put a burr in Cropper's back. Now, Rill was overreacting about it.

Juliana pulled her black shawl tighter around her shoulders. There was just enough of a pout to her full lips to make him want to grab her and kiss her until she melted in his arms like frost in sunshine.

"Get up on the wrong side of your bedroll this morning, did you?" she asked.

He didn't need her sarcasm. "I'm not fooling around about this."

"I can see that. I didn't realize I had to report to

you if I wanted some time alone." There was a defensive crispness to her voice.

"Nature calls are the only reason you leave camp, and then you tell me or Cropper, and you don't go far."

"I've already said I understand. I left camp without thinking. I agree it was a stupid thing to do, and I won't do it again."

He could see that her blue eyes sparkled with banked defiance. Even though he'd been hard on her, he hadn't made her angry.

Rill swallowed hard. Juliana looked so prim with her tightly buttoned blouse with the square of lace and the gold brooch pinned at the base of her throat. He couldn't help but remember how he'd felt that afternoon he'd unpinned it and how desperately he wanted to unfasten it again.

He rubbed his hands down his legs. His hands itched to touch her. He hadn't really had a conversation with her in several days, and he hadn't wanted their first to be an argument. He'd missed her companionship.

"How's the shoulder, now that the stitches are out?" he asked.

"Much better, thank you. It's not as tight, and I can move my arm with no pain whatsoever."

"I'm glad." The day brightened quickly. Her eyes searched his face.

"You must have done a good job sewing me up. It healed so quickly."

"I had a lot of practice on the trail."

"Do you miss being on a cattle drive?"

"No. It's just as well. In another couple of years, they'll be a thing of the past. The railroads are taking the place of cattle drives. It's cheaper, quicker, and a hell of a lot safer for ranchers to use the railroads."

"Why is it safer?"

"Stampedes, weather, deadlines, and men who want to steal your herds."

"Is that why you decided to buy a ranch now?"

He looked up at her and smiled. Over her shoulder, the sky was turning from dark to light blue. Sunrise spread across the horizon in soothing colors and morning wind blew vagrant breezes across their faces.

"Any particular reason you woke up with all these questions on your mind when you've barely spoken to me these past days?"

"You're the one who has been ignoring me."

"I guess you know why."

"No. Not really. I know we disagree about some subjects, but I enjoy talking to you, spending time with you."

"I thought you were angry with me about our kiss and what I said about your aunt."

"Maybe for a short time. But anger's not what I'm feeling right now."

Rill felt as if all his blood had rushed to his head. Did she know what she did to him when she made statements like that? "What are you feeling?"

"Frustration."

His lower stomach knotted. "Tell me about it," he said with an uneven leap of his breath.

"And disappointment that I've done a poor job of caring for Cassandra."

Rill felt as though a fist had hit him in the gut. He should have known her thoughts were on Cassandra, not on him. "I have to disagree with you on that. I don't know what more you could do for her."

She gazed into his eyes with such warmth that the chill went out of the air. "I feel that I haven't earned the trust Auntie Vic placed in me and that I won't until Cassandra is safe with her grandfather."

"You're putting a lot of faith in a man you've never met."

"I have to. There's no one else."

There was pain in her voice and that bothered Rill. "Then we'll have to see that happens."

She nodded. "I know you don't like gratitude, but I'm filled with it."

Rill ran a hand through his hair. "Juliana, it's difficult enough having a woman like you on a journey like this without you saying things like that."

"Because?"

He took a step closer. His voice lowered. "I lie in my bedroll at night and remember how good you felt in my arms and how sweet you taste."

She moistened her lips. "I've been remembering the same things about you."

His manhood tightened in his trousers. Maybe she did have more than Cassandra on her mind. "It's not a good idea to tell me that."

"Why? You told me, and it's true."

"Because it'll take my mind off what I have to do and that's keep you and Cass safe."

Juliana rose up toward him on her toes. "I feel safe with you."

The click of a hammer alerted Rill. He jerked around, drawing his Colt as he moved and pointing it in the direction of the sound.

"Don't try it, cowboy," a deep voice called out. "I'll gun you down before you get off your first shot."

Out of the darkness strode three men. Each one had his pistol drawn and aimed at Rill. He heard Juliana's intake of breath, and he instinctively stepped in front of her.

He recognized two of the men as Baxter and Nolen, the deputies who'd crossed their path more than a week ago. The new man was sporting a tin star, too.

He was younger and edgy. Instinctively, Rill knew the new man would be the one he would have to make a move on when the time came.

Over his years as a drover, Rill had met just about every kind of cowpuncher there was. He knew the best way to handle any man who had a gun trained on him was to relax, strike up a conversation, and catch the man off guard.

"What took you fellas so long to get here? We've been expecting you."

The young one laughed. "Yeah? You think we're fools? Looked to me like you were about to kiss that woman."

"Ease your finger off that trigger and throw your gun this way," Baxter ordered. "Don't even try to be a hero. I'm just looking for a reason to put a bullet in your gut for costing me almost two weeks in the saddle."

Rill flipped his Colt downward on his forefinger and gently threw it to the ground. He didn't want it landing too far away. He'd be needing it again. Now he knew Cropper's itch didn't have anything to do with Juliana. Cropper's feeling was right. Again. Rill was glad his old friend had left camp wearing his pistol.

"I had a feeling you were on to us. We were betting on outriding you."

"Hard to do in a heavy wagon like the Conestoga." Nolen spoke for the first time.

"I suspected you were hiding the woman and the girl," Baxter said. "Told Nolen so, as we left you that day. As soon as everyone in the posse checked in, and we had come up without a nibble, I knew I was right. Started after you that night. You've been making good time."

"We've been trying hard."

"Where's your partner?"

"In the wagon. Fell and broke his leg. Fever's got him addled," Rill lied, without batting an eyelash.

"How about the girl? Where's she?"

"She's asleep," Juliana said, stepping from behind Rill and facing the men.

"Let me handle this," Rill said low enough only Juliana could hear him. He took a step forward, closer to his gun. He couldn't count on Cropper getting back to camp in time to help him.

Juliana elbowed up beside him again. "Cassandra is my responsibility."

"Then I guess that makes you mine," Rill murmured. "Get behind me and stay there."

"I reckon you're Miss Juliana Townsend," Baxter said. His voice and his expression told how pleased he was to have the jump on them.

"I am."

The young man couldn't stand still. He was constantly shifting from one foot to the other, moving the aim of his gun each time. That made Rill nervous.

"You've made quite a name for yourself in these parts, young lady. You got guts, putting a goose egg on Mr. Cabot's head and kidnapping his daughter the way you did."

"His stepdaughter," Juliana said tightly.

He laughed. "I wouldn't want to cross Warj Cabot."

"That's enough, Harper," Baxter said to the youngest man. "You're talking too much."

"What I did was for Cassandra's welfare," Juliana insisted in a voice that held no fear.

"It doesn't matter to us none why you stole her," Nolen said. "We're taking her back."

"I didn't steal her," Juliana said sharply. "I protected her from a madman."

"Whoa, there, young lady!" Harper said. "Mind how you speak to a man of Nolen's stature. He's been deputized by a U.S. Marshal. We all have." He pointed to his badge and grinned. "Now, we're taking the girl back to her father, and you back to stand trial for kidnapping."

"Her stepfather," Juliana said contemptuously as she remained rigid.

"We've talked enough," Baxter said. "Harper, you go with the woman to get the girl. Me and Nolen will stay here and keep our eyes on the cowboy and watch for his partner. We don't want him sticking a gun out of the wagon and shooting us."

Juliana looked at Rill. Fear etched her features and touched his heart. He wished he could tell her he needed her out of the way so he could make a play for his gun.

"Go with him, Juliana."

She shot him a desperate look. "No, this is my fight. Not yours." Instead of walking away with Harper, she took a pleading step forward. "You can't take Cassandra back to Ward Cabot. He's a beast of a man. I only took her away because he tried to kill her."

Harper swung his arm wide and hard, smacking Juliana across the face with the back of his hand. She flew to the ground like a rag doll.

Rill had drawn his fist back to slam into Harper's face when a shot rang out. Harper jerked. A red stain appeared on his left shirtfront.

"Die, you bastard!" Cropper yelled as he came lumbering from behind the wagon, firing his pistol at the other two men.

"Stay down, Juliana!" Rill yelled and dove for the ground, sliding up to his pistol.

Baxter returned Cropper's fire.

Bullets plowed into the earth beside Rill, splattering his face and stinging his eyes with dirt. A child's shrill scream rent the air.

"Cassandra!" Juliana cried out.

"Don't get up," Rill called to Juliana, then yelled to Cassandra, "Stay in the wagon!"

Rill's hand closed around his gun, and his finger crooked around the trigger of the Colt. He heard Cropper grunt. Rill jerked his arm up and put a bullet in Baxter's chest.

The hired gunman grabbed his chest over his heart and fell to the earth beside Juliana.

From the corner of his eye, Rill saw Nolen running like a scared rabbit. Rill scrambled to his feet and started after him.

"Rill! Look out behind you!" Juliana screamed.

He spun around. Baxter had raised up on one elbow. He fired at Rill again. The bullet whizzed past his ear. Rill returned the volley, hitting the man twice more. Baxter lifted his face toward heaven, grunted, and fell to the ground again as another red stain appeared lower on his belly.

Over by the wagon, Rill saw his friend down. Fury rose up in him. "See to Cropper!" he yelled to Juliana and took off after Nolen.

In the distance far ahead, he saw the deputy climbing onto the saddle of a horse. Nolen fired at Rill, but the bullets fell harmlessly nearby. Rill stopped, dropped to one knee, took careful aim, and fired his last bullets at Nolen. He saw the man jerk and knew he'd been hit, but Nolen kicked the horse and galloped away.

Fear lodged in Rill's chest and winded him as he raced back to camp. He fell to the ground beside his friend. The old man lay on his back, blood pouring from his side. Juliana held his head in her lap and was desperately trying to tear a strip of cloth from her petticoat.

"What's wrong with Cropper?" Cassandra asked, running up to Juliana.

"I told you to stay in the wagon," Rill reprimanded her.

"Is he going to die?" Cassandra asked, as she stood holding Miss Watkins by the foot and looking over Juliana's shoulder at Cropper.

"No," Rill declared.

"I want my mama."

Juliana reached back and took hold of Cassandra's hand. "Oh, sweetie, I know you're upset. Please don't cry. Everything's going to be all right."

"Cass, stop crying," Rill said in a stronger tone. "We need your help." Softer, he asked, "You can help us with Cropper, can't you?"

"No," she whimpered and chewed on her doll's foot. "I'm afraid."

"No one's going to hurt you," Juliana said.

"Cass," Rill said, "Cropper needs some water. Can you get it for him?"

"I don't know."

"Get a canteen out of the back of the wagon. You can do it. Get the water now," he said.

"All right," she sniffled and hurried away.

"Let me do this." Rill whipped a bowie knife from his gun belt and sliced off a scrap of Juliana's petticoat.

"There's so much blood," Juliana whispered in a desperate voice.

"Has he spoken?"

She glanced up at Rill. "No. Rill, I don't know what to do. I'm so sorry this happened. I can't believe I brought all this trouble on you and Cropper. I never expected either of you would be harmed because of me."

His gaze caught hers and held. "What happened wasn't your fault."

"How can you say that? Of course, I'm responsible. Those men wanted me. Cropper is fighting for his life because of me. I shouldn't have asked you and Cropper to get mixed up in my problems."

"Cropper didn't do anything he didn't want to do. He wasn't going to stand by and let that man strike you and not do something about it."

Rill saw redness and swelling underneath Juliana's eyes. "Damn bastards," he muttered in a growling voice as she pressed the cloth to Cropper's side.

"Is that you swearin', Rill?"

"Cropper, you old goat." Rill couldn't believe the size of the lump that rose in his throat. "What'd you go and get shot for?"

"You all right, Julie?" Cropper asked, looking up at her with pain-filled eyes.

"Oh, Cropper, I'm fine. I'm just worried about you."

Rill glanced up at Juliana. He saw her swallow hard and knew she was holding back tears.

"How bad is it?" Cropper asked.

"Don't know yet. How do you feel?"

"Burnin', like I'm sittin' at the gates of hell."

Rill pulled the white cotton away from the wound. His stomach was caved in on his back. The bullet had torn a hole the size of a half-dollar in Cropper's side. He couldn't let his friend die. He hadn't been able to save his men the night Stedman stole his herd, but dammit, he intended to save Cropper, and he'd keep Cassandra and Juliana safe, too.

"I'm going to turn you over and see if the bullet lodged or if it went through."

"No need to. It's still there. I feel it. You're goin' to have to take it out."

Rill looked from Cropper to Juliana, to the wound. "Not if I can get you to a doctor by sundown."

"I won't make it," he said in a raspy voice. "You got to do it."

"I don't have the skill. I figure we're close enough to Hattersville that we can make it before dark. I'll bind you up tight to stop the bleeding. There should be a real doctor there. One who can get the bullet out and fix you up right."

"You can do it. I trust you."

Rill looked down at his friend. He'd met Cropper on his first drive. He didn't want to lose him. "It's bad, Cropper. I'm not taking a chance with your life. I'm going to lift you into the back of the wagon, and we're heading out."

"What about those men?" Cropper asked. "You can't leave them out here for the buzzards to eat. That ain't Christian."

"It might not be Christian but it's not my problem, either. Nolen got away. If he wants his partners to have a decent burial, he'll hang around until we're gone and come back for them."

"You don't believe he'll do that, do you?"

"No, and I don't give a damn either way. Right now, you're alive, and they aren't. You're the one I'm worried about."

"What we gonna do about Cass? I don't want her to see me all shot up like this."

Rill didn't have the heart to tell him she already had. "I'll keep her up front in the seat with me. I'll have Juliana take care of her until I can get you settled in the wagon."

"Wait, Rill. If I don't make it—"

"I don't want to hear that kind of talk. You make

sure you do. I'm going to need your help to get that ranch started."

Cropper grimaced. "We've known each other too long to start lying, Rill. We both know I'm not going to recover from a gut shot."

"I don't know any such thing. The bullet's more to your side. You have a chance, and that's all we need."

The old drover shook his head. "Naw. I was just holdin' on long enough to see for myself that Julie and the little boss wasn't hurt."

"Don't worry about us, Cropper. Just think about yourself," Juliana said.

Rill glanced up at her. "Go get Cassandra and keep her away from the wagon until I call for you."

Juliana looked down at Cropper and said, "Don't you dare die on us."

She gently laid Cropper's head on the ground, then rose and rushed away.

"Rill, I know how you've felt since that no-account stole your herd and killed your men. Put it behind you now, and get on with your life. You got to take care of Cass and Julie. You have your ranch waiting for you, too."

"I know what I have to do. You just do your part and stay alive. Now stop talking. You're wasting time."

Cropper grabbed the front of Rill's shirt with a trembly hand. "Dang-it-all, listen to me. If I don't make it, don't waste time on me, and don't go lookin' for the one who got away. Get my girls here to that ranch in Wyoming."

Rill took his friend's cold hand and looked down at him. "I'll take care of them for you."

❧ 12 ❧

It had been a frantic few minutes as Rill had carried Cropper into the doctor's office and placed him on the table. The young physician and his wife had set to work immediately to save Cropper's life.

Rill had wanted to be in the operating room, but the doctor forbade it, forcing Rill to stay in the outside office with Juliana and a fretful Cassandra.

Juliana tried to calm Cassandra but soft words only made her whine louder. "I want to go home."

"I know you do, sweetie," Juliana said, watching Rill out of the corner of her eye. He paced from the window to the door of the surgery room. She knew Cassandra's crying was the last thing he wanted to hear right now. "You know we can't. We have to stay here and make sure Cropper will be all right."

"I want to see him."

"No. The doctor's taking good care of him. Please don't cry. You'll make Rill sad, too." Juliana looked around the room and spotted a book lying on a desk. She hurried over and picked it up. Maybe it had enough drawings inside to keep Cassandra occupied for a few minutes.

"Here." Juliana handed the book to Cassandra. "Look through this while I talk to Rill a minute."

"I don't want to."

"It has drawings of animals in it. Here's a horse. See what else you can find, and I'll be back in a minute so you can show me."

Juliana walked over to Rill and said, "I know Cassandra's crying is upsetting you. I don't really want to leave you, but maybe Cassandra and I should check into that hotel down the street."

His mouth tightened. "No. I don't want you alone until I can check out the town. Cabot could have men all over the area."

"But I don't want to be a burden to you any more than I already have been."

"Do you have to argue with me all the time?"

"I don't. I just don't want her disturbing you."

"Right now, you are the one bothering me, not Cassandra."

Juliana sucked in her breath at the sting of his words. She felt his rage and understood it, but that didn't keep his caustic comment from hurting.

"Oh, of course," she mumbled, clasping her hands together in front of her. "I'm sorry. I was only trying to help."

"Well, you're not. You can't. And the hell of it is, I can't, either. Now if you want to do me a favor, leave me alone and stay out of my way." He turned and walked over to the window.

Tears watered her eyes. Juliana wanted to sob from the pain she'd caused him and Cropper. She knew the anger Rill directed at her came from his fear of Cropper's condition. She had to remember he was hurting, too, and forgive him. Slowly, quietly, she returned to Cassandra.

A couple of hours into their wait, Rill had told Juliana that he was going out and for her to stay away from the windows and door. She acknowledged him with a nod. A few minutes later, he came back carrying a loaf of bread, some cheese, and some fruit for their supper.

After Juliana had settled Cassandra down on a chair with her lap full of food, she walked over to the surgery room door and stood there staring at it, saying a prayer for Cropper's safety.

She sensed Rill's presence behind her and turned to face him. He extended a large red apple to her.

She barely glanced at him and shook her head. "I'm not hungry."

"You have to be. You haven't eaten all day."

"You haven't, either."

"I'll have something later," he said. "Take the apple."

Juliana looked into his eyes, and her heart swelled with appreciation of him. She took the apple and put it in the pocket of her skirt. "Thank you."

"I didn't mean to snap at you earlier. It's just that I'm angry, and I'm afraid for Cropper. He's a good man."

"I know. I understand how you feel, and you don't have to apologize for being human."

He nodded. "I rented a two-room suite for the night at the hotel." He reached into a trouser pocket and pulled out a key. "I'll walk you and Cass over whenever you're ready. The town's quiet. As late as it is, you should be safe there."

He avoided her eyes and that bothered her. She knew he was thinking that Cropper wouldn't be fighting for his life if not for her. "Thank you, but I don't want to leave until I know Cropper is all right. Rill, I'm so very sorry. I'd do anything, pay any penance, to go back and change what happened," she whispered.

"We've already been over that, Juliana. I'm in no mood to go over it again."

She swallowed hard. "I know you don't want to talk about it, but I have so many emotions burning inside me right now. I'm angry, and I feel helpless. I feel responsible and guilty."

He looked at her. A flicker of concern showed in his eyes as his gaze swept up and down her face. "You have no reason to feel guilty."

A lump rose in her throat. "How can you say that? Of course, I do. Ward's men were after me and Cassandra. Not you and Cropper."

Juliana clutched the front of her skirt with trembly hands. She was afraid if she didn't hold herself in check she might reach out and touch him. She desperately needed to feel his strong arms around her. She wanted to give him comfort and take solace from him.

"Cabot and his men are responsible."

"And they aren't going to stop hunting us until they have Cassandra. I understand that now." She took a deep breath. "Ward Cabot doesn't care how many people he has to kill to get to Cassandra."

"I'll see that he pays for what his men did to Cropper."

"No. I can't endanger your life again. I know you never wanted to help us in the first place."

"That was almost two weeks ago, Juliana. I didn't know everything then. I didn't know you."

It surprised Juliana how it tore at her heart whenever she thought of leaving Rill. She was attracted to him, had become attached to him, but she hadn't expected to feel this devastating loss at the thought of separating from him. The thought of never seeing him again burned a hole of denial into her heart and made her feel like weeping. The only way she could cope with the fear of never seeing him again was to convince herself that later, after Cassandra was safe with her grandfather, she would go to his ranch in the Wyoming Territory and visit him there.

"Rill, Cassandra and I are going to take the next stagecoach out of here," she said, her throat hurting with every word.

A wrinkle formed in Rill's brow. "The hell you are."

"I have to get to the Triple R before anyone else gets hurt. Even now, her grandfather could be in danger."

"We'll send him a telegram to warn him about Cabot and his men."

"I had wanted to do that, but we always bypass towns. But, Rill, that won't change the fact that I might have already caused Cropper's death. I can't worry about you—"

He grabbed her upper arms and pulled her up close to his chest. His tone was firm as he said, "First, Cropper's going to make it. Second, don't even think about striking out on your own. And third, the three of us are leaving together after we see Cropper in the morning."

His grip was tight, but she didn't mind. She needed to feel his strength, his anger, his frustration. "First, you can't leave Cropper. Second, I can't believe you'd want to continue with me and Cassandra under the circumstances, and third, don't you see that I have enough concerns without worrying about Ward's men shooting you, too?"

"Juliana, what's wrong?" Cassandra asked from the other side of the room. "Why are you shouting?"

"Nothing, sweetie. Everything's fine."

Rill let her go and took a step back. "It's my job to worry about Cabot's men, not yours. I promised Cropper I'd deliver you and Cass safely to the ranch, and I'll do it."

"But I feel so responsible."

"Your aunt didn't teach you to quit whenever things got tough, did she?"

Juliana stiffened, blinked. "Of course not."

"Good. That's something else we agree on. I don't desert someone just because the going gets tough. Now, I don't want to hear any more about guilt or about you and Cass leaving town without me. And, Juliana, I haven't forgotten you tried to run away on Doc. Don't try it again."

Juliana lowered her head. "I don't think I really expected Ward to go to such lengths to get us. I would have never begged you to let us travel with you, if I had thought one of you might be hurt."

"Cropper knows that. So do I." His voice softened. He reached over and brushed a strand of hair away from her cheek and let the backs of his fingers lightly brush across the swollen area under her eye. "It's a bad bruise. I'm sorry Cropper killed the son of a bitch who hit you. I wanted to do it."

"Don't talk like that." Her words choked in her throat. "I didn't want *anyone* to get killed."

"I know, but Cropper had to protect his own. He looks at you and Cass as the daughter and grandchild he never had. He told me when I was putting him in the wagon that he went crazy when he saw that man hit you, and he had to come out shooting."

A lump grew in her throat. "I'd like to think of Cropper as my father."

Rill looked at her with a questioning expression on his face. "How do you think of me, Juliana?"

His words caught her by surprise and caused a fluttering in her stomach. Suddenly, she was aware of how close she and Rill had become. Heat prickled across her skin and stunned her. Ward Cabot wasn't the only danger closing in on her. She was fast realizing that Rill was perilously close to capturing her heart.

"I'd better check on Cassandra," she whispered and turned away before he could see in her face all she was feeling for him.

An oil lamp burned softly in the quiet room. The only sounds Juliana heard were her own rapid breaths and her constant footsteps as she paced back and forth in front of the settee in the small sitting area off the two-bedroom suite Rill had rented for the night.

She and Cassandra had stayed with Rill at the doctor's office through Cropper's long surgery. As the night lengthened, Cassandra grew more and more agitated, but Juliana couldn't get her to settle down and fall asleep. Rill had tried to get Juliana to take Cassandra to the hotel earlier, but Juliana hadn't wanted to leave Rill alone until she knew Cropper had made it through the operation.

Rill had paced, as Juliana was doing now, the whole time Cropper was in surgery. Juliana had wanted to somehow take away the worry lines she saw in Rill's features, but all she could do was be there with him and try to keep Cassandra quiet.

Juliana knew that the gunfire and seeing Cropper shot had terrified the little girl. Juliana kept trying to calm her by promising that Cropper was going to be all right. When the doctor finally came out and told them Cropper had made it through the operation, she'd asked the physician if he could give her something to help calm Cassandra.

He gave her a vial of paregoric. Juliana had come straight to the hotel, given some of the medicine to Cassandra, and put her to bed. Her charge had been sleeping soundly since.

While she waited for Rill, Juliana filled the basin, took a wipe-off bath, and donned fresh clothes she'd washed in a creek a couple of days ago. She took down her hair and brushed it free of tangles before washing her undergarments and hanging them to dry. After whispering a prayer of petition for Cropper's life, Juliana had started pacing, pondering, and planning.

The first thing she must do in the morning was send a telegram to Cassandra's grandfather to alert him that she hadn't kidnapped Cassandra, but was bringing his granddaughter to him because her life was in danger from Ward Cabot. The second thing she was going to do was buy a pistol and bullets to keep in her reticule. She hoped that Rill would teach her how to shoot the gun.

A twister of emotions tore through Juliana while she paced. She picked up her hairbrush again and combed through her tresses. After she'd said another prayer for Cropper, her thoughts turned to Rill. It was true he hadn't wanted the responsibility of her and Cassandra, but he had changed after Ward's men first appeared. She knew he found her attractive and wanted to kiss her again. He'd told her so, but did he want to kiss her because any woman would do, or did he want to kiss her because she was Juliana Townsend?

Juliana decided she had to take Rill's advice and follow her own instinct. Staying away from men might have been what was right for Aunt Victoria, but it wasn't right for Juliana. She wanted Rill. She wanted him tonight. And it didn't matter that Auntie Vic wouldn't understand or approve.

At last, Juliana heard Rill's key in the door. She threw the hairbrush aside and rushed over to meet him.

"Why are you still up?" he asked, closing, then locking the door behind him. He swiped his hat off and let it drop onto a side table, then ran a hand through his shaggy hair.

The strain of the day and night showed in the lines around his eyes and mouth and in his clipped tone. She was sure he didn't want her to see or know how vulnerable he was at this moment so he had to mask it with anger and irritability. And she understood. Maybe she had no right to witness his despair over his friend, but she had no intention of leaving him alone tonight.

"I was waiting up for you. How's Cropper?"

Rill took a deep breath and threw the room key on the table beside his hat. "Bad."

She swallowed hard and asked in a husky voice, "Were you able to talk to him?"

Rill shook his head. "No. The doctor assured me he'd given Cropper so much medication he wouldn't wake up until morning. The doctor's wife insisted I leave and get some rest."

"She's a sensible woman," Juliana murmured, then added, "Cassandra should sleep through the night, too. The paregoric the doctor gave me calmed her almost immediately. I checked on her just a few minutes ago. She's sleeping peacefully."

His eyes were bright yet empty of vitality when he turned to her and said, "You should have gone to bed with her."

"I couldn't sleep until you returned."

"I'm here now," he mumbled as his gaze darted about the room as if searching for something lost.

Only part of him was there. His thoughts were with his friend.

Rill rubbed his eyes with the heels of his palms. "Damn, it's been a hell of a day."

Juliana was desperate to find a way to comfort him, a way to make him forget what had happened to Cropper, if only for a little while. "I know. Come over here and sit down and let me—"

"No," he cut in, then, as if realizing he'd been too sharp, he stared into her eyes and said, "You're not the kind of woman I need tonight."

His meaning was clear, but what surprised her was that she wanted to challenge his assumption. A lump of expectancy grew in her throat. "What kind of woman would that be?"

He chuckled bitterly for a moment. "The kind who wears cheap perfume and can drink a pint of whiskey without holding her nose."

Juliana saw weariness in his eyes and a reluctance to banter. Her heartbeat sped up, warning her she was getting in over her head, but it didn't keep her from saying, "I agree that it would be difficult to associate me with those two things. The only real experience I've had with men is what I learned from you." Her words were so breathy she wasn't sure he could catch them.

"And that was more than I should have taught you. Now, do us both a favor and go to bed." He walked back over to the table and picked up his hat and the room key. "I'm going out. Keep the door locked, and don't answer it for anyone. I'll be back in an hour."

She took a deep breath and stepped toward him,

fearful that she wouldn't be able to keep him from leaving. "Rill, I don't want you to leave."

"Juliana," he said softly. "I need to."

"I want to comfort you tonight. I don't want anyone else to do it."

"No." Rill backed away.

His answer didn't surprise her, nor did it deter her. Keeping her gaze locked on his, she took another forward step. "I need comfort from you, too."

He shook his head. "Not from me. Not tonight. Turn yourself around, go to bed, and leave me alone."

She took the key and the hat from his hand and replaced them on the table. "You need to talk about your feelings to someone who cares. A saloon woman might listen, but she won't understand. I do."

A growling sound preceded his husky, "No. Right now, I'm angry as hell, Juliana, and I need a woman who'll—"

Rill stopped, and Juliana wondered if she really wanted to know how he would have finished that sentence. She knew what kind of woman he thought he needed, but she wanted to change his mind. "I'm not afraid of what I'm asking for. I'm not afraid of you."

"You should be," he said, but there was no longer any anger in his voice. "You don't know what I'm feeling tonight."

"Yes, I do." Her stomach fluttered. "Kiss me, Rill."

His eyes widened, and he stepped back again. "No."

"Why not?" she answered in the same quiet tone he used, as her eyes searched his face.

"That's not a good idea, Juliana."

"Why?" She advanced on him.

"I don't need any more guilt tonight."

Her breath caught in her lungs. She understood him more than he knew. She had her own share of culpability to deal with—but not tonight. There would be plenty of time for that. There was something more pressing on her mind and in her heart, and she knew she was ready to share it with Rill.

She swallowed her fear of the unknown and said, "You need a woman who cares about you. A woman who can understand what you're going through, and who can make you forget. I'm that kind of woman."

"No." He backed away again. His head and the heels of his boots banged against the wall, sounding like thunder rumbling throughout the dimly lit room. His gaze locked on hers. "You're a virgin, and you want to remain that way all the days of your life because your dear, sweet aunt told you you must, remember?"

He was deliberately being cruel, but she easily forgave him. He was fighting his anger, his pain, his fear for Cropper's life.

She closed the distance between them, standing as near to him as she could without touching him. Her stomach quivered again, as if to remind her one last time she was treading on unfamiliar ground. "I've changed my mind and decided you were right. Auntie Vic didn't know anything about men."

"Don't tempt me, Juliana," he said huskily, as he touched the bruise underneath her eye.

"I'm not afraid of you—of us."

"I'm afraid of the way you make me feel."

She slid her arms around his neck and pressed her breasts against his chest. Not certain of herself, not certain how Rill would react, Juliana reached up and placed her lips on his. He stood motionless, allowing her to kiss him but not responding. Her heart almost stalled in her chest when he remained passive and seemingly unmoved by her attempt to force him to surrender to all she had to give him. How could she make it any clearer that she wanted him to show her how a man touches a woman?

Stunned, feeling rebuffed, Juliana didn't know what to do next. He had rejected her offer, and it cut her all the way to her heart. She ended the kiss.

Suddenly, his arms slipped around her waist, and he caught her up against him, his strong arms holding her like a steel band against his chest. "I have no willpower to resist you tonight, you know that, don't you?"

"I hoped."

"Don't make this hard on me. I want you. I need you the way a man desires a woman, but I don't want to destroy the beliefs your aunt instilled in you. And if I make love to you I sure as hell don't want you to regret it later."

His voice was ragged with passion, his eyes were hot with desire, his embrace was trembly with need. Juliana realized the power within her to ease and sate these vulnerable feelings inside this man.

"Auntie Vic taught me many things, and was right about all of them, but I want to find out for myself what these feelings I have for you are all about."

"I won't stop with just one kiss."

"I don't want you to." She reached up to him once again.

Rill groaned deep in his throat. "Don't tell me that if you don't mean it."

"Kiss me, Rill," she said again.

"You know that if you come to me now, I won't let you go."

"Yes."

With frantic movements, he caught her up in his arms and swung her off the floor. He twirled and changed their positions as he gently pressed her against the wall with his body. His lips came down on hers with hard, demanding pressure. Crushing. Clinging. Their tongues met. Their breaths merged.

She felt desperation in his kiss and welcomed it, answered it with her own urgency. She needed to feel his heart beating against hers. She wanted this night with him.

Juliana opened her heart and her life to Rill.

His tongue plundered the depths of her mouth as his hands expertly moved up and down her arms, across her breasts, and over her hips. He tasted of the clean spice of apple, and it made her hunger all the more for his touch. Her whole body shook with wanting.

Rill fumbled with the buttons down the front of her blouse, unfastening each one. He pushed the front panels aside exposing her undergarments.

Suddenly, he stopped and gazed into her eyes. "Damn, Juliana, forget what I said earlier. I want you and I need you, but if you say the word, I'll walk away from you right now before we take this any further."

Her body burned with a curling fire of need. "I don't want you to leave."

His lips seized hers in a fierce kiss. She had expected to be nervous, but she wasn't. There was a hunger in her soul, and she knew only Rill could satisfy it.

Her blouse fell off her shoulders and hung uncomfortably around her arms. Rill's kisses left her lips and moved across her chin, down her neck, over her shoulders to the top of her undergarments. He pushed the wide strap of her garment down her arms and stared at the fullness of her breasts rising above the cotton material. He reached into the cups of the corset and laid her breasts bare before him. He pushed the garment down and gently closed his lips around a rosy tip and suckled.

Juliana gasped from the thrill that shot through her. She moaned softly, sweetly. Desire was so intense she thought she might faint from the power of it. She had never experienced anything like the fiery sensations gnawing inside her.

Rill took his lips away long enough to lift her in his arms, all in one fluid motion. "Which room is Cass in?" he asked in a husky voice.

Juliana pointed at the door on the far side of the room. Rill took off toward the other one. He pushed the door open with one hand, then gently closed it. He strode over to the bed and laid her down. He reached for a pillow and placed it under her head.

She watched as he quickly unbuckled his gun belt and dropped it on the bedside table.

He placed one knee on the side of the bed and, keeping his gaze on her, as if he were afraid she might bolt, he took his time and untied the kerchief from around his neck, then flung it to the other side of the room.

Slowly, Rill unbuttoned his shirt, dragged it off his arms, and let it drop to the floor.

She took a deep breath as she stared at his powerful chest and arms, the slim firmness of his waist.

"Are you sure you want this?" he asked.

Juliana nodded.

He started unbuttoning his trousers, and Juliana realized why she wasn't nervous. She wanted this man. She wanted this night, and she wouldn't let him deny her.

With his trousers unfastened, he remained poised above her as if he were waiting for something. Juliana peeked at the flat firmness of his abdomen and her heartbeat quickened.

Her gaze strayed up to his eyes. He was staring down at her, questioning.

"If you're trying to intimidate me, you're not going to," she said. "I know what I want."

Admiration shone in his eyes. Rill placed his other knee on the bed, then stretched his body on top of Juliana.

Their lips met with fierce passion. His tongue entered her mouth and plundered its depth as his hands helped her shed her blouse, corset, and skirt, leaving her dressed only in her drawers.

With unsure hands, she stroked the smooth firmness of his back and shoulder and down the hollow of his spine. She kissed his cheek, along his jawline, and down his neck, occasionally letting her tongue graze his tangy skin and brush the trace of beard on his face.

"I have no patience for wooing you tonight, Juliana," he mumbled against her lips as his lower body pressed her into the mattress.

There was an urgency to his touch as his thumb brushed the taut tip of her breast and his palm cupped the fullness. Juliana's insides quivered.

"I know," she answered between frantic, moist kisses.

She had imagined gentle kisses, soothing words of love and a wedding night, but how could she be disappointed when what was happening between them made her feel like fireworks at a Fourth of July celebration?

"I didn't want it to be like this between us."

"I understand." She, too, had wanted time to savor

each touch, each breath, each sound, but she had known Rill's state of mind before he walked through that door. She hadn't wanted him going to any other woman for what she could willingly give.

She arched her pelvis against him and surrounded his back in her hands and arms. "Don't make us wait any longer, Rill."

With jerky movements, Rill finished undressing her, and yanked his trousers off and tossed them aside.

Juliana gasped at the suddenness of the hot pressure as he joined his body with hers.

There was a burning intensity that almost took her breath, but she forced that from her mind, determined not to let the discomfort keep her from enjoying every moment of this time with Rill.

She swallowed down her moan of protest and resisted the urge to push him away as he pressed harder and deeper into her. His kisses were wild, his hands frantic as his hips pumped. Within a few moments of beginning, his movements slowed, stopped. He fell against her and hid his face in the crook of her neck, gasping for breath. His body trembled as she held him.

Juliana's breaths were choppy, too, as she calmed from the intensity of what had just happened. There had been pain, but it wasn't unbearable. It had quickly vanished. His kisses had demanded that she participate and join him in the passion of their two bodies coming together. And, up to the point of penetration, there had been all kinds of glorious sensations to enjoy. That was what she'd wanted.

She felt wondrously content to lie beneath him, kiss him, touch him, and breathe in his scent. Now she knew why she had been ready for tonight and had insisted that Rill stay with her. She loved him, and she wanted to be forever in his arms and in his life.

A smile eased across her face.

She couldn't remember much about her parents. She must have loved them, but she couldn't remember what that love had felt like. And she had the greatest respect for Auntie Vic. Juliana must have loved her, too. But neither of those feelings had prepared her for the depth of love she felt for Rill. It consumed her, and made her happier than she could ever remember being.

"Sweet Juliana," he whispered against her neck. "This isn't what I wanted for you. For me. I should have left."

His breath fanned her heated skin, making it pebble with goose bumps. "Did I do something wrong?" she asked in a nervous voice.

Rill raised his head and looked deeply into her eyes. "No, of course not. I'm the one who was wrong. I should have had more control. It's just that—"

"What?"

"I've wanted to throw you down on a bed and love you since I first saw you in my wagon. I shouldn't have let what happened to Cropper—"

Juliana smiled and reached up and silenced him with her fingertips to his lips.

Rill felt like the worst kind of lowlife. He lay on top of Juliana, gasping for breath. His taking her was over far too quickly. In a way, he'd never felt more satisfied in his life, but in another way he felt that he could never have enough of Juliana to sate him.

He'd tried to be noble and push her away. He'd wanted to go elsewhere for his pleasure, but his mind, his body, his soul had demanded that he not turn her away when she offered herself. He was ready to accept any kind of denouncement from her when, in the shadowy light, he saw her face, her eyes sparkling, and a smile lifting the corners of her lips.

Moonlight spilled in through the white sheers adorning the two windows. She lay in quiet repose with her eyes heavily hooded with her dark lashes. Her hair spread out behind her in shimmering, wavy strands of golden blond. Her face, the color of her skin, the shape of her body were more beautiful than those of any woman he'd ever seen. How had he gotten so damn lucky?

A smile?

He thought his heart would beat out of his chest.

"I don't understand. I just had my way with you—a virgin—with no care for your enjoyment, just my own frustration and release, and you're smiling at me."

She nodded.

"You should be angry with me."

She reached up and brushed hair away from his damp forehead. Her touch felt like butterfly wings. "How can I when you made me a woman tonight?"

Rill moistened his lips. "Is that what you think?" He felt her stiffen beneath him.

"You did, didn't you? I mean, we made love, didn't we?"

"Sort of."

Her eyes searched his face. "What does that mean?"

"It means I did. You didn't."

Her eyes widened. "Yes, I did. I mean, even now you're—" She hesitated. "Your body is still joined with mine."

Rill felt his body coming to life again, and he began to slowly move his hips up and down. His desire was too great to be sated with just one desperate act of coupling. His need to satisfy Juliana rose up in him with demanding force.

"That's true, but you didn't experience what love-making is all about."

She moistened her lips. "I think I did. Your kisses, the way you touched me felt like—like a million stars falling on me."

He chuckled lightly. "You are so wonderful, and I'm so damn lucky." He reached down and lightly kissed her bruised cheek.

No other woman had ever lit such a fire of longing inside him. He wasn't sure what all the things he was feeling meant. He only knew he'd never had them for any other woman. Only Juliana.

He held himself up with one elbow and let his other hand lazily move up and down her breast, pausing to cup, mold, and squeeze the firm mound. His gaze stayed on her eyes, wanting to watch her enjoy his touch.

"What about what I'm doing now? Does it hurt?"

"Not when you touch me like that," she whispered.

"How does that feel?"

"Good."

He quirked an eyebrow. "Just good." His voice was low, seductive.

"No. Delicious," she managed to say and arched toward him. "Like you're sprinkling me with star-dust."

"That sounds more like it." He deliberately changed his position and pressed his body so that he pressed the center of her womanhood. He continued to caress her breasts, shoulders, and abdomen as he pressed against her, slowly moving up and down, joining his body with hers. He watched as her eyes closed, and her body lifted off the bed to meet him. She gasped, and her body trembled. He slid his arms around her and held her close while she labored to hold on to that fleeting feeling of her first climax. At last, she took a deep breath.

Rill smiled and looked into her eyes. "Now we've made love."

Her chest rose and fell with heavy breathing. "What happens next?" she asked, eager to discover more of these wonderful sensations.

He caressed her neck, her arms, and her breasts with a lightly callused hand. "We start all over again."

She frowned. "Except for the pain. We don't have to do that again, do we?"

He chuckled. "No. We won't do that again."

❧ 13 ❧

Early the next morning, Juliana was where she'd started last evening. At the doctor's office. Cassandra watched the horses and people pass by from the front window. It had not been easy, leaving Rill's bed and joining Cassandra when the sun's first rays stole into his room and robbed her of the night and his embrace.

Juliana took a deep breath and remembered. Their time together was a glorious night that wasn't meant to be forgotten. Ever.

A door opened, and she turned to see Rill walking out of the sick room where Cropper lay.

Their eyes met. She saw in his eyes that he remembered, too. But all that had to be put aside now. There would come a time later when they could talk about last night, and if she were lucky, about the future.

She hurried over to Rill and asked, "How is he?"

He looked down at his hat, which he held in his hand. "As long as he's alive, there's hope."

A bolt of pain electrified her body. Rill's tone and

187

his expression told her what his words didn't convey. The doctor had given Cropper no hope for recovery.

"Rill," she said earnestly, "you know I'd do anything to make Cropper better, to change what happened."

"So would I, but the past can't be changed. He wants to see Cass."

Swallowing down all the loving things she wanted to say to him, Juliana glanced over to where Cassandra was looking out the window of the doctor's office. "He was so worried about her seeing him shot. Do you think that's a good idea?"

He nodded. "She needs to see him without blood all over him. It might help her to talk to him, and I know it will help him to see her."

Juliana's eyes stared into his, and her heart ached for the man she loved. Rill needed to deal with what was happening, too. "Tell me the truth, Rill," she said softly. "What are Cropper's chances according to the doctor?"

"He's a tough old man. The bullet's out. He's alive. It doesn't matter what the doctor says."

She knew Rill was the one wanting to be tough. He didn't want her to witness his pain and grief. She wanted to take Rill in her arms, to hold him close and comfort him as she had last night. She wanted him to pour on her his grief for his friend and let her bear the burden, but she knew Rill wouldn't do that.

Juliana moistened her lips. "You shouldn't leave him, you know. He needs you. Cassandra and I will be all right. We can go it alone from—"

"Don't say it," he said calmly, firmly, looking deeply into her eyes. "We settled this conversation yesterday. You have a bad habit of stirring up what's already settled."

"You know Cropper needs you right now more than we do."

"No." His voice was filled with emotion that showed in his eyes and on the grim set of his lips. "That's the hardest part of this to deal with, Juliana. I can't do anything for him. I know it, and he knows it." He moved his hat from one hand to the other. "We need to head out. Cass, come here. Cropper wants to see you."

Cassandra turned to Rill, a smile beaming across her face. "He wants to see me?" Hugging Miss Watkins to her chest, she ran over to Rill. "I thought he was too sick for company."

"He's not too sick to see you," said Rill. "He wants you to know that he's going to stay here and get better. We need to go on to your grandfather's without him. He wants to say good-bye to you."

A pout formed on her lips, and she folded her arms across her chest defiantly. "I don't want to leave Cropper. If he stays, so do I. He's my only friend."

"That's not a nice thing to say, Cassandra," Juliana said in a stern but soft tone of voice. "Rill is your friend, and so am I."

"I don't care if it's not nice. It's true. Rill would rather talk to you, and you don't count as a friend. No one ever wants me to have friends."

Rill bent down on one knee in front of the little girl and grasped her small shoulders with his strong hands. Juliana's heart spilled over with love for him. He was so patient with Cassandra. It was easy to see that he'd be a wonderful father.

"You don't want Cropper to get worse, do you?" Rill asked.

"Of course not. I just told you he's my only friend."

"Then he has to stay here, and you have to go with

us." Rill rose and picked up Cassandra and held her in his arms. "Now you have to talk softly to him, and we can't stay long, all right?"

Cassandra nodded.

It pleased Juliana at how easily Rill handled Cassandra. He always seemed to know when to be firm with her and when to be gentle.

Juliana tiptoed into Cropper's room behind Rill and Cassandra. He lay clothed in a white nightshirt. He was covered from his neck to his feet by a plain white quilt. Juliana had to hold in her gasp when she saw Cropper. Her heart broke for Rill all over again. It was clear that Cropper's condition was grave. He was so white that she wouldn't have been able to tell the difference between his face and the sheet had it not been for the brown coloring still present in his graying beard.

Cassandra leaned over the ex-drover and softly whispered, "Cropper, it's me, Cass."

Eyes dull with pain popped open. A weak smile appeared on his pale, dry lips. "Hey, little boss," he managed to say in a raspy voice. "Are you all right?"

"I'm fine, Cropper," she whispered. "How are you feeling?"

"I'll be fit as a fiddle at a spring dance in no time." He coughed. "I want you to be good for Julie and Rill, you hear me?"

"I want you to come with us, Cropper."

"Can't, this time. I better stay here and do what the doctor says do."

She nodded.

He coughed again. "I'll come see you at your grandpa's ranch after you get there."

Cassandra's mouth drooped. "I don't want to go, Cropper. Can't we wait for you to get better?"

"Best not. You go ahead. I might even catch up with you before you get to the Wyoming Territory."

"I don't want to leave you, Cropper. You're my only friend."

Tears welled in the old man's eyes, and Juliana thought she was going to start sobbing. She glanced over at Rill. She knew what the grim set of his lips meant. He didn't think he'd ever see Cropper again.

"I'll always be your friend, Cass." He lifted a trembling hand and extended his harmonica to her. "I asked Rill to get this out of my pocket. I want you to have it. You keep up with your lessons, now. Just like I taught you."

Cassandra's eyes grew wide with surprise as she took hold of the instrument. "Are you sure, Cropper? It's your favorite."

" 'Course I am." His voice grew raspy, his breathing was loud and labored. "I'll be expectin' you to play a tune for me next time I see you. You go on now. Long way to go. I'll see you soon."

Cassandra reached down and kissed the old man on the cheek. She then took Miss Watkins and placed the doll in the bed beside the old man. "I'll leave Miss Watkins here to look after you. She'll see you get better."

Juliana was desperate to hold her tears at bay. She was angry for Cropper's life being stolen from him, sad for Rill losing his friend, and so proud of Cass for giving up something that was very dear to her.

Cropper winced. "You best keep her. I ain't never had a woman to worry about, and I don't need one now."

Cassandra giggled and reached down and kissed his cheek again. "That's silly, Cropper. You know Miss Watkins isn't a real woman. You can bring her back to me when you come to see me at Grandpapa Rake-field's."

Rill walked up behind Cassandra and placed his hands gently on her shoulders. She looked up at him, and he nodded that it was time for them to go.

"Good-bye, Cropper," she said, then followed Rill to the door.

Juliana reached down and took hold of his hand and gently squeezed his fingers. She remembered the night Cropper told her he was going to build a house on a corner of Rill's land. She was so afraid that wasn't going to happen.

She sniffed before she managed to say, "Is there any way I can repay you for what you did for us?"

He looked up at her. "Don't let Cass's stepfather get my girl. Help Rill keep her safe."

"I promise."

"I'll ask the doc to mail her doll to the Triple R for me."

"Don't you dare. If you don't bring Miss Watkins to the ranch yourself, I'm going to come looking for you. You have a place waiting for you at Rill's ranch, remember?"

He closed his eyes for a moment but didn't answer her. "Take care of Rill for me. He's got family, but they've never been close. I don't want him to end up going through life a loner like I did."

"I will."

Rill placed a gentle hand on Juliana's shoulder. "Go to Cass. I'll be out in a minute."

With heartfelt regret, Juliana rose and quickly left the room.

Cropper motioned for Rill to come closer, so he knelt by the bedside. It tore at his insides to see his friend in such grave condition. "I told the doctor what you wanted and gave him the money."

The old man nodded. "Now there's no use worryin' 'bout me, but you know those men will be after you again."

"I know. I'll be careful."

"I ain't never minded your business."

"That's right."

"Julie would make you a fine wife. And if things don't work out with her grandfather, Cass's going to need a strong pa like you."

Rill nodded. He'd already been thinking about both those things, but they weren't on his mind right now. The doctor didn't expect Cropper to see another sunrise, and Rill was trying hard to keep up a good face for his friend. "I'll take care of them, Cropper." He paused. "I'll stay if you want me to."

"No. You just put my worries to rest. Now get on out of here. I don't want you to see me die."

Rill's throat closed up tight. He didn't want to leave, but knew he couldn't stay. He took hold of Cropper's hand and squeezed it. "Good-bye, my friend." A lone tear trickled down his cheek. He rubbed it away with the back of his hand.

Clear blue skies led the way as Juliana, Rill, and Cassandra started the journey to Cheyenne with Doc tied to the back of the wagon. With the horses fed and rested from their overnight stay in Hattersville, they made good time out of town.

Rill was in a sorry state of mind. The doctor hadn't given him any hope Cropper would make it through another night, and it tore at his insides not to be there for him.

He wanted to stay, but Cropper insisted he wanted Rill to go. He understood the old man not wanting anyone hanging around waiting for him to die. Hell, he wouldn't want that, either. Still, it wrenched his gut to leave his good friend to die alone.

Juliana sat quietly beside him on the wagon seat, and he felt comforted to have her occasionally brush against him.

"When will you find out about Cropper? I mean if he—how he's doing," Juliana asked shortly after they left the outskirts of town.

"I left money with the doctor. If Cropper lives, he'll join me at the ranch. Otherwise, the doctor will use the money to give Cropper a Christian burial."

"I hope you know how much I want him to live."

Rill glanced at her and knew exactly how she felt. "I know."

Juliana was silent for a moment or two, then asked, "Do you want to talk about last night?" she asked.

For him, it wasn't a day for talking about anything, but he realized Juliana might need to. He turned to her and asked, "Do you?"

"No—not necessarily." She paused. "I mean—I just wanted you to know that I'm glad that we—that it happened between us, but—"

He knew what she was trying to say. "But now we have to think about Cass, not ourselves."

"Yes."

As the day wore into late afternoon, his thoughts turned from his friend to last night and Juliana's sweet-tasting lips, desirable body, and the way she'd loved him. He didn't know how he was going to keep his hands off her. He hungered for her. He admonished himself for not having kept her at a distance, but she'd been so damn compelling, so appealing, so innocent, and so courageous that he'd folded like a house of cards.

Rill couldn't let that happen again. They had three or four weeks of hard riding ahead of them, and he had to stay watchful at all times. He wouldn't be caught unawares by Cabot's men again.

"I've been thinking," Rill said, as the afternoon shadows started creeping in. "Cabot's men know we were following the old Pony Express trail across Kansas. I've decided we're going to change our direction and head north into Nebraska and hit the Oregon Trail just below Fort Kearny."

"Will that trail take us into Cheyenne?"

"It'll bring us close. We'll have to cut south."

"Will it take us longer to get there?"

"I don't think so. We're traveling light. Most of the wagons heading north are traveling in groups and loaded with supplies, furniture, and personal belongings. Some of them even have livestock to care for. Our horses aren't pulling a heavy load, and we aren't traveling on anyone else's timetable. The only thing that can slow us down is snow or rain."

"Well, then, let's head that way, and I'll pray we won't face either one."

"By the time Nolen can get back to Cabot and tell him what happened, and they look for us on this trail, we'll be more than halfway to Cheyenne."

She smiled at him. "I trust you to make the right decision. I'm prepared for long days and short nights."

He nodded and turned the horses north.

They were quiet again for a while. Cassandra played inside the wagon. The only sounds on the spacious prairie were the horses' hooves, the wagon wheels as they rolled over parched, uneven ground, and the clink and clanging of the harness holding the ill-tempered mares together.

"Rill, I have a favor to ask of you."

He glanced over at her and gave her a wry smile. "What's that?"

"I always seem to be doing that, don't I? Asking something of you."

Remembering how he'd felt when she'd asked him to stay with her last night, he said, "That's all right. Sometimes I like what you ask."

Juliana looked away from him and said, "I want to learn how to shoot a gun."

"What?"

"When I went to the mercantile this morning to pick up the things you asked me to buy, I—I purchased a small pistol for my reticule and two boxes of bullets to go with it, but I'm afraid I don't know how to use it."

Her words hit him hard, staggering his ego. She didn't trust him to take care of her. She knew about his last trail drive, and she'd seen what happened to Cropper. Determination rose up within him. He had to prove to her he could keep her and Cass safe.

"Women shouldn't know how to use a gun," he declared, still stinging.

"That may be, but should the need arise, I want to be capable of defending Cassandra from Ward Cabot."

"I'll take care of him," he said huskily. His gut twisted. "I won't let Cabot near you or Cass."

She touched his arm, but he refused to look at her. Something more than his honor was at stake here—his manhood.

"Rill, listen to me. I know you can protect us. I trust you to take care of Cassandra—of us. I've felt that from the first day we met, and I don't want you thinking I don't, just because I want to learn how to shoot."

Rill thought of last night and the sweet, loving,

giving woman who'd lain so expectantly beneath him. He thought of how she'd sought him out, how she'd known what she wanted, what he needed, and how she wouldn't let him deny her their night together.

Juliana was a woman of rare courage and strength. How could he deny her anything she wanted? Besides, she was right. It made good sense for her to know how to shoot and for her to carry a gun in that purse that she wore around her wrist.

"All right. I'll teach you how to shoot."

❧ 14 ❧

There wasn't much change in the terrain after they crossed from Kansas into southern Nebraska. The land remained a flat windblown sea of earth mixed with empty hillsides and grassy mounds with an occasional clump of trees to break the monotony.

It seemed to Juliana the only thing that changed was the sky. Usually it was filled with stationary puffs of white clouds or wispy windswept clouds that sailed lazily overhead. Sometimes, the sky was a perfect, solid sheet of pale blue that faded into a deep azure color as darkness crept upon them at dusk and turned the bright sunshine of day into night.

The first two days of their journey went quickly as Rill kept the team of horses clipping along, not allowing them to graze except when they stopped in the late afternoon. The few minutes Juliana spent at the mercantile the morning they left Hattersville had proved a lifesaver for her and Cassandra.

Not only did the child have Cropper's harmonica to keep her busy during the seemingly endless hours of the days, but Juliana had bought her a bag of colorful marbles, two books, a small slate, and a box of chalk to practice her letters, her numbers, and to draw. Cassandra was eager to learn how to write, and the slate and chalk kept her occupied for hours.

Juliana spent most of her days inside the wagon with Cassandra, alternating between teaching her the alphabet and how to make her numbers and reading from the primer Juliana had also purchased.

Sometimes, she and Cassandra would sit at the back of the wagon and stare back through the opening, watching the wind sweep through the tall golden blades of grass or imagining shapes formed by passing clouds.

But more often than not, more often than she should, Juliana found herself looking through the opening at the front of the wagon, staring at Rill's broad shoulders and firm back, thinking she'd rather be sitting beside him on the driver's seat, watching him, talking to him, and drinking in his essence.

Occasionally, they would pass other wagons, but on their westward rush, Rill never stopped to talk. He knew time wasn't on their side, and it seemed to Juliana that he didn't waste a minute.

Rill kept his loaded rifle at his feet and his Colt in the holster at his hip at all times. In the late afternoons after they made camp, Rill would backtrack to make sure no one was following them, but he always returned before nightfall. Juliana slept peacefully each night, knowing that Rill made his bedroll under the wagon.

Juliana enjoyed the time she spent sitting on the wagon seat with Rill and by the campfire in the evenings. Sometimes she would catch him staring at her, and knew that he, like she, was thinking about their night together in the hotel room. Though neither of them had mentioned it since the morning they left Hattersville, it was never far from her thoughts. It seemed to be an unspoken rule that what had happened between them must be put on hold until Cassandra was safe with her grandfather.

One evening after Juliana had washed and put away the pot and plates from their dinner of boiled potatoes and ham, she walked over to the campfire with her reticule dangling from her wrist and eased down beside Rill.

There was just enough of a nip in the air to make the fire feel good to her exposed skin. Stars twinkled from the black velvet sky, and a misshapen moon floated overhead.

He looked over at her and smiled. "This is a surprise. You usually sit beside Cass in the evenings."

"You and I have business to take care of." She opened her purse and dug inside it for her gun and bullets.

"I miss Cropper sitting with us. Don't you, Juliana?" Cassandra asked. She sat on her blanket rolling her new marbles around on the blanket and watching them glimmer in the firelight.

Juliana cut her eyes around to Rill as she spread her blue-striped skirt over her boots and said, "Of course I do." She knew Rill thought about Cropper, even though they didn't talk about him.

"How about you, Rill? Do you miss him?" Cassandra asked him.

He glanced at Cassandra. "Hard not to. We've been riding together for years. I met him on my first cattle drive."

"Juliana and I remember him in our prayers every night, don't we?"

Juliana nodded.

A thoughtful quality shone in his eyes, and he

glanced from Cass to Juliana. He gave them a sweet smile and said, "That's a nice thing for you to do. Cropper would like that."

Juliana's throat tightened. She so wanted him to live and join Rill. She would never forgive herself for forcing her troubles into the lives of these two fine men, if Cropper didn't make it.

"Would it make you feel better to talk about him or would you rather not?" Juliana asked in a soft voice.

Rill looked into her eyes, and her heart warmed to him. "It's best not to. Talking about him won't change the outcome." His voice was low with a hint of regret in its tone.

Juliana took a deep breath and watched Rill's handsome face. She would have liked to take him in her arms and hold him, kiss him tenderly, and let him know that she cared about him, about his good friend.

They had agreed not to talk about what had happened between them, but nothing could keep her from thinking about their night together and how Rill had made her feel special. She went to sleep each night remembering the taste of his lips on hers, hearing his soft moans of pleasure, feeling the fullness of his body joined with hers.

"I guess you're ready to learn how to use that." He motioned to the small caliber pistol nestled in the folds of her blue-striped skirt.

A quiver of longing trembled through her, but she had to brush it aside and concentrate on the reason she had the gun. "It's intimidating, but necessary." She picked up the small wooden-handled pistol and box of bullets. "I didn't need to learn how to use one of these in Chicago. Auntie Vic never would have allowed it anyway. But out here on the prairie, I think it's best that I know how."

"All right, tonight I'll teach you how to load and

unload it. You can practice pulling the hammer back and squeezing the trigger. You need to get used to the feel of the weapon in your hand. Tomorrow afternoon when we make camp, I'll teach you how to aim and shoot."

He picked up the pistol and said, "Come closer."

Rill looked into her eyes, and her stomach fluttered. She knew it would always be that way, and she no longer wanted to fight the way Rill made her feel. She intended to enjoy the sensations that being with him stirred within her, even if she couldn't act on them.

She scooted closer to him and immediately felt the heat, the power from his body. It drew her, making her want to put her arms around him and press her face into the warmth of his neck and become one with him again.

"Why don't we start by you telling me what you know about a gun," Rill said.

Juliana cleared her throat, then tried to clear her mind of making love with Rill. "Let's see. I had never actually held one until I bought this the other morning. I know that when you give someone a gun you always extend it handle first, like this." He nodded and took the .22 Colt from her. "I know they are dangerous. Not much else, I'm afraid. Auntie Vic told me if I came across a gun in a home where I was working that I was to leave it alone unless it was where a child could get to it. If that were the case, I was to bring the pistol to someone's attention immediately."

"Another thing your aunt and I agree on. All right, we'll start at the beginning. Press this, and the gun will break open to give you access to the cylinder. Insert the bullets pointed-end first, like this. When all six chambers are filled, snap it shut." He opened the gun again, shook the six bullets into his palm, and refastened the cylinder to the barrel. He extended the gun to her handle first. "Now you try it."

He made it look too simple.

"What are you doing, Juliana?" Cassandra asked from the opposite side of the campfire.

"Rill's teaching me how to load a gun."

Cassandra jumped up, sending her marbles rolling in all directions. "Oh. I want to learn, too."

"No," Rill said, holding out a hand to stop her. "You stay over there on your blanket and play with your toys. Guns are not for little girls."

"Juliana's a girl," she pouted, sticking her bottom lip out as far as it would go.

"Yes, but she's older than you are. You'll have to wait until you're her age."

"Juliana gets to do everything, and I don't. That's not fair." She plopped back down on her blanket. "I want Cropper to come back and play with me. Go get him, Rill."

"You know that's not possible. Cropper has to get better before he can travel," Juliana said, trying to appease her.

"But I want him here. He'll play with me, and you and Rill won't."

"I'll tell you what. I'll help you write him a letter tomorrow, and we'll post it the next time we go into town. Would you like that?"

Her eyes brightened, and she started reaching for the marbles. "Will he answer it?"

"If he's feeling better. If not, maybe the doctor will help him write to you."

"Let's do it now."

"No. I have to do this right now. You can be thinking about what you want to tell him so it won't take so long when we get started."

Within a moment or two, Cassandra went back to

moving her marbles around on the blanket, and Juliana turned to Rill. He was watching her.

"You handled that very well."

She smiled as a warmth stole over her and made her stomach quiver again. She had never been more aware of how much she wanted Rill in her life forever, helping her teach their children.

"Just hold the gun for a few minutes and get used to the feel of it."

With Cassandra quiet, Juliana took the gun and looked it over. The pistol was cold, heavy, and uncomfortable in her hand at first. She palmed it, placing her finger on the trigger and her thumb on the ribbed hammer a few times before she popped it open. One by one she picked up the bullets from Rill's hand and inserted them into the cylinder, then snapped the gun shut.

A smile of admiration made his eyes sparkle with appreciation. "Good. It didn't take long for you to learn how to do that."

"I'm sure that's the easy part."

Rill nodded. "The hard part will be if you ever have to point it at anyone."

"I understand. I don't think I'll ever be comfortable carrying a gun, but I want to learn enough to know how to protect Cassandra. If Ward's men come back, they'll have to kill me to get to Cassandra."

His eyes hardened, and a wrinkle formed on his brow. Juliana wasn't sure if his expression was one of anger or pain.

"They'll have to go through me to get to either of you," he said, a bitterness she hadn't noticed before lacing his voice.

She smiled at him fondly. "I know, and I don't want you thinking I don't trust you to take care of us. I do. I'm just being cautious."

"I haven't seen any sign of anyone following us," Rill continued. "I'm hoping that changing trails will throw them off long enough for us to get to the Triple R. There's a better than fair chance someone will be waiting there for you. Are you prepared for that?"

She took a deep breath and nodded. "Yes. At least this way, I'll have the opportunity to tell my side of the story. I have to believe Cassandra's grandfather will help me. I don't think anyone would have if I'd stayed in Kansas City and gone to the authorities there."

"All right. We'll start practicing tomorrow. I want you to put the gun in your pocket. Keep it loaded and with you at all times. Take it with you on nature calls, and sleep with it. Most of all, don't hesitate to use it."

She didn't like the idea of always being armed, but remembering how Ward's men had sneaked into their camp with guns drawn, she knew it was the best thing to do. "I'll speak to Cassandra. She has to know that—"

"Know what?" Cassandra interrupted.

"Are you listening to our conversation?" Juliana asked.

"What do you want me to do?" Cassandra asked, not bothering to look up. "Cover my ears?"

"That might work," Juliana said, then turned back to Rill. "I'll put it in my reticule and wear that on my wrist at all times."

"That should work better than putting it in your pocket."

Juliana nodded, catching Rill's gaze with her own. His eyes searched her face. She felt as if he were trying to tell her he wanted to be alone with her, and that did crazy things to her insides.

She would have liked to talk with him about the way she felt about their night together, about the way she felt about him, but with Cassandra's little ears so close by she knew they'd made the right decision not to discuss their feelings.

Rising from the blanket, Juliana said, "I think we should go to bed. Daylight comes early."

The first day of their second week on the Oregon Trail Rill woke to early morning skies the color of mulberry wine. He hurriedly built a fire, hoping to make a pot of coffee and hit the trail before the clouds opened up. If they were lucky, they'd be able to put a few miles behind them before the ground became too soggy for the wagon wheels to pull through it.

If the rain set in, it could be days before they would have enough dry kindling to make a fire. As soon as Cassandra and Juliana woke up, he had them out collecting twigs, small limbs, and dried brush to store in the wagon to keep them dry—while he hitched up the team.

He watched the two working together, and his heart swelled with love. How could he not love Juliana? She used this time of work as an opportunity to teach Cassandra her numbers. Cass counted the twigs as she picked them up from underneath a nearby pine.

Every time Rill looked at Juliana, he wanted to take her in his arms and hold her, kiss her, touch her soft skin, and make love to her again. He forced himself to keep his distance and to stay away from conversations that led to their one night together. Cassandra was too sharp not to pick up on every word that passed between him and Juliana.

Long days in the wagon didn't bother him with Juliana beside him. He'd never felt so welcomed by a woman. He no longer felt threatened at the thought of settling down with a wife and children. Cropper was right. He needed Juliana and Cass as much as they needed him. And that was a good feeling.

Rill's only fear was that he might not get them to the Triple R safely.

When they were ready to leave, Juliana stopped Rill at the back of the wagon and said, "The gray skies have made inside the wagon almost as dark as night. Do you mind if we sit up front with you for a few minutes this morning?"

Do I mind?

Hell no!

Do I think it's a good idea?

Hell no!

Do I have the strength to deny you?

Hell no!

Rill knew the folly of having her so close he could touch her but didn't want to deny himself the chance to enjoy her company, be near her, and occasionally let his arm brush up against her.

He laid his hat on the back step of the Conestoga and shrugged into his slicker. "You can, but I don't know for how long. Looks like the rain could start any minute."

"Thank you. I promise I'll keep Cassandra quiet and not let her bother you."

"Is that why you've spent so much time in the wagon? You thought Cass would bother me?"

"I know how talkative she is, and how quiet you are, and I don't want us to be any more trouble than we've already been."

His eyes swept up and down her face. His hands ached to touch her cheek, to lift her chin, to lace through her hair.

"I don't think of you as trouble any more."

A pleased smile stretched across her face. "That's nice to hear."

They were silent for a few moments, then he asked, "You think of me as quiet?"

"Most of the time. Out here on the prairie, everything is quiet except the noise from the wagon and the horses." Her gaze left his face and scanned the landscape. "When you ride on Doc or on the wagon seat, you seem quiet and very much—alone."

She was right. He'd felt that way since his first drive, but since Cass and Juliana had stolen into his life, all his feelings had changed. Now—for the first time in his life—Juliana had him thinking about being a husband, and Cass had him thinking about being a father. At first, his protectiveness of them had astonished him, confused him. Now he was beginning to understand it.

"What do you think about me the other times?"

Her gaze darted back to his eyes, and she questioned him, "What do you mean?"

"You said I'm quiet most of the time. When am I not?" He saw her swallow hard. Her eyes blinked rapidly.

"When you're in bed. You talked more than I'd ever heard you say at one time before."

"Did that bother you?"

"Oh, no," she whispered. "I loved every word, every touch that passed between us."

Excitement grew inside him. "So did I. I want to make love to you again."

She drew a sharp intake of breath, and it pleased him.

It thrilled him to know she wanted him as much as he wanted her. He knew she would come to him again once they had Cass settled. Until that time, he had to restrain his feelings, the things he wanted to say to her, until Cass was safe.

He needed to touch Juliana. He reached out and

put his palm to her soft cheek. Juliana leaned into his hand and slowly rubbed her cheek against his skin.

Rill was about to pull her into his arms when Cass stuck her head out of the wagon and said, "What's the matter, Juliana? What's wrong with your face? Do you have something on it?"

Juliana jumped back. "Ah—nothing," she stammered. "Rill said we could sit in the driver's seat with him. Go on, and I'll meet you up there."

Her eyes darted back to his face. Rill said quietly, "We have many things to talk about when we get to the Wyoming Territory. Sit with me. I'd like the company, and don't worry about Cass talking. Sometimes, I spend too much time alone."

She nodded, and headed for the front of the wagon. Rill wondered if he had the strength to stay away from Juliana. He knew he had to stop thinking about making love to her again or he wasn't going to make it through these last three weeks on the trail.

It struck him as an awesome surprise. He had never had the desire to be a part of a woman's life until he met Juliana. He'd never given any thought to love, a home, or children. His brothers must have felt this way about their wives. That was why Web was always telling him to find a nice woman and settle down. But Web should have known he couldn't—not until he found the right one. And Rill was beginning to believe he had.

Rill placed his black hat on his head and followed Juliana. With the fast pace they were traveling now, he risked pushing the horses too hard. It was impossible to travel faster, but now he had more reason than ever to get Cassandra under the care of her grandfather.

"I want Juliana all to myself," he muttered and strode to the front of the wagon.

An hour later, Rill was smiling to himself. Juliana was right. Cass, who was sitting between them, hadn't stopped talking. She could find more questions to ask than he or Juliana had answers for.

The chatty little girl had asked him to tell her a story, the way Cropper had, but shortly after he started telling her about crossing a swollen river with fifteen hundred head of cattle, she stopped him and told him that story wasn't interesting enough and to start another. She wanted to hear about Indians or grizzly bears.

By midmorning a light drizzle fell, and rumbling rolls of thunder sounded in the distance. To the south of them Rill watched jagged streaks of lightning spit across the darkened sky and drive into the ground.

"You and Cass crawl into the wagon," he said. "No use in all of us getting wet."

"We're not afraid of a little rain, are we, Juliana? I want to stay out here with you, Rill," Cass said.

Juliana looked at him over Cass's head. "That's not a good idea, Cassandra," Juliana said, brushing her brown hair away from her shoulders. "If you caught a chill or a fever, it could delay our journey, and we don't want that. Off you go."

Cass looked up at Juliana. "One time before you came to take care of me, I played in the rain with Miss Watkins. We didn't get sick."

"That may well be, but you're not going to do it today."

"I don't want to go inside. It's too dark in there, and I can't breathe."

"Cassandra, remember when we discussed there were times you could argue and times when you couldn't. This is one of those times you can't. I'm not going to let you get wet. That's my final word."

She huffed loudly and clamped her hands on her hips. "You're coming inside, too, aren't you?"

"Yes. Crawl in, and I'll be right behind you," Juliana said, then turned to Rill. "What will we do? Are we going to stop for the day?"

"No. We'll keep going for as long as we can. If the lightning gets too close, we'll try to find a group of trees and stop near them."

"Isn't that dangerous?"

"Not if we don't get under them. Lightning strikes the tallest object. I'd like for that to be a tree and not us."

Juliana shivered. "I've never seen it so dark in the middle of the day."

"The prairie's known for violent storms. Nothing to stop the wind from building up across the plains. Don't worry. We'll be all right."

He saw that the rain was saturating her skirt and collecting in her hair, but he didn't want her to leave. The heat of her next to him warmed him like a fire on a frigid night.

"You're getting wet. Go inside with Cass."

"I'd rather stay out here with you."

She looked into his eyes, and he wanted her so badly he swayed toward her. A loud clap of thunder split through the air, and the horses whinnied and jerked against the reins, forcing his attention back to his driving. "When it stops, you can come back out. Look in the trunk. There're two ponchos in there. Hand me one of them."

Juliana nodded.

By midafternoon Rill felt chilled and in desperate need of a hot cup of coffee. The raincoat hadn't helped much. He felt as though there wasn't a dry thread of clothing on him. He'd been through many storms during his cattle drives, but it had always been hot. Today, the air had a crispness that left him cold.

The rain had stayed steady, but not heavy, for most of the day. Several times, Rill had fought to keep the skittish horses from bolting when loud thunder rumbled across the skies and rent the air.

Black storm clouds blossomed and roiled across the wide expanse of sky, darkening the prairie in every direction. Bright, forked lightning illuminated the distant horizon. Occasionally, there were so many bolts flashing at one time that it looked as if the electrical phenomenon was shooting up from the earth like a parade of fireworks.

"Rill!" Juliana exclaimed, crawling out of the wagon and onto the seat with him.

He threw a glance her way. Rain rolled down the collar of his slicker and ran down his neck. It took all his attention to hold the horses in check. "Juliana, get back inside. The rain will ruin your coat."

She grabbed hold of his forearm. "No, stop the wagon. We're in trouble."

Rill heard fear in her voice. Her hand trembled against his arm. He snapped around to look at her.

Rill caught sight of Juliana's eyes and knew immediately something was wrong. Dead wrong. He stiffened. Not bothering to ask what, he pulled the team to a halt and set the brake. He jumped down from the wagon, pulling his pistol free of his holster. Instinct took over, and he flattened his body against the wagon as he eased toward the back.

That old familiar feeling of weakness struck him in the gut. Fear for Juliana's and Cassandra's safety knotted in his chest, closing off his breath. What if he failed them? What if Cabot had sent more men? More guns? Rill's stomach jerked. He broke out in a cold sweat.

He shook his head and blinked rain from his eyes. Damn, he couldn't live with the fear of failure any more. He had to act.

If Ward Cabot has sent more men—I'll have to kill them.

Rill hurried to the back of the wagon. "Oh, shit!"

Twirling straight toward them at an alarming rate of speed came a funnel-shaped, violent gray swirl of cloud, dirt, and debris.

❧ 15 ❧

Juliana jumped down and ran over to Rill. Staring at the dark gray funnel bearing down on them, she gasped in horror, in awe. It looked bigger, more threatening, now that she was out of the wagon and could see the entire length of the tornado twirling up into the sky. A gripping fear froze her.

"Can we outrun it?" she asked Rill.

His mouth tightened. "No time, but I don't think we're directly in its path. I have to get the horses loose before they see the funnel. They'll go crazy."

"I'll help."

"No. Where's Cass?" He strode over to Doc and untied him. He slapped him on the rump with his hat, and the stallion took off.

"Asleep in the wagon."

"Get her out," he said, as he pushed his hat down on his head and tightened the strings snug under his chin. "Make her lie facedown under the wagon. There's two extra canteens in the back left corner by the trunk. Fill them with water, then get under the wagon with Cass while I unhitch the horses."

She couldn't take her eyes off the swirling destruction coming toward them. Rain stung her eyes, and a fierce wind whipped viciously at her hair, tearing down her chignon.

"Do what I told you." Rill turned and started toward the mares. *"Now,* Juliana!"

His command was clipped and urgent, snapping Juliana out of her mesmerized state.

Fighting her fear, Juliana climbed into the back of the wagon, quickly found the two canteens, and placed the straps across her shoulders. She crawled over to Cassandra and gently shook her.

"Wake up, Cassandra. Wake up!" Juliana lifted the sleeping child's head and raised her to a sitting position.

Cassandra jerked. Her eyes flew open, and she struck out at Juliana. "No!" Cassandra screamed. "I can't breathe. I can't see. I can't breathe."

Juliana grabbed her hands and held her close. "It's all right, Cass, I'm here. Look, I'm right here. You were dreaming."

"I couldn't breathe," she said again, tearfully.

"Shhh—don't think about that, sweetheart. I'm here," Juliana tried to soothe her. "And you're awake now. See, you're all right."

Cassandra's lips trembled. Her small hands made fists under her chin. "I want my mama."

Juliana's heart broke for Cassandra, but there was no more time to comfort her. "Come. We have to get out of the wagon immediately. Follow me."

"Why? What's wrong?"

"There's a storm coming. Hurry, we haven't much time. You have to get under the wagon."

Tears rolled down Cass's cheeks. "No! I'm afraid," she cried. "I don't want to."

Juliana jumped down and reached back inside. Cassandra fell into her arms. The wagon began to shake.

Juliana rushed to the water barrel and threw off the top. She unscrewed the cap and dipped one canteen inside, letting the water rush into the spout. "Get under the wagon now, Cass! I'll be right beside you as soon as I get the water."

"No!" Cassandra ran to Juliana and grabbed her around the waist, burying her face in Juliana's skirt, sobbing loud and pitifully.

The wind picked up suddenly, whipping at her hair and skirt. Goose bumps of fear popped out on Juliana. She decided to let Cassandra stay with her. It would take more time to force her to get under cover and, with the way the wagon was shaking, she wasn't sure it was the best place to be anyway.

Juliana glanced toward the front of the wagon. She couldn't see Rill but heard the rattle and clanking of the harness. With cold, trembly fingers she replaced the cap on the canteen and exchanged it for the empty one on her shoulder.

The wind and rain became more fierce, plastering her hair and clothes against her body. Juliana heard the distant sound of a train. Her breath lodged in her throat. She'd heard that tornadoes sounded like the long freight trains that roared in and out of Chicago every day.

She dropped the second canteen into the barrel and grabbed Cassandra's shoulder. Knowing the best way to get her to obey without question, Juliana turned her toward the fast moving funnel. "Look! You are in danger. A tornado is heading straight for us. You must get under the wagon now and lie with your face to the ground."

"Don't leave me, Juliana," she cried.

"I won't. I have to help Rill, then I'll join you. Take the canteen, and get under the wagon. Do it now, Cass!"

Whimpering, Cassandra fell to her knees and crawled under the wagon as Juliana demanded.

Dirt blew in her eyes and mouth as Juliana held on to the wagon. The roaring sound of the swirling wind grew louder as she edged toward the front of the wagon.

Through the cloud of dust, she saw Rill working furiously with the horses. They'd already sensed the danger and were fighting his efforts to free them.

"Rill!" she shouted into the wind. "Come now! There's no more time!"

"I'm— co—ing. Get —der wa—!"

At last the horses were free and ran off. Rill grabbed hold of Juliana as the wagon started shaking violently. The wind took her breath. The locomotive of swirling terror grew louder.

Suddenly, Juliana realized there was no safety on the prairie. The Conestoga would be little protection from the evil bearing down upon them. She and Rill fell to the ground and crawled to Cassandra, flanking her.

Juliana threw one arm around Cassandra and the other over her head. She felt Rill's arm across her back pulling her closer to Cassandra, closer to him.

His touch calmed Juliana. Rill was with her, and she knew that somehow he'd see they made it through the storm.

The sound became deafening, bearing down on them with the fierce intensity and power of a runaway freight train. Her skirt blew up and around her head.

The earth shook violently. Juliana thought the ground would split in two and swallow her.

Wind whipped at Juliana's clothes with amazing force. Her feet and legs lifted off the ground. She was going to blow away. The sound was ripping her from the earth. She couldn't open her eyes.

Filled with terror, Juliana screamed.

Something strong, warm, and powerful fell on top of her legs and held them to the earth. She realized it was Rill. Stinging bits of dirt and wind beat against her. Cold rain felt like buckets of water washing over her. Mud splattered her face.

Juliana trembled.

The stupefying sound ebbed.

The terrifying wind died.

The horrifying rain slacked.

Tentatively, gasping, Juliana raised her head. Rill had raised up, too, and was looking around. Cassandra lay in the mud with her face hidden by her arms, crying.

The storm had passed.

The wagon was gone.

"Rill?"

He turned to her. "Are you all right?"

She nodded.

He reached over Cassandra and took hold of Juliana's dirty hand. His eyes glistened. "I heard you scream and saw you lifting off the ground. I was so damn scared the tornado was going to capture you in its wind."

"So was I. I felt your legs on mine, holding me down. Thank you." Juliana managed a trembly smile as she squeezed his hand, drawing comfort from his touch.

"Thank God you're safe."

She nodded, wiping dirt from her face as the rain fell upon her and helped her wash. "Where's the wagon?"

"I don't know." Rill scrambled to his feet. "Take care of Cass while I look around."

"Come here, Cass," she whispered, taking hold of the small girl's arm and pulling her into her embrace.

Cassandra scrambled into Juliana's arms so fast she almost knocked Juliana over. The child was wet and coated with black dirt and grass, her hair tangled and matted against her head. She clutched the strap of the canteen Juliana had given her.

Juliana hugged her tightly. For a moment, she wondered if she'd done the right thing in taking Cassandra from her stepfather's home, leaving her vulnerable to the dangers on the trail.

"Shh—Cass, it's all over. The storm has passed, and you're fine. We all are."

"I—I w—want my m—mama."

"I know you do, sweetheart. I wish she were here with you, too. She would do a far better job of taking care of you than I do." She kissed Cassandra's wet forehead, wondering why so many things were going wrong when all she wanted was to do the right thing.

"I want Cropper, too."

"I know."

Juliana felt weak and trembly. How had she managed to get Cassandra into so many dangers? It was as simple as going to sleep one night and before the next morning, Juliana was on the run for her and Cassandra's lives. She was trying so hard to protect Cassandra, and it seemed all she did was end up putting the girl in danger.

It would be so easy to think that fate was deliberately being cruel to her—except for Rill. She trembled from guilt. It was a deplorable thought, but she wouldn't have met Rill if Ward Cabot hadn't attempted to kill Cassandra.

Juliana looked around as she comforted her charge. A fierce wind sent the terrifying, destructive dark gray funnel stampeding across the sky in the distance ahead of them, twirling, swirling, like a child's top. Juliana shivered from the leftover wind and chilling temperature. The rain had saturated her winter coat, leaving her clothes wet and dirty against her skin.

Rill walked over and knelt down beside them. He reached over and lifted Cassandra from Juliana's arms and placed her on his lap. She looked so small and protected in his strong arms.

Rill kissed the top of her head. "How's my little girl?" he asked fondly. "Are you all right?"

Cassandra threw her arms around his neck and whimpered, "I didn't know what to do. I was afraid."

"I know, but it's over now, Cass."

He held the child, but stared at Juliana. Her heart overflowed with love for Rill. When they first met him, he wouldn't even call them by their names. Now, he was calling Cassandra his little girl and comforting her the way a father would. Juliana's throat tightened with tears of admiration. How could she not be filled with pleasure, because she loved this man?

Rill's gaze swept up and down Juliana's face as he gently patted Cassandra's back. "You're wet, you're dirty, and you've never been more beautiful."

His eyes told her so much more than the words he spoke. Excitement danced through her senses. Suddenly, she didn't feel the cold or the wet clothes against her body. Rill had warmed her.

"Am I beautiful, too?" Cassandra asked him.

Rill laughed. "Yes. You're beautiful."

Juliana smiled at Rill and brushed her dripping hair away from her face with the back of her hand. "It was so terrifying. It won't come back this way, will it?"

"I don't think so. I've never heard of a tornado turning around and heading back to where it came from."

"Do you think there's another one behind it?"

"Not likely. Storms as fierce as this one usually happen in the spring and early summer. The warm weather we've been having probably caused it."

"I don't want it to come back, either," Cassandra said.

Juliana shivered again and rubbed her hands together to warm them. "What are we going to do? The horses are gone, and the storm blew the wagon away."

"I spotted the wagon." He pointed in the direction of the fading tornado. "About two hundred yards from here. Looks like the canvas top is shredded. I'm hoping it's in one piece and that at least some of our supplies are still inside."

Juliana rose and looked in the direction he pointed to. Through the mist of rain, she spotted the ragged canvas top of the Conestoga flapping in the wind.

"Dear mercy, you're right. It is the wagon. How can that be? I thought it would be a broken pile of wood, if we even found it."

"I don't know. Miraculous things can happen during a tornado. I've heard that a storm like that can pick up a whole house and move it more than a mile away, then put it back down without toppling the first piece of furniture inside."

Having heard similar stories, Juliana could only nod her agreement. It was a miracle that the storm hadn't taken their lives.

"And what about the horses?" Juliana asked, picking up the canteen Cassandra had dropped when Rill took her in his arms. "Can we find them?"

"I hope so. I don't see them anywhere right now, but they shouldn't be too far away. Let's head toward the wagon. I think Doc will pick up our scent and find his way back to us as soon as the rain stops."

"You can whistle, Rill," Cassandra said, lifting her tear-streaked face from his shoulder and rubbing her eyes with chubby little-girl hands. "That will bring Doc running back to you."

He looked down at her, then laughed. "If he's close enough to hear me, he'll come. Let's head for the wagon and see if we have anything left in there. You and Juliana need dry clothes, if we can find them."

"So do you," Cassandra said. "You're wet, too."

Rill rose with Cassandra in his arms, then stood her on the muddy ground.

"Carry me, Rill," she said, reaching back up to him.

"All right, I'll carry you on my back." He bent down. "Hop on."

Cassandra laughed and climbed up on his back. He reached out his hand to Juliana.

She smiled and took it.

By the time they'd reached the wagon, the tornado was out of sight. The rain had slowed to a mist, and the sky had started clearing in the east behind them. Strident rays of sunshine poked out of the dark gray sky overhead.

The tornado was gone as quickly as it had come.

The storm had wreaked havoc on the Conestoga, but by some miracle it was upright. Rill inspected their transportation closely, and it appeared the wheels hadn't been damaged. The tools and Cropper's cast-iron Dutch oven had been stripped from the sides, and the water barrel had been splintered. Some of the supplies had been swept away by the spinning wind while others had been tossed about and scattered.

Juliana felt lucky that the rain hadn't penetrated her leather satchel. Their extra clothes were dry. Rill had a dry change in the ox-hide chest, which had been left unscathed by the storm, too. He suggested that Juliana and Cassandra change into the dry clothes while he went looking for the horses.

The rain had already washed away a lot of the dirt from their faces and hair. As soon as they had dressed, and their hair had been brushed and properly pinned away from their faces, Juliana took the driest fuel they could find from around the wagon and made a fire.

She knew she needed to dry their blankets and Rill's bedroll so they would have a place to sleep. They were lucky the canvas top had held as long as it had, so the rain hadn't completely soaked through all their belongings.

Juliana put Cassandra to the task of collecting more twigs and pieces of wood torn off the wagon to lay by the fire, hoping they would dry enough to burn without putting out the flames.

While she waited for the coffee to bubble and the beans to heat, Juliana held the blankets up in front of the fire, drying them. She worked without allowing herself to think about the near disaster that chilled her to the bone. She kept repeating to herself that as long as Cassandra was safe and Rill was with her she could handle anything. She had to be strong and believe that.

Cassandra found a large tree limb the terrible wind had left behind, and the two of them dragged it over by the fire where Juliana hung Rill's bedroll on it to dry.

It was close to sundown by the time Rill returned. He hadn't found the horses. After they'd eaten, all three of them held blankets up to the fire until Cassandra became fretful. Knowing Cass was still shaken from the storm, Juliana told her the story of a princess, a fairy godmother, and a handsome prince while Rill held Cassandra in his arms and soothed her until she fell asleep.

Juliana helped Rill put her in the wagon and cover her with one of the dry blankets, then they walked back to the fire and sat down.

The wind had died down, and the air that was moving in seemed to be warmer. A veil of darkness covered them.

Weary, Juliana said, "I can't believe we made it through that storm alive. We were so lucky."

Rill threw more sticks onto the fire, then moved closer to her. "It was a close call, all right."

She looked up at him with worry on her face. "What are we going to do now?"

"Don't worry, we'll make it."

"How?" She tried to rub the tension out of the back of her neck. Now that Cass was asleep, she felt free to show her concern. "We have no horses. The wagon is damaged. We have only a few cans of food and mere ounces of water."

"Juliana, don't worry. We're going to be all right. I'm not going to pretend I'm not worried. We're in one hell of a mess, but the map shows a town a few miles from here. We should be able to restock our supplies there."

"That won't help us right now, Rill. What will we do if Ward's men find us?"

"The same thing we'd do if we had our horses. We

have our guns. We'd fight." His eyes softened. "Juliana, trust me. We're going to be all right."

A calming feeling flowed over her, and she remembered she'd given her trust to Rill a long time ago. Now, she had to put that faith into action. "I do trust you. It's just that the storm left me with a lot of anxiety."

"I know. But it would be foolish to start walking tonight. We'll start out at first light and carry only food and water. I'd be more worried if there wasn't a town nearby. Even if we don't find the horses, we should be able to walk to the town in a couple of days."

"I guess I'm too tired to think straight. I think I'll go check on Cass. I want to make sure she's all right."

The night was dark, and there was no lantern to light inside the wagon, but it appeared Cassandra was sound asleep. For now, they were as safe as they could be under the circumstances.

Juliana felt her body relax for the first time since the tornado hit. She walked the few steps back to the campfire and dropped down beside Rill. "Cass is sleeping peacefully," Juliana said.

"I'm not surprised," he said. "She was so tired she should sleep all night without waking."

Juliana brushed a strand of hair away from her face. "Cass is such a bright and beautiful child. It's so hard to believe anyone would want to hurt her."

"We're going to keep her safe, Juliana," he said. "What I want to know is, when did you start calling Cassandra Cass? That is new."

Juliana looked at him and saw amusement lurking in his eyes. He smiled so cunningly that Juliana pushed her dark feelings aside and responded to his light mood.

Rill's hair was ruffled and at some time during the

storm something had scratched his cheek just below his eye. Even though fatigue didn't show on his handsome face, she knew he wasn't getting enough rest and had to be tired.

She was intensely aware of Rill and of how their conversation had turned.

"I think it was during the storm. There wasn't time to say her whole name. Cass is so much quicker." She smiled at him. "And I have to admit that Cropper was right. Cassandra is a big name for such a little girl."

Rill's smile slowly faded. He drew his knees up and wrapped his arms around them. "Cass fits her personality better, anyway."

"I'm sorry," she said, touching his hand. "I didn't mean to remind you of Cropper."

"I don't mind talking about him. He's been my friend for close to fifteen years."

The light tone of the conversation had gone as quickly as it had come. A sadness settled over Juliana. She'd never forget that it was her fault that Cropper was no longer with Rill. She wondered if she would ever forgive herself for what had happened to him.

Her mind drifted quickly over her lifetime as she stared into the fire. "That must be a wonderful feeling. Having such a good friend to depend on for that many years. I've never even known anyone for that long. It sounds like forever to me."

"How's that?"

"I was eleven when my parents were killed and Auntie Vic took me into her home. Living with her meant moving to a completely different section of Chicago than the one I was used to. When I left, I never saw the people from my old neighborhood again."

"There was no other family?"

"No." Suddenly, she felt very alone as memories

from the past swept over her. "My mother and Auntie Vic grew up in an orphanage. If my father had family anywhere, he never spoke to me about them. I have to admit that I've wondered how you could move so far away from those who love and care about you. I think I would love to live close to my family—if I had any."

He shrugged. "Just because I didn't want to make Texas my home doesn't mean I won't ever see them again. My mother will visit me at the first hint I give her. And once I get my ranch working, I'm sure my brothers will have to come and take a look at it if for no other reason than to tell me all the reasons I should have settled in Texas."

"Will that bother you?"

"No. I'll want them to come."

"Even though you don't want to admit it, it sounds like you have a close family. I envy you."

Juliana's sadness turned into a longing to love and be loved and to belong to someone. Cassandra had her grandfather. Rill had his family, but Juliana had no one.

"You'll have a family some day, Juliana."

Her heart skipped a beat. Was he making her a promise or only making a statement?

An overwhelming need to be touched by Rill filled her. She wanted to love him and be a part of his life, a part of his family. There was something possessive about the way she was feeling about him tonight.

She looked at Rill. He watched her with his dark gray-brown eyes. A raw tension exploded between them. Her breath came quickly as she realized what was happening. Their journey had been too hard, the storm too frightening, to spend this night without him beside her.

She leaned toward him. "Rill, I know I have no right to ask you, but could you hold me?"

Without a spoken answer, he reached and pulled her into the circle of his strong embrace. His breath fanned her hair as he rubbed his cheek against the top of her head.

Juliana slipped her arms around his neck, laid her head on his shoulder, and sighed contentedly as his arms wrapped around her back. The warmth that covered her came from Rill, not the campfire. She felt protected in his embrace. She wanted to be cradled by him forever.

"This is dangerous, Juliana. This makes me want to hold you all night, not just a few minutes."

"I know." She kissed the side of his neck and heard his intake of breath, felt his muscles tighten under her touch. Waves of pleasure radiated through her. She liked the taste of his rain-washed skin. Her hands roamed over his wide shoulders and down his muscled back.

"Mmm— You're tempting me, Juliana," he whispered in her ear.

She shivered with anticipation. She wanted Rill to love her again. Just as Rill had needed her the night of Cropper's surgery, she needed him tonight.

"I know."

"Your breath is warm against my neck. Your hair smells fresh, like rainwater," he said, his fingers tangling in her chignon as he pulled the pins out of the bun.

Juliana lifted her head and looked into eyes lit with desire. He wanted her as much as she wanted to be in his arms and his bed. In an unusually husky voice, she said, "I'm cold tonight and only you can warm me."

He cupped the side of her face with a callused hand. "Are you sure you know what you want? Do you know what that means?"

"I know."

She brushed her lips against his in a tender imploring kiss and heard a soft moan deep in his throat. They clung together, each understanding the other's need.

"You're so tempting," he murmured, then pulled her up tight and caught her lips with his in a soulful kiss meant to let her know how deeply she stirred him. She opened her mouth as the kiss turned into a fierce expression of all the passion that flared between them.

She traced the line of his top lip, then sucked the soft fullness of the lower one into her mouth.

Rill moaned with satisfaction and returned the intimate gesture.

Juliana's heart beat wildly, her blood rushed through her veins in a heady sensation that made her dizzy. The first time they'd made love she hadn't known what to expect, and her body took all its cues from Rill. Now she felt eager, ravenous to touch him, to join her body to his and become part of him. Her need for him was too sharp, too keen, to be denied.

Rill's lips left hers and traced a pattern over her eyes, her chin, her nose, with moist featherlight kisses. His hands caressed her breasts, shaping and molding them with such loving tenderness that she wanted to cry out from the naked pleasure he gave.

He raised his head and gazed deeply into her eyes. She saw firelight dancing in his pupils, glowing on his cheeks. She felt his hunger for her exploding in the way his body trembled beneath her open hands.

Gently, he tumbled her down onto the blanket in front of the fire and with exquisite slowness covered her with his body. Juliana felt excitement growing inside her as he whispered her name over and over again. She concentrated on the lush feelings spiraling through her.

The hotness of the flaming fire couldn't match the heat searing inside her. Through their layers of clothes she could feel his hard maleness pressing against her. Desire flew through her like the uncontrollable tornado that had ripped across the prairie, and she welcomed it.

She shuddered, and her hands slid up his chest to snake down the front of his shirt. Spirals of heat curled and tightened in the pit of her stomach. She was aware of every touch, every sound, he made. With all her heart, body, and soul, she knew she loved this man.

She needed to tell him how much she wanted to be the woman in his life, but knew he had to be the one to speak of love and commitment first. He was the one who wasn't ready, and until he was she would wait and continue to show him how much she loved him.

With eager fingers she worked the buttons of his shirt as he helped with her blouse. She lifted her lower body and pressed against him, enticing him to hurry with the process of undressing them.

"Juliana, you are tempting me beyond my control. I want you naked beneath me. I want to drive deep inside you and make you mine once again."

Rolling away, he quickly shucked his boots, and flung off his clothes. Juliana gasped with anticipation when she saw that he was fully aroused. She turned so he could help remove her skirt and drawers, leaving her dressed only in her chemise. He pulled the bodice of the plain cotton garment below her breasts and pushed the tail of it up so that the material bunched at her waist.

Poised over her, he let his gaze sweep up and down her body as she lay before him with only firelight and moonlight shining upon her. She relished the hot feel of his eyes upon her.

Finally, his gaze met hers. Juliana smiled and reached up to him. "Come to me."

Rill moved against her. "From this moment on, you are mine."

Rill woke to bright sunshine heating his face. He rolled and hit something soft. He tensed. Juliana lay peacefully beside him. He looked over at her. Most of her body was covered by the blanket but their clothes and shoes were strewn about the cold campfire.

He looked up at the sun and judged the morning to be well past dawn. He needed to wake Juliana and get her dressed before Cassandra woke up and found them together, but he hated to when Juliana lay so warm and soft beside him.

Propped up on his elbow, he stared down at Juliana, the woman he loved, sleeping so peacefully. As he watched her sleep, he remembered last night and how eagerly, how passionately, how unconditionally, she'd given herself to him.

By the firelight, he'd loved her with his eyes, with his lips, with his hands, with his shaft. Those masculine sensations she'd stirred then flickered, fluttered, and built inside him until again he was wild with wanting her.

He thought over last night, and how she'd arched her back and moved sinuously against him. He'd liked the way her firm yet soft breasts felt in the palms of his hands. Worshiping her, he'd slid his hands down past her waist, around her hips to the center of her womanhood. She had been moist with need for him. He'd joined his body with hers and felt a love for her that he knew he could never feel for another woman.

Prickles of heat danced in his loins even though he knew he had never been so satisfied, so complete, with any other woman. Juliana had welcomed him into her arms, and just as he had the other time he had made love to her, with Juliana he felt like he was home.

All through his thorough loving, he'd tried to convey his commitment to her, even though he knew it wasn't the right time to tell her how he felt—that he wanted her in his life forever.

The wind rustled the torn canvas on the wagon and disturbed Rill's musing, reminding him that he didn't want Cassandra to catch him and Juliana undressed and under the blanket together.

He quickly stepped into his trousers and shoved his arms into his shirt. As he fastened the buttons, he bent down and kissed Juliana on her closed eyelids.

Her eyes popped open. "Rill." She smiled and reached for him.

"I hate to wake you but Cass will be up soon. You need to get dressed."

Juliana bolted up, holding the blanket over her breasts, and immediately started reaching for her clothes. "Dear mercy! Rill, you shouldn't have waited so long to call me. Cass could have seen us together."

"I haven't been awake too long myself." He smiled and winked at her. "I didn't get much sleep last night, if you remember. You get dressed. I'm going to check on Cass."

He reached over and kissed her soundly on the lips before he rose.

Rill caught himself whistling, and he chuckled as he walked the ten or so yards to the Conestoga. He couldn't remember the last time he had felt like whistling. He couldn't believe how two females had changed his life and had him thinking about a home, a wife, and children.

He peered into the back of the wagon and saw the rumpled blanket Cass had slept on, but not her. A shiver of foreboding stole over him. Rill shook himself free of the feeling and crawled up into the wagon and looked around the supplies to make sure Cass wasn't hiding inside. He jumped down and walked around the wagon, making sure she wasn't underneath it.

"Cass," he said in a calm tone, even though his stomach had started to cramp. "Cass, where are you?"

Anger at himself stabbed through Rill as he moved away from the wagon and searched the landscape. He looked quickly the first time, making a complete turn-around, hoping to spot her. A tight knot formed in the pit of his stomach. He had to think. He couldn't become alarmed. He turned again, slowly so as not to miss any possible movement in the near or far distance.

"Cass!" he called again, louder.

"Rill, what's wrong?" Juliana asked, walking up beside him as she buttoned her blouse.

He tried to keep the worry that swamped him off his face as he turned to her and said, "Cass isn't in the wagon. She's gone."

❧ 16 ❧

Juliana stared at Rill. A thread of unease slithered up her back like a snake. "What do you mean, gone?"

"Cass!" he yelled. "Answer me. Where are you?"

Alarm shot through Juliana like a bullet out of a gun. Rill was serious. She turned and ran to the wagon. She climbed up on the back step and looked inside. A rumpled blanket and a few supplies lay scattered about the wide-planked floor.

"Oh, no!" She dropped down from the step. Barely able to breathe, she called, "Cass!"

Rill strode up to her. "I've looked. She's not here."

"Don't tell me that. It can't be true." She grabbed the front of his shirt in desperation, needing to feel his strength once again. "Rill, what's happened? Oh, my! Did Ward's men steal her from the wagon in the middle of the night?"

"I don't think so. They wouldn't have missed an opportunity to take us in to the authorities."

Intense fear shook her. "Indians took her! I've heard they steal white children and make them slaves.

Oh, my Lord, what have I done!" Juliana gasped and covered her mouth with her hand.

Rill took hold of her shoulders and forced her to face him. "Juliana, get hold of yourself and calm down. Listen to me. We're not in Indian territory right now, so it's not likely that happened."

"You don't know that!" she shrieked, unable to bear the thought of Cassandra kidnapped.

"I don't know for sure, but—"

"Then where is she?" Juliana asked wildly.

"I don't know. It's my guess she woke up early and found us together and—"

Could it be her fault that Cass was missing? "Oh, my, no! Cassandra!" Juliana tore away from Rill and started running away from the wagon.

Rill caught hold of her arm and stopped her a few steps away. "Juliana, get hold of yourself."

"No, let me go!" She struggled against his hold.

"Stop fighting me."

"No! I have to find her." Tears formed in her eyes, and her legs trembled. She tried to pull away, tried to push him away.

He gently shook her. "Juliana, listen to me. We must have a plan."

"Plan!" She was breathless. "All we need to do is look for her. Rill, please let me go so I can find her."

"You're wasting time arguing. We'll find her, Juliana, but you have to calm down first."

All of a sudden, Rill's face faded from her sight and she saw Auntie Vic standing in front of her, that formidable, stern set to her thin lips and eagle eyes. Juliana lifted her shoulders, her chin, and relaxed.

You must never let anyone or anything fluster you. It is your duty to remain in control of yourself and your charge at all times. If there is a crisis or an emergency, you have to remain calm and handle the situation with haste and efficiency. Your job, your reputation, demands it.

"Are you all right, Juliana? Can you hear me?"

Juliana blinked and saw Rill. She looked up at the pale blue sky. "Yes, I hear you. I'm sorry I lost control for a moment, but I'm fine now."

"Good. It's two, maybe three, hours at the most past sunup. Cass can't have wandered too far away in that length of time."

"I agree. I don't believe she would have left camp in the dark."

He let go of Juliana. "Look." He swung his arm wide and made a complete circle with his body. "Which direction do we start?"

Her breath caught in her throat as she followed the wide arc of his arm across a sea of grass. Her knees weakened, and for a moment she thought she might crumple to the ground. Only knowing that Cassandra was her responsibility kept her from it. It was her job to find her, and she would.

She took a deep calming breath and said, "I see what you mean." She could allow her emotions to be torn apart on the inside but outwardly she must appear calm and levelheaded.

"The first thing we do is look for tracks."

"Yes. That should be easy enough. The ground is still damp from all the rain."

"That's right. And we know that she left the wagon."

At the back of the wagon, Juliana's gaze flew to the ground. She and Rill had already disturbed the muddy earth beneath their feet.

"Yes," he said, reading her mind. "We won't get any help there. We've made a mess of the ground. If seeing us together made her leave, then she must have walked closer to the campfire."

They hurried over to where their bedroll still lay by the cold campfire.

"All right, let's start here," Rill said. "You take east and I'll take west. If we don't find her prints leading away, we'll come back here and search north to south. Careful before you take each step. You don't want to cover her tracks with your own."

"I will. And," Juliana added, "remember, she was walking all around this area late yesterday looking for firewood. Her prints could be everywhere."

He looked at her and nodded. He touched her cheek with the backs of his fingers. "We'll find the ones leading out of camp. Let's go."

Bending low over the ground, Juliana and Rill started walking and looking for signs of Cassandra's small feet. A few minutes later, and more than a dozen yards from the campsite, Juliana spotted a clear trail of footprints leading away from the fire.

"Rill, over here. I think I have something."

He ran over and she showed him the pattern of shoe indentations she'd discovered. "It's her," he confirmed, looking up at Juliana with relief showing on his face. "She's heading back the way we came," he said.

"How would she know to do that? Why would she?"

"Again, it's only a guess, but I think she's going back to where we left Cropper. If she saw you with me, then maybe she needed to go back to the person she considered *her* only friend and wanted to set out to find him."

"That's right." Juliana's spirits lifted. "Let's run."

"No, wait. The best thing we can do is continue to follow the prints. It's hard to walk in a straight line. She could veer left or right at any time, and—"

"We don't want to have to backtrack," she finished for him.

He smiled. "You're learning. I'm getting my rifle and canteen. You need to get your gun, too, remember? It should always be on your wrist."

"I'll remember from now on."

It was a painfully slow ordeal following Cassandra's footprints. Every time Juliana looked up from searching the area, the landscape looked more desolate, more barren, more lonely, than before. Occasionally, she and Rill would stop and call Cassandra's name several times. The longer they went without finding her, the harder each step became.

"Rill, I can't believe she's traveled this far," Juliana said after they had been walking about an hour.

"Don't worry, we'll find her soon."

Juliana wiped her brow with the back of her hand. Her heavy reticule dangled before her eyes. "I'm not so sure any more. We haven't seen a footprint for quite some time now. I'm afraid we've lost her."

"No, Juliana," Rill said in a frustrated tone of voice. "We haven't lost her, do you understand?"

"What will we do if we don't find her?"

"Don't even think it. That's not going to happen."

"I can't believe I let my emotions for you control me and my duty to care for her. I should have stayed away from you. I should have—"

"Don't say it, Juliana," Rill said on a ragged breath. "What we did was natural, and there was nothing wrong with what happened or when it happened."

She looked away from him to the wide open plains before her. Rill was wrong. There had been something blameworthy with their timing last night. Now, she knew why Auntie Vic had told her that her own feelings of loving a man and wanting to have a family had to be forgotten. She wanted to love Rill and be diligent in her responsibility to Cassandra, but last night, love got in the way of duty. She wouldn't let that happen again.

"Auntie Vic said it's not unusual for kids to run away when they get angry with people they love. She was right about that, and she was right when she said a man would only interfere with my duty." She turned and started walking again.

Rill stopped Juliana by grabbing her forearm. He glared down at her. "I thought you decided your aunt didn't know everything."

"I was wrong. She wasn't."

"Let's get one thing straight right now, Juliana. I'm not going to let you regret what happened between us because of your aunt or Cassandra."

"It's not your decision to make. It's mine." She jerked her arm away from his hand. "This isn't the time to think about me and you." Her voice was husky. "Cassandra is lost out there, and from now on *she* is the only person who is important to me."

A fierce gleam showed in Rill's eyes just before a strange expression stole over his features. He reached up and readjusted his hat on his head. "Understood."

Regret filled Juliana, but she forced it down and started walking. She had a job to do.

Half an hour later, Rill stopped. "Look!" A smile spread across his handsome face. "It's Doc."

"Thank God!" Juliana whispered. "Now we can travel faster to find Cass."

Rill put his two middle fingers to his lips and whistled.

The stallion turned toward Rill and nodded his head up and down, but didn't move from his spot.

Rill's smile faded.

Juliana's chest tightened.

Rill whistled again. Doc remained where he was.

No one knew better than Juliana how well-trained the horse was. "Maybe he didn't hear you."

"He heard."

"Why didn't he come to you?"

"I don't know." Rill started walking again.

Juliana hastened her step to keep up with Rill's longer strides. "Do you think he's hurt and can't walk?"

"Could be."

"What can we do if he's lame?"

"Nothing," he said in a raspy voice, then immediately said, "Look. It's Cass lying at his feet."

Juliana's heart lurched. Rill started running, pulling ahead of Juliana.

Rill fell on his knees in the dirt and Juliana plowed in behind him. He lifted a sleepy Cassandra up in his arms and hugged and kissed her and asked, "Are you hurt?"

"Cass! Dear God, thank you! Are you all right?" Juliana said through tears of joy as she patted the child's back.

"Rill," Cass said, pushing away from him. "You're squeezing me too tight. I can't breathe."

Juliana beamed with relief and wiped the tears from her cheeks. "We were so worried about you. Why did you run away from us?"

Cassandra stuck out her bottom lip. "I saw you sleeping with Rill instead of me. You like him better."

"No, I—" Juliana stopped and glanced up at Rill. For a moment she thought she saw hurt in his eyes, but it was so fleeting she couldn't be sure.

Cass brushed hair away from her face with her small hand. "I want Cropper to come back. He likes me, and I like him. I was going to get him."

A pang of guilt ripped through Juliana. She glanced

at Rill, then back to Cassandra again. "I was so tired from the storm that I fell asleep by the fire," she admitted, knowing that was the truth. She'd had every intention of joining Cassandra in the wagon before daylight.

"You're not supposed to leave me alone. You promised you wouldn't leave me."

"I know. And I didn't leave you. I was by the fire. You're the one who left, and you shouldn't have. That was a very bad thing for you to do." She turned and stared at Rill again.

"I was angry you were with Rill and not me."

"I realize that now. It won't happen again," Juliana promised.

Rill met her gaze. She saw a hardness in his face.

"Juliana is right," he said to Cass. "It won't happen again."

A dark feeling possessed Juliana. She felt as if she were losing Rill, and she couldn't do anything to prevent it. She turned back to Cassandra. "Tell us how you found Doc."

"I was walking, and he just came trotting up to me. I patted him on the nose like Rill does. I was too tired to walk any more, so I lay down to rest."

Juliana reached for Cassandra. "Come here and let Rill take a look at Doc to make sure he's all right."

Rill didn't look at Juliana as he gave Cassandra to her and rose to see about his horse.

"Cass, I've made a promise to you that I won't leave you alone. You need to make one to me."

Cassandra stared at her with those big brown eyes. "Do I have to?"

"Yes. I don't want you to ever run away again. That's a very dangerous thing to do."

"I won't do it again. I was scared when I looked back and couldn't find the wagon."

"I'm sorry you were frightened. We have to stay together, remember." She kissed Cassandra's cheek.

"Doc's fine," Rill said as he walked up to them. "Come on. I'll help you two up on him and walk you back to camp. With Doc's help, I should be able to find the other horses, and we'll soon be on our way."

Rill lifted Cassandra onto the horse's back, then turned to Juliana. "The way I see it, we're halfway to the Wyoming Territory. We've got a lot of ground yet to cover."

Juliana stiffened, as his terse tone reminded her he hadn't asked for the job of seeing them safely to the Triple R.

"I'm aware of that."

"The next town we come to we're going to trade the wagon in and go the rest of the way by horse."

Her eyes widened. "Horse? Ah—we don't know how to ride."

"You'll learn, the same way you'll learn to shoot. By horse, it will take less than half the time to get there than if we stay on the Conestoga."

She stiffened. Her chin lifted. He was telling her he was ready to be rid of them. "And you're anxious to get there."

"You're damn right I am," he said as he reached under her arms and lifted her onto the horse.

❦ 17 ❦

It was a long, tiring day for Juliana in the small town of Windyfield, Nebraska, but she would have bitten her tongue off before complaining. Rill wanted to get rid of the two of them, and the fastest way to do that was by horse.

Rill had no trouble trading the wagon, his tools, the ox-hide trunk, and a few other things for two horses—one for Juliana and Cass to ride, and the other to be a packhorse to carry their supplies. He chose mares that were young enough to make the hard trip to the Wyoming Territory, but old enough to have lost most of their jumpiness.

Juliana couldn't help but notice that the only personal items Rill kept were his shaving mug and brush, which he stuffed in his saddlebags.

He didn't sell the four mares that were just beginning to learn how to pull together as a team. Instead, Rill paid the liveryman two months' board and told him he'd be back for them in a few weeks.

Knowing they couldn't ride comfortably wearing

dresses and petticoats, Juliana told Rill she was going in to the general store to buy riding skirts.

"I don't have any ready-made riding clothes," the owner said. But not wanting to miss a sale, she added, "I have five boys. I think I can fit both of you in trousers and shirts if you don't mind used clothing."

"That will be better than riding a long distance in our dresses," Juliana told her. "What about hats and gloves? Do you have those?"

The woman's eyes brightened. "Plenty of hats, and I can probably spare a pair or two of gloves. Come with me. I think I can bundle you both up nice and warm."

Soon, Juliana and Cass were outfitted in long underwear, trousers, and long-sleeved shirts. Their bonnets were exchanged for brown felt hats. The resourceful saleswoman found a pair of fur-lined leather gloves to fit Juliana that would help protect her hands from the cold wind and the constant rub of the reins on her palms and a pair of mittens for Cass.

Juliana stuffed their dresses and petticoats into a bag and tied it on the saddle of the packhorse. She folded her square of lace and carefully wrapped it in a handkerchief together with the gold brooch Auntie Vic had given to her for her first job interview. She put the packet in the bottom of her saddlebag, vowing to herself that she would wear the gold heart again after she had delivered Cass safely to her grandfather.

When Rill first saw Juliana and Cass in boy's clothing, his eyes narrowed and a frown crossed his face. Juliana thought he was going to object, but he remained quiet. She didn't know if he decided they didn't have the time to argue about it, or if on second thought he saw the common sense in the way they were dressed.

Juliana wasn't surprised that Rill remained terse with them. They had turned his life upside down, and she didn't know how to make up to him for all that had happened to him and Cropper.

In the corral at the back of the livery stable Rill gave Juliana a quick course in riding and handling a horse. He put Cass on the saddle in front of Juliana and showed her how to turn and manage the horse. He told Cass to hang on to the saddle horn.

Pleased with all the money she'd made from the threesome who'd ridden into town that morning, the store owner treated Rill, Juliana, and Cass to a full meal of boiled chicken, potatoes, cornbread hash, and a large slice of fresh-baked peach pie.

Before they left, Juliana talked the woman into selling the rest of the pie, a loaf of fresh bread, and two quart jars of peaches she had canned that summer. Juliana stuffed one jar in each side of her saddlebags. She knew a slice of the fruit would be a special treat each evening for Rill and Cass, and she hoped to make the dessert last until the end of their journey.

They mounted by midafternoon, and within minutes it was clear to Juliana how much faster they could travel by horse than on the slow, heavy Conestoga.

They rode at a steady but not fast pace, and no one talked, not even Cass, who managed to move her position and the way she was sitting on the horse every few minutes. All three of the horses carried two filled canteens around their saddle horns. Also, the packhorse carried a leather pouch containing an extra gallon of water.

When the sun lowered beneath the hazy blue horizon, a chilling wind nipped across their faces. They found a grassy knoll and stopped for the night.

Rill dismounted, reached up, and helped Cass down from the horse. "Your job each evening when we stop is going to be to collect wood, twigs, cow chips—anything we can use to build a fire. That tree over there," he pointed to a small cottonwood, "should be a good place to start. Pile it all in the area here." He pointed to the spot where there was little grass growing.

Cassandra kept her hands in the pockets of her winter coat. "I don't want to. That's work, and I don't have to work. I'm only a child, and I'm cold, too."

He looked down at her. "On this trip, everyone has a job. You're not going to get any warmer until the fire's built. We can't build it until we have the wood. Get busy."

"Why do I always have to do everything?" she complained, huffing as she stomped away.

Rill reached up to help Juliana. "No thanks," she said, swinging her right leg over to the left. "I need to learn how to do this. I'll be all right." And she would be.

Juliana wrapped her reins once around the saddle horn and jumped down. When her feet hit the ground, she thought her legs wouldn't hold her. Her inner thigh muscles stretched taut with pain. Juliana gasped as she straightened.

"I guess I forgot to tell you that you'd be sore the first few days."

A smile teased at the corners of his mouth, infuriating her, even while she was drawn to him. He hadn't shaved in a couple of days, and the slight growth of beard only added to his appeal.

"It seems you did," she retorted, trying to put on a brave face to hide her reaction to the dull ache in her muscles.

"I have some liniment on the packhorse. It doesn't

smell very good, but it'll help relieve the soreness if you rub it in each morning and night."

"Don't you think it might have been a good idea to warn me so I could have put the liniment on before we started today and not be so sore now?" Her voice carried a slightly scolding tone, which to her consternation made his smile more apparent.

"Cass may be sore, too."

"Not likely," Juliana fussed. "She wiggled this way and that all afternoon like a worm in a freshly dug flower bed. I'm the one who sat in one position without moving." As soon as the words were out of her mouth, she was sorry.

"You'll get used to it, and you'll be all right in a day or two." He walked over to the packhorse and started digging through one of the drawstring bags tied to the saddle.

"Now I know why most women ride sidesaddle."

A soft, masculine chuckle floated on the air. Juliana had to keep reminding herself that Rill wasn't helping them for payment or because he wanted to. He was taking them to the Triple R only out of the goodness of his heart. He wasn't under any obligation to her or to Cass. Juliana hadn't even asked for any kind of promise or commitment after the two nights they'd spent together. How could she ask for any more than she already had? Juliana had to remain hopeful that, after she and Rill no longer had the worry of taking care of Cass, he would realize she loved him.

He'd stopped complaining about feeling responsible for them; now she had to stop complaining, too.

"What is Juliana going to do?" Cass called from where she stood underneath a tree, her arms laden with small sticks.

"She's going to practice shooting her pistol," Rill answered.

Cassandra threw down her armload of twigs and started to run over to them. "I want to learn, too."

"No. Stay right there, Cass," Rill said, stopping her in her tracks. "You're not coming anywhere near this gun. You're too young."

"You say I'm too young for everything I want to do. I'm not, and I'm almost as big as Juliana."

"Well, almost isn't good enough. Now get the firewood like I told you, and don't come over here where we're firing. Stay behind us. Understand?"

Cass folded her arms across her chest and stuck her bottom lip out as far as she could.

Juliana was struck again at how Rill could be firm with Cass when he needed to be, yet at other times he could take her in his arms and comfort her as if she were his own child.

Rill's gaze swept across Juliana's cheeks and up to her eyes. She wondered if he'd seen in her face the admiration she had for him.

"Let's go over toward that tree," he said to Juliana. "It will be dark soon."

She nodded. With some difficulty in moving her legs, she followed Rill.

He looked down at her reticule. "Always use care when taking your pistol out of your purse. Make sure you touch only the handle. Grasp it lightly with your fingertips. Never use strength or squeeze it. There's always the possibility you could put your finger on the trigger instead of the guard. You don't want to shoot yourself in the foot."

The lines around his eyes crinkled with his smile. He was teasing her again, and Juliana felt herself relaxing and warming to him. She couldn't help but respond to him, because she loved him and enjoyed being with him, even when he teased her.

Keeping the velvet bag around her wrist, with her other hand she eased the gun out the way he'd told her to.

"Now hand it to me."

Rill's easy expression, his provocative tone of voice, and the way his eyes searched her face left Juliana feeling as if she'd just been touched by him, and that set her senses on fire for more.

Forcing down the distraction he created for her, she extended the pistol handle first.

"Good. Now that tree is about the size of a man's chest. I want you to aim at it and shoot. When you fire, the only thing I want you worrying about is hitting the trunk. It doesn't matter where on the tree the bullet lands as long as it hits. All right?"

Rill moved behind her, and Juliana tensed. He took hold of her arm, lifted it, then stretched it out straight. He placed the handle of the gun in her hand and positioned her index finger around the trigger and her thumb on the ribbed hammer. Juliana stood rigid as a tin soldier.

"Relax. You're too stiff."

Relax! How could she relax when the man she loved was standing so close. His hands touched her, sending spicy tingles of desire darting through her?

"Loosen up like this." He moved his arm up and down to show her what he meant.

Juliana tried to do as he did, but the gun felt awkward in her hand. Rill's touch had already flustered her.

"You don't have to be afraid that I'll touch you."

"I'm not," she fibbed.

"Yes, you are, but nothing's going to happen between us."

"I know that." Her stomach quivered. "I don't

want to touch you." She fibbed again, trying to come to terms with the fact that Rill could turn her insides into a weak, quivering, uncontrollable mass of desire.

"Yes, you do."

She snapped her head around to stare at him. He was too perceptive. Juliana opened her mouth to deny his words, but when she looked into his knowing gray-brown eyes, she slowly brought her lips together.

"Don't look at me like that." A tender expression settled on his face. "We're not going to get into that because it leads to trouble neither one of us wants, and we don't have the time to deal with it."

She didn't know why, but his words stung like grains of sand in her eyes. "And you've had all the trouble you want from me, right?"

"Trouble? Yes. Have I had all I want from you? No. But Cass has to be our only concern for now. I promised Cropper I'd get her safely to the Triple R, and I will."

"That's what I want, too."

"Right now, you pose the greatest threat to my accomplishing that."

"I do? How?"

"Because all I have to do is look at you, and I forget what I'm supposed to be doing. I start thinking about holding you and kissing you—" He stopped. "See what I mean? Trouble."

"I know," she answered. Juliana took a deep breath and focused on aiming her gun at the tree.

She had to forget about the warmth of his hand, the feel of his body so close to hers that she heard the beat of his heart. Until Cass was safe with her grandfather, they wouldn't be free to think about their own feelings. Rill had just given her hope that they might have a future together and, for now, that had to be enough.

He stepped away from her. "Now, aim the gun at

the tree and pull back the hammer, then immediately squeeze the trigger. And always shoot twice, Juliana."

She cut her eyes around to him again.

"Always. The only reason you should ever pull out this gun is if a man threatens you or Cass. Shoot twice before you stop. If the first shot doesn't hit him, maybe the second one will. Do this every time you shoot, even when you're practicing."

"I understand."

"Chances are, if you ever need to use this, you won't have time to take aim. Go for a wide area like the center of his chest or stomach."

"All right."

"And keep this in mind, Juliana."

She looked at him, and his gaze roamed ever so lightly up and down her face, conveying the message that he'd rather be doing other, intimate things with her. A shiver of anticipation shook her.

"Most men are not afraid of a woman with a gun."

She blinked. "What do you mean?"

"Men know the average woman doesn't have the nerve to pull the trigger and shoot them because— well, women are just made differently from men. What about you, Juliana? If you point this pistol at a man, are you capable of firing it?"

The night Juliana fled the Kansas City mansion flashed across her mind. She remembered how she'd felt seeing Ward Cabot stand over Cassandra, trying to kill her. The anger and outrage bubbled up inside her again.

"Yes, I can do it," she said calmly. "If Cass's life is in danger, I know I can shoot." She also knew she could shoot if Rill's life was in danger, but she didn't want to tell him that, and she hoped she never had to prove it.

"I believe you would. Now let's try some practice shots. We'll shoot a couple of rounds every morning and afternoon until we get to the Triple R."

"Should I be a fairly good shot by then?"

"Let's hope we don't have to find out."

The days ran together. Juliana no longer knew the day of the week. Most mornings, they rose before sunup and were on their way by first light, stopping only long enough to give the horses a rest and to water them. Rill, Juliana, and Cass ate little during the day. Since Juliana wasn't as good a cook as Cropper, Rill helped her prepare their evening meal. Juliana always laid a peach slice on Rill's and Cassandra's plates, hoping the treat made up for her lack of skills at campfire cooking.

The nights were always cold now, and the days could be downright chilly when the wind blew incessantly and the sky remained gray, refusing to let the sun peek out from behind the dreary clouds.

Rill kept the fire going most of the night, and Cass slept right up against Juliana's back, keeping her toasty warm. But not a night passed that Juliana didn't wish that it was Rill lying beside her.

The closer they came to the border of the Wyoming Territory, the more the terrain changed. Even though they were scattered, there were more trees to supply wood for the fire in the evening. They rode up small hills and down into valleys covered with a rusty-colored sand.

In the distance, the shadowed, hazy outline of craggy mountain peaks rose up to pierce the sky. Some days the sky was so blue and seemed so close, Juliana felt like she could reach up and take a big chunk out of the fluffy nothingness.

Cassandra complained a lot. The newness of riding

on the horse had worn off, and there was no time to let her stop and play. Juliana knew the little girl was tired of the traveling. They all were.

One night after Cassandra had gone to sleep, Rill called to Juliana and asked, "Are you asleep?"

Alarmed, the first thing Juliana did was check her reticule. It lay beside her hand. Finding the strings, she slipped it over her wrist and slowly, so as not to disturb Cass, Juliana sat up and faced Rill. The small campfire had burned low, but there was enough light for her to see that his hair was attractively rumpled.

"What is it? Did you hear something?" she asked, tucking the blanket around Cassandra. They had traveled without incident since Windyfield.

"No. Everything's fine. I thought we should discuss a few things while Cass is sleeping."

"All right." She brushed her tangled hair away from her face, then buttoned her coat against the chilling night wind.

"The way I see it, we're only a few days from the border. Probably less than a week."

Juliana's stomach quickened. Always at the back of her mind was the fear Ward's men would find them again before they reached Thomas Rakefield.

"Do you have any idea where the Triple R is located in connection with Cheyenne?"

She shook her head. "I never heard. It could be north, south, east, or west."

"I have a feeling that Cabot or his men already have every one in Cheyenne on the lookout for us. We don't want to walk into their trap. I'm thinking it would be best to stop in a small town before we get to Cheyenne and ask around. If the Triple R is a good-sized spread, someone there will have heard of it, and we can go directly to the ranch."

"I think you're right. Your plan sounds good to me."

"There's something else we need to talk about. What about Cass's grandfather? What if he doesn't want to get involved, or what if he believes Cabot and wants to send Cass back to Kansas City with him? What are you going to do?"

His questions brought a long moment of silence. Juliana closed her eyes and forced herself to consider that possibility. The wind whipped at her hair and blew it in her face. She swiped at it with the backs of her fingers.

"I've tried not to think about that. Surely, if Thomas Rakefield believes there's *any* chance Ward would hurt Cass, her grandfather won't let her go back to Kansas City with that man."

"People will fool you, Juliana. And you've admitted you don't know Rakefield at all."

"I know. Ward fooled me and everybody else in Kansas City." She paused and looked deeply into his grayish-brown eyes. "You sound as if you're talking from personal experience."

His eyes gleamed in the firelight. "I could be, but what man likes to admit he made an error in judging another man's character?"

Juliana found herself moving closer to the fire, closer to Rill. "None, I suppose." She stared at Rill's solemn face. "Are you thinking about the man who stole your herd? Did you misjudge him?"

Rill chuckled softly, and it made him so very appealing.

"You amaze me, Juliana. How did we get from discussing Cass, Cabot, and Rakefield to talking about me?"

She felt her eyes, her lips, her face soften as she looked at him. He stirred things inside her she didn't understand. All she could do was attribute them to her love for him.

"You've told me only tidbits of information about what happened on your last trail drive, but I have a feeling it's shaped your life more than your brother Web trying to, as you put it, control you."

He eyed her warily for a moment. "You're too smart sometimes, Juliana."

"Thank you." She smiled at him as the cold air whipped across her cheeks. "What happened, Rill?"

He looked deeply into her eyes. "It's a long story, best told over a shot of good Kentucky whiskey, and it just so happens I left mine with the liveryman."

"Sounds to me like it might be the kind of story that's best told on a dark, lonely night when there's plenty of time. We certainly have that."

At first, she thought he wasn't going to relent, but suddenly he said, "Mark Rolson had been with me for three years. He was as good a cowhand as I've seen. Never gave me any trouble until I signed on Lee Stedman. The two of them hatched a plan to steal my herd, drive it to Montana, and set up their own ranch."

"One of your men betrayed you."

His eyes turned the color of burnt silver. Intense pain crossed his face as he looked into the flames of the campfire. "Yes, but it was more than that. Five of my drovers were killed that night."

Juliana drew in her breath with a sharp gasp. "That's horrible. Tell me what happened."

"It had been a hard drive. Bad weather. Near the end of the trail, one of my men was killed in a stampede that was caused by lightning. We were close to a small cow town, so I told the men we'd take a break and spend a couple of nights outside the town. It wasn't something we usually did, but the men were edgy. I let half of them go into town the first night. All of them were back by noon the next day. Then the rest of us headed into town. As soon as we were on our way, and far enough away that gunshots couldn't be heard, Rolson and Stedman shot my other men and started driving the herd north."

"You were with the second group going into town?"

Rill's face hardened. "Yes."

"Cropper, too?"

His lashes lowered over his eyes, but they couldn't conceal the pain she saw in his features. Her heart hurt for him, and she wanted to comfort him.

"Yeah, we both went in the second night. Stedman had the whole thing planned well. When we started to head back to the herd the next day, the sheriff stopped us and threw all of us in jail. He said a saloon girl was found dead, and he wasn't going to let any of us leave until one of us confessed to her murder."

Juliana listened intently. "Dear mercy!" she whispered. "This man had a woman killed just to keep you in town—"

"So he could kill my men and steal my herd."

"And you felt responsible for all of them, didn't you?"

"Wasn't I? They were my responsibility. I was their trail boss."

He sat silent for a moment, staring at the smoking embers. For the first time, Juliana understood why he had been so determined not to get involved with her and Cass in the beginning. She longed to hold him.

Rill continued in a low voice. "A couple of days later, I finally got the sheriff to ride out to the herd. I was worried because no one from the outfit had come looking for me."

"He found the cattle were gone."

He nodded. "And he found the bodies of four of my men."

"The sheriff let you out, and you went looking for Stedman and Rolson?"

"That's right."

"You found them and your herd?"

"It took me a while. I thought they were driving the cattle to market. That's the quickest and easiest way to get rid of a herd, so I searched the towns with stockyards and railroad connections before it hit me that they had never planned to sell the cattle. They were halfway through Colorado before I caught up with them."

She knew the answer, but still she asked, "What happened when you found them?"

A faraway gaze crept into his eyes as he continued to stare into the fire. "It was a night like this. Quiet, dark. I slipped into their camp and told them I was taking them to jail."

"Did you?"

"No. Stedman went for his gun first, and Rolson followed him." He cocked his head toward her. A bitter smile touched his lips. "It was a stupid thing for them to do. My pistol was already aimed. It was like they'd rather die than go to jail."

"Maybe they didn't think you had the nerve to shoot."

"I guess that could be the answer."

Juliana knew it wasn't right to make him relive a time he wanted to forget, but she was glad he'd trusted her enough to tell her what stirred inside him.

"I understand more about you now."

Rill looked at her. "What's that?"

The fire warmed her face and knowing Rill better warmed her heart. "Oh, now I know why you didn't want to have to worry about Cass and me. I even think I know why you spent so many years on the trail drives."

"Yeah?"

"Yes. You didn't want to settle down, because your brother Web wanted you to. And you decided not to buy a ranch in Texas because that's what Web would like you to do."

Rill chuckled. It pleased her to see the tension of the conversation of moments before erased from his face.

"You're wrong. I stayed on the trail because I liked being out on the range herding cattle, and because I'm good at managing men. I'd probably still be on the trail, but the railroad is faster for the rancher and better for the cattle. And I admit there was a time when, if Web told me to do something, I'd do the opposite. As for Texas, I'll always consider it home. But I don't want to live in the shadow of my father or of either of my brothers. I want to make my own place in this land."

Juliana smiled. She was so filled with love for Rill she wanted to cross the small distance between them and wrap him in her arms. She wanted to be a part of his life at his new home. She wanted to be his wife. But all she said was, "I can't imagine you living in the shadow of any man."

"You don't know my brothers."

"No, but now I know you."

Something awakened Rill. He stiffened. His hand went immediately to the gun by his side. He lay quiet, listening. It was dark, with the barest tint of pink in the sky—just before daybreak. The perfect time for anyone to attack.

The shuffling of feet and heavy breathing sounded

close. Rill bolted upright and pointed his gun in the direction of the noise. By shadowed moonlight, he saw a large bear lumbering straight for Cass and Juliana.

Rill's action startled the bear. It stopped, growled, then leaped over Juliana and Cass and lunged for Rill. He fired one round before the bear's paw slapped him across the chest. The power of the blow knocked the gun from his hand, slamming him to the earth with such force it stunned him.

Cassandra screamed. Juliana called his name. He was too addled to move. The weight of a paw landed on his chest. A feral growl roared above him. Fear for Juliana and Cass forced Rill to stay lucid. He blinked rapidly and shook his head.

"Over here!" Juliana yelled.

The bear growled loudly. Rill's ears rang. The animal reared up on its hind legs and started walking toward Juliana and Cass. Juliana stood in front of the bear with both hands on her gun. The weapon shook.

"Shoot!" Rill yelled, scrambling over to his saddle. "Shoot!" he yelled again, knowing her twenty-two wouldn't kill the bear, but hoping it would slow the animal and give him time to get his rifle.

Juliana fired two quick shots, just the way he had taught her, into the bear's large chest. The animal didn't jerk, but it stopped and pawed the air and growled again. Juliana shot again. She didn't stop until the gun was empty and made only a light clicking sound as the cylinder turned.

Rill rose to his feet and grabbed the rifle all in one fluid motion. He aimed for the back of the bear's head and pulled the trigger. The wounded animal jerked and roared with pain. Its front feet fell to the ground. Rill cocked the rifle and fired again.

The bear stumbled backward, then dropped to the ground so hard the earth shook.

Rill lowered his rifle and staggered over to Juliana and Cass, throwing his arms around them. "Are you all right?" he asked breathlessly, shaking with the fear of what almost had happened. His ears rang. His legs were weak.

"Yes, we're fine," Juliana whispered. "Rill, I was so frightened for you."

She slipped her arms around his waist and held him tight. Her body trembled next to his. He'd been so damn frightened for her. It felt good to touch her again and know that she was all right. He glanced over at the bear again to make sure the animal wasn't moving.

Cassandra wrapped her arms around Rill's legs and clung to him, crying. He patted the terrified little girl's shoulder and said, "It's all right now. Don't cry any more."

Juliana pushed away from him. "I saw blood on your chest. Let me see about you."

He gazed into her eyes and cupped her cheek with one hand while he continued to pat Cass with the other. "I'm all right. Just thankful you two aren't hurt."

"Is it dead?" Cass cried.

Rill looked around at the bear. The fierce animal's mouth and eyes were open but not moving. "Yes. It's dead. Don't worry. It can't hurt you." Rill pressed her closer to him.

He looked at Juliana, a feeling of pride filling him. "I'm not happy you got the bear's attention. That was damn dangerous with that small gun you carry. A couple of shots to the chest might stop a man, but not a bear."

"I couldn't let it maul you."

"You saved my life," he said softly. "You used the gun without hesitation."

"You were in danger."

"I'm impressed. Remind me to never be on the wrong end of the barrel of your gun."

A smile spread across her face and lit her eyes. "I don't think there will be any danger of that happening. Now, let me have a look at your chest," Juliana said, spreading the front panels of his sheepskin jacket.

He wanted to pull Juliana back into the circle of his arms but she wouldn't let him, so he stood still and let her look at his wound. He liked the feel of her gentle hands pushing back his clothing and touching him.

She glanced up into his eyes. "The scratches aren't deep. I don't think you'll need stitches. A good washing should take care of them."

He looked down at the red marks across his chest. "I think my ribs would be showing right now if I hadn't had my coat on, or if the bear had been any bigger. By its size, I don't think it was full grown."

"Thank God," she whispered.

When she looked up at him with those big blue eyes, Rill wanted to kiss her. "It's too bad I don't need stitches," he said with a smile. "I bet you're good at sewing."

"Not as good as you."

"Let's get away from here, Rill," Cass complained. "I don't like looking at that bear."

Rill forced his attention to Cass, bending down and hugging her close to him for a moment. She was so small and depended on him for so much that that funny feeling of wanting a wife, a home, and children filled him again.

"All right, little one, we'll break camp and leave this place. It's almost light, anyway. Get your blanket, and I'll saddle the horses."

Cassandra went for her blanket, and Rill's eyes met Juliana's. He reached for her but she moved away. His chest constricted, even though he knew why she rejected him and that she was right to do so.

"What do you think made it attack?" Juliana asked, walking over to look at the bear.

He stood beside her, looking down at the big furry animal. "I don't know."

"I think I'd still be shooting if the gun had had more bullets. My heart was pounding so fast I thought I was going to faint."

Rill chuckled. "It takes a lot of firepower to bring down a bear. I think we can stop your shooting lessons. You know what you're doing."

The night had lightened into day, and Rill saw that her face beamed with appreciation as she said, "Thank you. I'm glad I did a good job. That makes me feel better."

Rill looked back to where Cassandra was reaching for her blanket. On the ground near her, he saw an empty peach jar. He walked over and picked it up. A sweet scent reached him, and he frowned.

"How did this jar get left out in the open like this? It should have been rinsed out and broken up like the other one."

"It wasn't empty when I put it away," Juliana said.

Both Rill and Juliana turned their attention to Cass. Her bottom lip quivered as though she was going to cry. "I didn't mean to eat all the peaches, but my tummy was still hungry."

"This is what brought the bear to our camp. It smelled the sugar from this jar and was after it.

That's why we have to be careful how we put our food away."

Cass wiped her wet cheeks with the back of her hand and said, "Well, I'm glad we ate all the peaches and didn't leave any for that mean old bear."

Rill looked at Juliana. He saw a smile tease the edges of her mouth. He relaxed and laughed. "So am I."

❧ 18 ❧

From the rise where Rill and Juliana sat on their
horses, she gasped as she looked down to the valley
below and saw the faint outline of the Triple R Ranch.

Silvery moonlight fell from the heavens, spotlight-
ing a corral with several horses inside and a large barn
nestled behind an L-shaped house. Warm, welcoming
light glowed from the front windows.

Rill hadn't wanted them to reach the ranch before
dark. If they were going to be riding into a trap, he'd
just soon do it at night so they'd have a better chance
of getting away. They had stopped midafternoon,
prepared a meal, and rested before continuing their
journey.

A strange feeling swept over Juliana. She realized it
was more than relief that she was less than a mile
from Cassandra's grandfather. It was a feeling of
accomplishment surging through her, too. Within a
matter of minutes, she would deliver Cassandra, who
lay sleeping against Rill's chest, to her grandfather's
house. She'd had faith all this way that he would help

her. Now, she prayed harder than ever that she hadn't been wrong.

"If the man in the town where we stopped a couple of days ago is right, that has to be the Triple R," Juliana said.

"And with all those lamps burning, it appears that whoever is inside is awake," Rill said, his gaze continuously scanning the far-reaching landscape surrounding them.

Emotion filled her throat like a lump of clay, and Juliana swallowed hard. "I can't believe we've made it this far without one of Ward's men trying to stop us. Maybe he gave up."

"Not a chance. We just evened our odds when we changed from the wagon to horses."

"I'm sure you're right," she admitted truthfully as their eyes met. "Where do you think Cabot's men are?" she asked.

Rill stared down at the ranch again. "Hard to guess. Cabot or his men could be inside that house."

Juliana shivered. The glowing lights that at first had appeared friendly and welcoming now looked menacing. She wasn't sure of the time, knowing only that it should be well past anyone's suppertime.

"I was thinking the same thing." She took a deep breath, summoning courage from deep inside for what she must now do. "The way we should handle this is for you to stay here with Cass. I'll go down to the house and check it out—see if Ward or any of his men are there. If they aren't, and it's clear, I'll signal you by dimming the light in the last window on the left, then brightening it again."

"I don't like that idea." His voice let her know he didn't want to argue.

She stared at him. Just looking at him gave her

strength to do what she had to do. "It's the only thing that makes sense."

"No," he stated firmly. "We stay together. The way it's been from the start."

Juliana lifted her shoulders. "Rill, if Ward's men are waiting for us inside, you have a better chance of escaping with Cass than I do. You can take her to your ranch and hide her there. Ward's men don't know your name and only Nolen can identify you."

"What about what's best for you, Juliana?"

"I can't worry about that at all. My obligation is to Cassandra."

"Right," he said in a growling voice, then looked away from her. "How could I have forgotten that your one and only desire is her safety?"

And yours! her heart cried out silently. "I didn't come all this way to think about myself now that I've reached the end of my journey."

"Well, I have a problem thinking about you, and I'm not letting you go down there alone. Cabot might be there or the sheriff might be there."

Inside, Juliana shook. "I'll have to accept whatever the law requires of me. I won't deny I took Cass from her home. But there's no use in discussing any of that until we find out who's in that house. We didn't bring Cass this far only to turn her over to Ward Cabot the moment we step foot inside that house."

"I'm not going to risk your getting caught."

"Rill, I've been risking that since the night I fled Kansas City. If I get caught, I want you to keep Cass safe until Ward is forced to account for what he tried to do to her."

"Juliana, you know that even if Cabot agrees that Cass can stay with her grandfather, he'll want you charged with kidnapping and thrown in jail. He'll have to do that to save face."

She wouldn't allow herself to think about jail or hanging. "I'm prepared for that."

His eyes remained hard and unrelenting. "Well, I'm not."

He started to move his horse forward. Juliana reached out and grabbed his reins, stopping him. Her velvet bag dangled from her wrist. "Rill, this isn't your decision to make. It's mine, and I made it before I met you. I know I couldn't have gotten this far without you. You'll never know how grateful I am to you and Cropper, and I—"

"Dammit, Juliana, I don't want to hear another word about your gratitude."

"And I don't want you to stop me. My mission hasn't changed since the day we met," she said sharply. "Everything I have done was for Cassandra's safety, and I'm not going to stop now that I'm half a mile from her grandfather's house."

A muscle ticked in his neck.

"Trust me on this, Rill. It's the best thing for Cass."

"You're asking too much."

His voice was low, encouraging her to deny her own plan and turn everything over to him. She weakened. Rill was bigger, stronger, bolder. He wanted to take care of her. Shouldn't she let him?

But instead of giving in, she tamped down those feelings of wanting to rely on him and said, "No. My way is the way this has to be."

A deep furrow formed between Rill's eyebrows. "Ride."

She let go of his reins and straightened in her saddle. Conscious of how loudly her heart was pounding, she said, "Promise me you won't come in search of me if I don't signal."

Rill shook his head once. "No promises, Juliana. Now go, before I change my mind."

Juliana's heart swelled with love for Rill. She didn't want to leave him. She wanted to touch him, hold him, kiss him again. She trembled. Once she rode down that hill, she could very well be parted from him forever. If Ward and his men were in that house, she would go to jail. She started to reach over and touch his face one last time, but instead, she whipped the horse around and started down the long, lonely hill toward the Triple R.

The only thing that gave her the courage to keep going was knowing that Rill's eyes would stay on her, watching her until she entered the house—if she got that far.

Cold wind chilled her cheeks and chapped her lips. A coyote howled in the distance, and Juliana shivered. A stray cloud covered the moon, making the way so dark she couldn't see anything ahead of her. Fear of the unknown grew inside her as the house disappeared from her view when she dipped into a small valley.

Maybe she hadn't been spotted. There was time to turn around. Juliana could take Cass and run away with her to somewhere where no one would find them. Yes. That would work. She loved Cass and would always take care of her. Cass could be Juliana's little girl forever.

The house came into view again. Reality returned. No, she couldn't run away with Cass.

She reined in her horse near the front porch. Juliana's legs trembled as she dismounted and her booted feet hit the ground. She threw the reins over the hitching post in the yard. The front door swung open. A large man stepped out. He carried a double-barreled shotgun pointed directly at Juliana.

Alarmed, she stumbled back against her mare, making her snort and sidestep away from Juliana.

"You have two seconds to state your name and your business before I empty both shells into your gut."

Dear mercy! His words took the breath from her lungs but she managed to mumble, "Juliana—Townsend. I'm here to see Thomas—"

"The woman who has Cassandra?" He cut in quickly. "Where's my granddaughter?" the man barked. "Why are you sneaking in here dressed like a man?"

She'd been wearing the trousers so long, Juliana had forgotten she looked like a cowboy. Trying to regain her balance and her senses, she stepped forward and said, "Mr. Thomas Rakefield? Is that you?"

"It's me all right, but where's Cassandra? Your telegram said you had her with you. Is she all right? What in God's name is going on? You and that bastard Cabot—pardon me—have a lot of explaining to do."

"Yes," she said, trying to calm her breathing. "That's why I'm here. Cassandra is fine. Where is Mr. Cabot?"

"First, you tell me where my granddaughter is."

Juliana hesitated, but he was the one holding the gun. She stepped closer to him. His large size and graying beard reminded her of Cropper and sadness swept over her. "I came alone. I didn't know if Ward Cabot or some of his men might be here. I don't want to turn Cass over to them."

The rancher lowered his shotgun. "They came all right, but they've gone. I hear that Cabot and some of his men are in Cheyenne. Took rooms there. My workers have seen Cabot's men snooping around the ranch all times of the day and night."

"But none of them are inside your house tonight?" she asked, wanting to be sure she could trust this man.

"I wouldn't have met you with this," he held up the

shotgun, "if I knew where his men are. I wouldn't be surprised if one or two of them aren't out there somewhere watching us right now."

"Let's go inside. I'll get your granddaughter on the way. I have a lot to tell you."

After signaling to Rill, Juliana and Thomas walked back to the front porch to wait. Juliana filled the robust man in on what had happened that had made her take Cassandra from her home in Kansas City.

"Never did like the son of a bitch—pardon my language. I went to the judge and tried to get Cassandra away from him. Thought I might win since I'm her only living blood relative. Judge wouldn't even listen to me because Kay had left Ward in charge of all of Cassandra's money. I told him I didn't give a damn—pardon me—I didn't care about the money. He could have it. I wanted my son's daughter."

"He never spent any time with her. I wonder why he wanted her, if he could have had the money without her."

"Well, there you are. The will might have said he couldn't. If he didn't keep Cassandra, maybe he couldn't keep control of the money. I never saw the will."

"Why?"

"Cabot's lawyer said the only copy was accidentally burned along with some old documents, and the judge let him get by with it." His voice was filled with accusation. "When Cassandra's nanny telegraphed me about Kay's death, I had a feeling Cabot was somehow involved. 'Course they hung another man, you know."

She nodded. "I heard."

"What happened to the nanny? Did she die, too?"

"No. I was told Mr. Cabot considered Cass too old for a nurse, that she needed a governess to start teaching her and preparing her for boarding school. I applied for the job."

The sound of approaching horses reached them, and Thomas lifted his shotgun again, until they saw Rill ride into view. Cassandra was still asleep in his arms.

"Here, take this," Rakefield said, handing Juliana the heavy shotgun. "I want to hold my granddaughter."

It took both hands for Juliana to hold the heavy weapon. Thomas met Rill in the front yard and took Cassandra from him. The little girl stirred, but didn't wake up. Thomas hugged her close and hurried toward the door.

"You satisfied it's clear?" Rill asked Juliana as he dismounted. He threw the reins of Doc and the packhorse over the hitching rail.

"Yes. Mr. Rakefield feels the same way I do about Ward. He and his men have been around here. Mr. Rakefield thinks they are staying in Cheyenne."

Rill took the shotgun from her, and they followed the older man into the house. Rill propped the weapon by the door, then threw the latch, locking them inside.

"I keep the coffee hot until bedtime," Thomas said. "It's in the kitchen. Help yourself while I put Cassandra to bed. I have a room ready for her."

He headed up the stairs, and Rill and Juliana walked into the kitchen. She knew a cup of coffee would help take the chill off her bones but that it would do nothing for the chill she felt coming from Rill. She knew he was upset that she had forced him to handle this her way, but she hadn't expected coldness from him.

She took two cups off a shelf, and Rill checked to make sure the back door was bolted.

A sudden sadness swept over her. Cass was safe with her grandfather. That was all she'd ever asked of Rill. His part in this ordeal was over. Would he leave them now? Would he leave her forever?

Auntie Vic's face swam before her eyes. That stern, ever-present, lecturing face. She thought her aunt would be happy now. Juliana had done her job, had delivered Cassandra safely to her grandfather. He would have to take over now.

Juliana shook her head and rubbed her forehead.

"Don't worry, Juliana. I'm not going to let Cabot's men take you to jail."

"That's not what I was thinking about. I told you I'm prepared for whatever the law deems proper. I can't deny I kidnapped Cass. I was just wondering what Auntie Vic would have done if she'd been in my position that night in Kansas City. I believe she would have fled the house, as I did, but—"

"You're wondering if she would have gone to the authorities, or whether she would have struck out on her own like you did," Rill finished for her.

"Yes."

"Cassandra hardly stirred," Thomas said as he lumbered into the room. "Good. You found the coffee." He reached out his hand and Rill took it. "Thomas Rakefield."

"Rill Banks."

"I owe you for bringing my granddaughter to me. Name your price."

Juliana snapped around to look at Rill.

He glanced at her before saying, "I'll be needing directions to a ranch called the Double Horseshoe. Ever heard of it?"

"Sure have. I hear it was sold a month or so back."

"That's right." He took a cup of coffee from Juliana. "I bought it."

Thomas smiled. "Then we'll be neighbors. It's about a day and a half's ride west of here."

Rill sipped the coffee. "That's all the payment I need."

"If you need an extra hand until you get settled in, let me know and I'll send one of my cowpunchers over to help you."

"I'll keep that in mind, but Juliana is the one you really need to thank. It's because of her that Cass is here."

Thomas turned to her. "I'm grateful, and I'll see you get whatever you want. Just name it."

"Cass's safety is all I want."

"Me, too. Well, I'm going down to the bunkhouse and put my men on notice to watch for Cabot, in case one of his men saw you ride in tonight. I'll send another into Cheyenne to get the sheriff." He turned to Rill. "Bring your coffee. I'll show you where you can bunk down for the night."

Rill hesitated. "If it's all the same to you, I'd rather stay in the house, between the front door and Cass's door until we hear from Cabot. I know what his men are capable of. If he has been watching the house, we can expect a visit from him first thing tomorrow morning."

"Or sooner," Juliana added.

Thomas looked from Rill to Juliana, and back to Rill. "All right."

"Mr. Rakefield," Juliana asked, "what will happen when Ward shows up to take Cassandra?"

"I'll tell him the same thing he told me when I was in Kansas City—Cassandra is staying with me. This is my country. The law here respects me and what I have to say. He doesn't have a chance. I'm going to tell him he can have the damn—pardon me. He can have the money, but not my son's girl. From now on, she's mine."

A weary smile crossed Juliana's face. "I'm so thankful that I made the right decision in bringing her to you. I've worried about how you'd react—if you'd believe me."

"You're damn right you made the—pardon me again. Now that Cassandra is here, I guess my language and the lack of womenfolk around here will have to change. I'd be beholden to you, Juliana, if you'd stay on with us."

Juliana's gaze flew to Rill. His eyes searched her face but he remained quiet. The moments stretched by. He didn't say a word about wanting her to go with him to his ranch, to be a part of his life. She wanted his love, his commitment, forever—but Rill didn't say a word.

Her heart broke.

She turned to Thomas Rakefield and said, "I'm sure we can work something out."

"Glad to hear it. I'll be back in a jiffy or two. Juliana, there's room in the bed with Cassandra. Upstairs, second door on the right. You two best get some shut-eye. I have a feeling tomorrow will be a long day."

Rakefield walked out, and Juliana turned her back to Rill. She didn't want him to see her face. She was having a difficult time holding back her tears.

"You don't have to wait until Mr. Cabot arrives. Cass will be fine now."

"I know."

"I only asked that you help me get Cass here safely. I don't expect you to do anything else."

"I know."

Maybe she should swallow her pride and tell him she loved him, that she wanted to go with him and be his wife. She turned and looked into his eyes again, but the words faltered on her tongue, and she whispered, "A simple thank-you doesn't seem near enough for all you've done. It seems so inadequate for all you gave up to get us here."

"It's all I want."

His words were like a knife in her heart, dashing her last bit of hope that he might ask her to go with him to his new ranch. A thank-you was all he wanted. She didn't know why it hurt so bad. She'd known from the start that he wanted no responsibility and no commitment, but she'd thought that had changed. He'd held her, loved her, and made her a woman! At times, she'd felt that he cared for her.

"Well, I think I'll go upstairs. I'm sure Mr. Rakefield is right about tomorrow."

Juliana hurried past him, disappointed that he didn't try to stop her, thankful that she got past him before the first tear hit her cheek.

It happened before anyone had finished the morning meal. Rill, Thomas, and Cass were all seated with Juliana at the kitchen table eating biscuits fresh from the oven when the sound of horses' hooves hitting hard-packed ground startled everyone.

Juliana's stomach knotted as they all glanced at one another.

Rill went into action, pushing back from the table. "Juliana, take Cass upstairs." He looked down at Juliana's wrist. "Where is your purse?"

"Right here." She pulled the velvet bag from her lap where she'd held it while she was eating.

"This is no time to be worrying about a purse," Thomas said, his chair legs scraping the floor as he rose.

Glancing at Thomas, Rill said, "It is if it's Juliana's. She has a loaded six-shooter in it."

Thomas grabbed the belt circling his rounded girth and pulled up his trousers. "In that case, pull it out, and get upstairs."

"I left your shotgun by the front door last night," Rill said. "Let's go."

"What's wrong?" Cassandra asked. Her hands shook, and her gaze darted around the room.

"Nothing you need to worry about, sweetie," Juliana said, taking hold of her hand. "Let's go upstairs."

"Why do you need your gun, Juliana?"

The sound of the horses came closer. Juliana didn't have time to explain. "I'll tell you as soon as we get upstairs. Now, let's go."

"No! I want to stay here with Rill and Grandpapa Rakefield."

"Go with Juliana," Thomas said.

"You can't stay down here right now, Cass," Rill said at the same time Thomas spoke.

They headed for the doorway that led into the front room of the house.

"We have to go now."

"No!" Cass jerked away from Juliana and ran to the corner of the room and stood there crying, frightened, shaking her head.

"Pick her up and carry her, if you have to," Rill said. "Just get her upstairs."

"I'm scared, Rill," Cass cried, holding her hands together under her chin, her bottom lip trembling.

Juliana grabbed Cassandra's arm and started to pull her toward the doorway. Cass fought her by dragging her feet and screaming. They entered the living area and had started up the stairs when the front door was kicked open, knocking Thomas to the floor as he reached for his shotgun.

Rill drew his Colt. Four men burst through the opening with guns drawn.

"I'm a federal marshal," one of the men called out. "Drop your guns."

Juliana's gaze darted from Rill, who remained frozen in place with his pistol pointing at the men, to Ward dressed in his expensive suit and hat, to Nolen with his bushy eyebrows and small deep-set eyes, to the marshal with his shiny badge and another man she'd never seen before who was trying to help Thomas stand up.

"Mr. Rakefield, I tried to stop them but the marshal just pushed me out of the way and busted down the door."

"It's all right," he said to the ranchhand. "Go to the main gate and watch for the sheriff. When you see him riding up, get him here as fast as you can." Thomas turned to Ward. "Where's the rest of your men?"

"Keeping your cowboys busy and making sure they don't bother us."

"If any of my men are hurt, you'll answer to me."

"Be glad to." Ward smiled, then turned his gaze on Juliana.

A fighting spirit settled over Juliana and gave her peace about what must be done. Her purse hung heavy from her wrist. She took a deep breath. With the U.S. marshal by Ward's side, Juliana wasn't as sure as Thomas had been that he would keep Cassandra.

Her fingers scratched the palm of her hand. She had no doubt what Ward Cabot was capable of. She had seen the demon inside the man. Watching him, she vowed that she would rather die than let Cassandra go with him.

* * *

Rill immediately started planning how to get Juliana and Cass out of the room without either of them getting hurt. He knew which man was Ward. His confidence, his smugness, his cocksure attitude showed in his face, in his clothes, in the way he stood so bold and arrogant.

There was no way Rill was going to let Juliana or Cass go back to Kansas City with that man.

"Come to me, Cassandra," Ward said and held out his hand for her.

"No, Papa Ward! Go away. I don't want you here."

"You've poisoned her against me, you bitch." Cabot spit the words at Juliana.

"Calm down, Ward," the marshal said. "Name-calling isn't going to help."

"Marshal, the sheriff of Cheyenne should be here any time now. I sent for him last night after they arrived. I'm sure he'll tell you that we don't have to turn Cassandra over to you. We're not in Kansas City."

"No, but I have papers here signed by the governor saying she has to come with us," the marshal said.

Thomas turned to Ward. "You can keep her money. I don't need it, and I know that's the only reason you want Cassandra. Go back to Kansas, and I promise you'll never hear from us again."

"That's easy for you to say now that Cassandra is only six years old, but what about when she's sixteen or seventeen and wants to marry?"

"Is that what her mother's will said?" Rill spoke for the first time. "You'll have to give up control of the money when Cass marries?"

Cabot's eyes narrowed on Rill. "So you're the man Juliana teamed up with to kidnap Cassandra."

"That's right. Because you tried to kill her."

"Is that what she told you? Cunning bitch, isn't

she?" Ward pushed back his fancy jacket and drew his pistol.

"Put the sidepiece away, Ward," cautioned the marshal. "I'll handle this with the sheriff when he gets here. We don't need any more guns out. No use in giving anyone else itchy fingers."

Cabot swung his gun to the side and shot the marshal in the chest. The man fell to the floor.

Cassandra screamed.

Juliana gasped.

Rill pulled back the hammer of his Colt. Ward aimed his weapon at Cassandra, who watched in terror as she held onto Juliana's waist.

"Drop the gun," Cabot said, "or I'll put a bullet in the brat where she stands."

Rill took the order as a challenge. "Do it and my first bullet goes in your heart."

"Drop the gun, Rill," Thomas said. "He'll kill Cassandra."

Ward shifted his gaze from Cass to Rill. He chuckled, but he didn't sound as confident as when he'd first walked inside.

Rill heard Cass sniffle behind him on the stairs, but he didn't dare take his eyes off Cabot to look at her and Juliana. "He's going to kill her anyway. Besides, he just shot a marshal. The sheriff won't let him go."

"Maybe and maybe not," Thomas said. "The shooting could be ruled accidental. I'm willing to attest to anything or sign any kind of paper that will say Cassandra is forever giving up any rights to her inheritance. I don't care what he does with the money, where he goes, or what he does, as long as Cassandra is safe."

The rancher was grasping at straws. Rill understood the man wanting to do anything to save Cass, but what Thomas wasn't willing to see was that Cabot didn't intend to let her live—no matter what Thomas promised.

"He wants her dead," Rill said. "If I keep my gun on him, at least he dies, too."

"Don't be foolish, either one of you," Thomas said. "Nobody else in this room has to die."

"Mr. Cabot."

Rill tensed, but didn't look back at the sound of Juliana's voice until he saw the surprise register on Cabot's face. He then slowly moved to the side and took one step back so he could see Juliana and keep an eye on Cabot, too.

She stood on the third stair with her pistol pointed directly at Cabot's chest, Cassandra crouched behind her whimpering. Fear leaped inside Rill. Juliana was going to get herself killed!

"Where's the girl?" Ward barked.

"Behind me. Sometimes, she actually obeys me. You'll have to shoot me to get to Cassandra. By the time I fall and expose Cass, Rill will have shot you. Either way, you lose."

Juliana's voice was strong, her face determined, leaving no doubt she meant what she said. She'd always told Rill nothing was more important to her than Cassandra.

He finally believed Juliana.

❧ 19 ❧

Juliana's hands shook. Moisture quickly dampened her palms and the back of her neck. Ward Cabot was as big a threat to Cass as the bear had been to Rill.

"You're bluffing," Ward said. "I'm not crazy. I know you don't want to die."

"No, but I'm prepared, if I have to. I've been told that most men aren't afraid of a woman with a gun." She took a calming breath. "I will shoot you. My first responsibility as a governess is to keep Cassandra safe. I intend to do that."

A muscle under Ward's cheek twitched. "If that's the way you want it."

"Don't do it, Cabot," Thomas said, taking a step forward. "What's to be gained if you and Juliana die? Cassandra will have her money, and you'll burn in hell. Take the inheritance and get out of here before the sheriff gets here. You have time to get away and keep the money, too."

"Oh, it won't be just me and Juliana who die," Cabot said. "You with me, Nolen?"

"Yes, sir."

"I'm in this too far now to change my plans. If one of us dies, we all do." Ward chuckled bitterly and looked at Rill. "I can take out Juliana and the girl. Nolen will get you and the old man."

"You forgot my bullet is for you," Rill said.

"Damnation! Why won't either of you listen to me?" Thomas's voice growled with anger and frustration. "If you and Cassandra are both dead, the money won't do either of you any good. Take the money and get the hell out of here. Be sensible," Thomas exclaimed. "For God's sake, take the money and sail to Europe if you're afraid we'll come after it."

"He can't," Rill said. "He's not a reasonable man. He's a murderer."

Ward's eyes narrowed. He took a step closer to Rill. Juliana realized she was more worried about Cass and Rill than she was about herself.

"Reasonable? You don't know anything about me. Let me tell you how sensible I've been. I started planning to get my hands on this fortune the moment I saw Kay." He glanced at Thomas. "She wouldn't give me the time of day because of *your* son. She married him. She had his child, and I still wanted her and her money every time I saw her. So I devised a plan to get her and her inheritance. Your son's carriage mishap was no accident."

"You bastard!" Thomas started forward.

"Stay back, Rakefield," Rill yelled. "He wants you to come after him so he can kill you. Think of Cassandra. She needs you."

Thomas stopped.

Juliana listened, hoping someone would talk Ward into leaving or giving up his gun. She didn't want to have to shoot him, but felt confident she could if he continued to threaten Rill and Cassandra.

"You killed your wife, too, didn't you?" Rill asked.

"I was patient. It took two years of dancing attendance on her to get her to say yes." He chuckled lightly, but his eyes appeared wild. "The thing I like best about this whole story is that after I married Kay and bedded her a few times, I realized I only wanted her money. Not her. It was easy to squeeze the life from her body."

"He's a madman," Juliana whispered to herself. He had to be stopped.

"I see now that I should have waited longer to try to kill Cassandra."

"You had control of Cass's money. Why kill her?" Rill asked.

"Because it wasn't mine. It still belonged to her. I wanted it. I'd worked to get it." He looked directly at Juliana. His eyes pierced her with an evil glare. "And I'd have it now if not for you."

She shivered. She knew now he'd meant it when he'd said they would all die. Ward Cabot had to be stopped before he shot Cassandra or Rill. Juliana knew what she had to do. It would take every ounce of her courage. Rill had told her most men didn't believe a woman would shoot them. That gave her the advantage over Ward. She knew she would.

Juliana tried to quell the trembling in her legs, but she was too fearful of what she must do. In her mind, she went over all the steps Rill had taught her about firing a gun.

Go for the chest with two rapid shots.

"You were so perfect for what I wanted," Ward said to Juliana. "You were from out of town, no money to speak of, no family to come to your aid when the murder was blamed on you. Perfect." His voice became a high-pitched whisper. "Why did you have to awaken that night and spoil all I'd worked for?"

"Because of what *I've* worked for." Aiming straight for his chest, she pulled back the hammer.

A shot rang out. Ward's eyes widened. He jerked. Nolen fired his gun at Rill and Juliana, missing both. Nolen snapped backward as two of Rill's bullets hit him in the chest. He fell to the floor. At the same time, Ward crumpled to his knees before falling facedown.

The U.S. marshal had raised up on an elbow—a faint whiff of smoke still curled from his gun—blood covered his chest. "I had to shoot him," he said in a raspy voice. "He would have killed her."

"I'm damn glad you did," Rill said, rushing over to the lawman and kneeling beside him.

"Cabot and his man are dead." Thomas held his arms out to Cassandra. "Come to Grandpapa."

Cass pushed away from Juliana's protection and ran into his waiting arms. Juliana was so weak with relief she could hardly stand. When the first shot was fired, she thought she'd been the one to pull the trigger. She looked at the pistol she held in her trembling hand. Her gun hadn't been fired, but she knew she would have shot Ward if the marshal hadn't. She shoved the gun back into her reticule and ran to help Rill with the marshal.

Later that afternoon, Rill left his shaving mug and brush on a chest in the guest bedroom of Rakefield's house and walked down the stairs with his saddlebags thrown over his shoulder. He'd thought long and hard the last hour about what to do.

He knew it was selfish of him to want Juliana all to himself when Cassandra needed Juliana to give her guidance and stability while she adjusted to her new life. Cass had cried for more than an hour after the shootings. That didn't keep Rill from wanting Juliana with him.

Rill walked into the large living area and saw Thomas sitting at a desk in the far corner. He rose from his chair when Rill entered.

"Is Cass still asleep?" Rill asked.

"Yes. That medicine Juliana gave her must be strong stuff. It took a while, but she's sleeping like a baby now."

Rill nodded. He remembered the night the doctor had given the paregoric to Juliana for Cassandra, and his stomach tightened.

"When she wakes, tell her I had to check on my own ranch, but I'll be back to see her in a few weeks."

"All right, but I don't want to tell her that if you don't mean it. I don't want to start out lying to her."

Those fatherly feelings that had plagued him since the day he first saw Cass hit him in the chest. As much as he wanted Juliana with him, he knew her duty right now was still to Cass. Juliana had taught him that you didn't run from or deny responsibility. You should meet it head-on and take care of it. That's why he couldn't ask her to leave with him today.

"I'll be back to see her."

Thomas smiled. "That's what I wanted to hear. One of my men just came back from town. Looks like that marshal might make it."

"I was hoping he would. Somebody needs to explain to the people back in Kansas City what happened here."

Thomas strode over to Rill and held out his hand. "I'm beholden to you. When you get to your ranch, let me know if I can help."

"Just take care of Cass," Rill said as he shook the rancher's hand. "She's had more than her share of hard luck to deal with."

"Juliana's out front if you want to talk to her before you go."

Rill nodded and headed for the door.

She turned and looked at him when he stepped outside. He stared at her for a moment. She was wearing her blue skirt and blouse with her lace and her brooch pinned at the base of her throat. Her hair was tidy. Her blue eyes sparkled like sunshine on water. She was the perfect picture of a governess. Her aunt would have been proud of her.

His spurs clinked as he walked over to where she stood at the end of the porch. He wanted to pull her into his arms, hold her, and tell her how much he wanted to have her in his life as his wife and the mother of his children. But now wasn't the time.

Not only did Cass need her, but Rill knew Juliana needed to settle some things in her own mind. She had to decide if she wanted to be like her aunt, always taking care of other people's children, or whether she wanted to be a wife and take care of her own. Juliana had to decide if she could step away from her aunt's shadow and be free to live her own life.

Rill had told Rakefield he'd come back, and he would, after he'd checked on his ranch and seen if there was word from Cropper. That would give Cass time to adjust, and Juliana time to make some decisions, too.

She loved him. He knew that, but he also knew she'd never leave Cass right now. Not after all the little girl had been through. And Rill wasn't going to ask her to, but he would come back for Juliana. He'd give her a couple of months—no, he'd give her one month, then he'd be back.

"Are you all right?" he asked.

Juliana nodded and looked out over the rolling hillside dotted with trees. "It's quite a shock, realizing I would have shot Ward Cabot. I was pulling back the hammer when the marshal killed him. I still feel the weight of the gun, the cold touch of the metal."

"I'm glad you didn't. I wouldn't want you living with that on your mind. I finally realized today how much Cass and your job mean to you. You are your aunt's niece."

She cleared her throat. "I accept your compliment, but I don't think Auntie Vic would have ever pointed a gun at anyone, and I don't believe she would have approved of my doing it, either."

He nodded. "You're probably right about your aunt. She wouldn't have approved of your running away with Cass that night, either."

"No?" she questioned.

He shook his head. "No. She would have played it safe and gone to the authorities. I'm sure of that. She didn't have your courage."

Doubt crossed her face, and it bothered him that she'd misunderstood him.

"Going to the sheriff would have been the wrong thing to do. Cabot would have seen to it that you were jailed, and he would have found some other way, at some other time, to kill Cass. You did the right thing. Because of you, she's safe now."

"I'm glad you think I did the right thing. That means a lot to me." She looked him up and down, then said, "I hope those saddlebags hanging over your shoulder don't mean you're leaving."

Suddenly her voice was husky with emotion, and it touched him. A quiver of longing shook Rill. She didn't want him to leave. That gave him hope that, when he returned, she'd be ready to leave Cass and go with him. Her eyes were bluer than he'd ever seen them, her face more beautiful than ever. He didn't want to leave her, but for now, he had to do what was right for Cass. She needed Juliana, too.

"That's what they mean." He shifted his hat to the other hand. "There's a lot of daylight left."

Juliana looked into his eyes, and his heart melted. A gentle breeze sent the sweet smell of lilacs sailing past him. He weakened. He wanted her to go with him now, not next month, not next week.

"Of course, you have your ranch to see about. You've been delayed much too long as it is."

"You plan on staying here?"

"How could I leave Cassandra now, after all she's been through?"

She looked into his eyes with a sadness that gripped his heart, letting him know he'd made the right decision—to give her some time before asking her to leave. "I was thinking the same thing myself, but—"

A hopeful gasp passed her lips. "But?"

"Maybe one day she'll be all right without you, and you'll decide if you want to be a governess the rest of your life, like your aunt, or if you want to be a wife someday?"

She moistened her lips. "Does that mean you might come back here for a visit?"

"I promised Cass I would."

She nodded and looked out over the rolling hillside again. "It will take her a while to adjust to her new home and to get over seeing her stepfather killed."

Rill's chest tightened. He thought he saw tears in Juliana's eyes. He reached out and touched her cheek. He wanted to feel her in his arms one more time before he left. "Juliana?" he whispered.

"No. Just go, Rill. I don't like good-byes any more than Cropper did."

To hell with good-byes. Rill opened his mouth to tell Juliana he loved her, that he wanted her to come with him now and be his wife. Cass could adjust on her own without Juliana, but those fatherly feelings struck him hard, and he knew he couldn't do that to the bossy little girl who had won his heart. Not yet.

He put his hat on his head and walked down to where Doc and the packhorse were tied. He threw his saddlebags over the back of his horse, mounted, and rode away.

❧ 20 ❧

Juliana was pregnant. There was no denying it any longer. She hadn't noticed that she'd missed her first monthly flow until the time for the second had come and gone. For the last several mornings, she'd felt queasy when she awakened. She was filled with a strange mixture of the wonder of having a child of her own and the fear of knowing she was alone.

She stood outside the barn, trying to muster the nerve to go in and talk to Mr. Rakefield. The cold Wyoming wind whipped at her cheeks and ears as she stood in the winter sunshine.

It had taken her a few days to come to terms with her condition, and then another day or two to decide what to do. She certainly couldn't stay at the Triple R and allow Cass to know that she was going to have a baby out of wedlock. She'd never forgive herself if that happened. Juliana had already failed Cass too many times when it came to the proper behavior for a young lady.

Juliana had also worried about whether to tell Rill

about the baby. She didn't want to force him into any kind of commitment or responsibility when he'd made it clear on more than one occasion that he wasn't interested in settling down with family ties. But she couldn't keep this news secret from him. She'd make it clear to him that she wasn't expecting anything from him, but he had a right to know he was going to be a father.

It still hurt to think about him leaving that day without asking her to go with him. She'd desperately wanted him to tell her that he loved her and wanted her to be his wife and help him build a home at his ranch. When he'd left without saying any of those things, she'd worried that maybe he'd decided that a family was more responsibility than he wanted.

She had some money left from taking care of Cass in Kansas City, and Thomas Rakefield had been more than generous since she'd come to the Triple R. After she'd talked to Rill, she'd find a quiet town to raise her child.

Juliana took a deep breath and walked into the barn, where Mr. Rakefield was saddling his horse.

"You're up early," he said, a concerned expression on his face. "Is something wrong with Cassandra?"

"Oh, no—yes—I mean there isn't anything wrong with Cass, but there is something important that I need to discuss with you, if you have the time?"

"Well, if it's not about Cass, it must be about you," he said, then held his hands over his mouth and blew warm breath onto his palms.

She nodded and pulled her winter coat tighter about her neck to keep out the chill of the windowless barn. "Cass is doing very well here. She loves you, and she is so happy on the ranch."

"I agree, but I thought you wanted to talk about you, not Cassandra."

She cleared her throat and met his eyes. "I do. It's time for me to leave."

He turned away from his horse and looked directly at her. "You've given this a lot of thought?"

It shocked her that he didn't seem surprised by her announcement.

"Yes."

"Where are you planning on going?"

"I'm not sure where I'll eventually settle."

"That doesn't sound like you've given this idea the thought you said you had."

"Well—what I meant was that—" Juliana stumbled over her words.

"I think I know what you mean. You're planning on going to see that fine young man who helped you bring Cassandra to me."

Her lashes fluttered. "Yes."

"And if he looks at you the way he did when he was here, you might stay with him."

Her heart constricted at the thought. "I'm not going to hope for that much, but yes, I plan to go and see him before I make any final decision."

"What do you plan to say to him?"

"Oh, well, I'm—working on exactly what I'll say." She wasn't exactly lying to the man. She wasn't sure how she was going to tell Rill she was going to have his baby. She only knew that she had to tell him.

"I think I have something that might make your showing up at his door in the dead of winter a little easier to explain than the fact that you love him, that you've been lonely without him, and that you want to be his wife."

Juliana gasped.

"I've been holding onto it just in case Rill ever made it back here like he promised. You can take it to him for me." Thomas Rakefield smiled and said, "I'm right, aren't I? That's what you'd like to say?"

She relaxed, knowing he already knew how she felt about Rill. "I didn't know it showed."

"It's written all over your face. You haven't done much the past month but look out the window as if you were expecting Rill to come back."

"I'm sorry, I didn't mean to neglect—"

"I'm not complaining," he said, interrupting her. "I expected this. From the night you two arrived, I thought something was going on between you. I didn't know what it was, and I didn't want to interfere."

"Then you understand why I have to go?"

"Of course I do. I was married once myself. The truth is, I've been half expecting him to show up here to get you any day."

Juliana took a long breath of relief. "Do you think Cass will be all right without me?"

"She's come a long way in the past few weeks. I think she can handle your leaving now better than she could have when she first got here. She'll miss you. I will, too, but I'm glad you stayed as long as you did."

A lump of emotion swelled in Juliana's throat. "I couldn't love her more if she were my own daughter. You know that, don't you? It breaks my heart to leave her."

Thomas clamped his lips together. He nodded. "She loves you, too. No matter what happens or where you go, I hope you'll come back and visit her."

"How could I not? I feel like she is a part of me." Juliana took a steadying breath. "My Aunt Victoria always said that children need to feel safe and secure. I know Cassandra has had very little of that in her life. It will be important for me to come back and visit, so she'll understand that not everyone she loves leaves her forever."

"When do you plan to go?"

She managed to swallow past the tight mass lodged in her throat. "By the end of the week. I think it will be best if I stay around for a few days after I tell her and give her time to get used to the idea. I'll ask her to help me with packing, choosing my traveling dress and things like that, so my leaving won't seem so sudden and cold. I want her to have time to adjust."

"It'll be hard on her, either way. A new pony for her to take care of might help, too. I'll get what I want you to take to Rill for me while you break your news to Cassandra." He shook his head. "I don't envy you. It's going to upset her."

Thomas walked toward the tack room, and Juliana's stomach quaked. Suddenly, she was hot instead of cold. Yes, the sooner she told Cass, the longer the little girl would have to get used to the idea. And Juliana had to do it now, while she had the courage to go to Rill.

With her purpose in mind, Juliana turned and left the barn. The hard-packed snow crunched under her feet as she forged a path from the barn to the house.

She stopped in the foyer, unbuttoned her cloak, and hung it on the coat tree by the door. She tamped the snow from her boots for so long, she realized she was delaying the mission she didn't want to carry out.

You'll know when it's time for you to leave a household and find other employment. It won't be easy, but it must be accomplished with grace, dignity, and respect. You must remain in control of your emotions and not let your feelings show on your face or in your attitude.

Juliana rubbed her watery eyes. Auntie Vic must have been made of stone. There was no way Juliana could remain unmoved by what she had to do. She would never forget her aunt's training, but Rill had helped Juliana discover that Victoria wasn't right about everything. In fact, her maiden aunt knew very little about matters pertaining to the heart.

After taking some deep breaths, Juliana climbed the stairs to the cheerful schoolroom Thomas had set up for Cass on the second floor. She sat at her desk practicing her numbers.

She looked up when Juliana's shadow fell across the room. Cassandra's face brightened with a smile of accomplishment. "Come look at what I've done, Juliana."

The cold lump in her throat grew. Juliana loved Cassandra and was going to miss seeing her every day and watching her grow up. They'd been so close, been through so much together. The parting would be heart-wrenching.

Juliana walked into the room and knelt in front of Cass. Sun streamed in through the parted drapery panels and bathed the room in a soft white light that sparkled off Cass's chestnut-brown hair. She held up her small chalkboard and showed Juliana her work.

Her numbers were large, tilted, and very much the writing of a beginner. Juliana smiled at her and took the slate. "You did an excellent job. I'm very proud of you—for so many reasons."

"I can write as good as you, can't I?"

"I believe you can." Juliana laid the tablet aside and took hold of Cass's warm, soft hands. "Turn around here and face me. I have something to tell you." Juliana's voice shook. For a split second, she contemplated stealing away in the dark of the night and avoiding this conversation, the pain of looking into Cassandra's eyes, the sorrow of saying good-bye. Yes, an abrupt, unexplained departure would be better for Juliana, but she couldn't do that to Cass. She deserved an explanation.

"What is it, Juliana? You look like you're going to cry."

"I think I might," she said, as the first tear spilled over her bottom lid and tumbled down her cheek.

Cass looked at her with big brown eyes. "Why? Do you hurt?"

"No, I'm sad. Because I have to go away and leave you."

"I'll go with you," Cassandra said quickly and started to stand up. Juliana stopped her.

A heavy tightness pressed against Juliana's chest. "You can't. You must stay here with your grandfather. I have to go alone."

Fear leapt into Cass's eyes. "No, Juliana. I don't want you to leave me," Cass said and threw her arms around Juliana's neck with such force she almost knocked Juliana over.

"I have to, sweetie."

"Don't go! I won't let you. I won't." She squeezed harder and buried her face in Juliana's shoulder. "I'll tell Grandpapa, and he'll make you stay with me. I know he will."

Juliana almost changed her mind about going. But how could she? She was expecting a baby. She could leave now with dignity or wait until she was found out and have Mr. Rakefield throw her out of his house.

"No. Your grandfather can't this time. I have to go."

"Why?" she cried.

Wiping the tears from her own cheeks, Juliana whispered, "You have to make a new life on the ranch here with your grandfather, and I have to make a new life for myself, too."

"Why can't you stay here with me? I'll be good, I promise."

Juliana's heart ripped as a sob tore from her throat.

"Oh, sweetheart, you are a good girl. You're smart and beautiful, and I wish you were my daughter. My leaving has nothing to do with you. It's just time for me to go. You're with your grandfather now. And this is where you belong and where you'll be happy. He loves you very much."

If only Cassandra wasn't so young, Juliana thought. If only Cassandra hadn't been through so much in her short lifetime. "I'm not leaving forever, sweetheart. I'll be back to visit."

"No, you won't. You won't ever come back."

"I will. I promise."

Juliana held her tightly for a few moments while Cassandra cried. When her sobs had softened and melted into an occasional sniffle, Juliana said, "You're going to be seven years old in a matter of weeks, aren't you?"

Cass merely nodded.

"All right. I promise I'll be back and spend a few days with you for your birthday."

Juliana knew that if she was careful with the style of clothing she chose, she might be able to visit for a couple of days without arousing suspicion of her condition.

She slowly pulled Cassandra's arms from around her neck and forced the child to look at her. Juliana wiped Cassandra's tears away and then her own. "I won't break my promise to you. I will be here for your birthday. Besides, I'm not leaving right now. I'll be here a few more days. I'll leave you plenty of work to do on your numbers and your alphabet, and I'll grade it when I return so you must do your best."

Cass stuck out her lips, then folded her arms across her chest. "I don't want to do schoolwork if you're not here."

"How will you send me letters if you don't learn to write?"

"I won't write you because I don't like you. If you go away, I don't want you to come back."

A knife-sharp pain sliced through Juliana—even though she realized Cassandra was expressing her hurt the only way she knew how. "Well, I hope you change your mind about that because I don't want to miss your birthday."

Cassandra pushed away from Juliana and ran from the room.

Thomas insisted on one of his men driving Juliana to the Double Horseshoe in his enclosed carriage. She stayed warm bundled on the long trip in a woolen blanket and velvet dress and cloak. They spent one night in a boardinghouse near Cheyenne and arrived at Rill's ranch the next afternoon.

From a distance she saw the house, nestled in a valley that had sloping hills on either side. At the back of the property stood a chain of craggy mountains with snow-covered peaks. Juliana loved the location immediately, but forced herself to tamp down her feelings. She wouldn't allow herself to believe Rill would want to marry her. If he didn't, the disappointment would be too great. She had to think of her child.

The door was unlocked, but no one was at home. The driver didn't want to leave her, but Juliana insisted she would be fine by herself. Only after building her a fire in the front-room fireplace to keep her warm, and in the woodstove so she could prepare something to eat, did the man agree to leave her alone at the ranch.

As soon as he had left, Juliana took the opportunity to look over Rill's house. She liked it. It had a large living area, with a kitchen in the back and a bedroom on each side of the front room.

She tried sitting in a chair by the fire where it was nice and warm, but being idle made her too nervous. She went into the kitchen and looked in the pantry. If Rill were out feeding his cattle, or mending a fence, he'd be cold and hungry when he got in.

Juliana found coffee, some winter vegetables, a smoked ham, and a side of bacon in the pantry. She peeled and cooked squash and sweet potatoes. She fried some bacon, then set it off to the side to keep warm while she went back to sit by the fire to wait for Rill to come home.

A few minutes later, Juliana heard a noise. She rose from her chair by the fire and turned toward the door. Rill slowly walked into the house and closed the door behind him.

He was as handsome as she remembered. Her abdomen tightened, and she wanted to smile. It felt wonderful just to look at him again.

If he was surprised to see her, it didn't show on his face.

"Hello, Juliana." He took his hat off and dropped it on a side table.

"I hope you're not angry that I—I decided to wait for you here at your home. I mean—I could have gone back into town and rode back out tomorrow, but—"

"It's all right." His voice was gentle, his expression tender. "I'm glad you stayed."

"You are?"

He nodded and took his gun and holster off and laid them on the table by his hat.

She was nervous, and she shouldn't be. She'd told herself a hundred times she didn't want anything, didn't expect anything, from him, but now that she was looking into his eyes, she knew how foolish those thoughts had been.

She cleared her throat. "You don't seem surprised that I'm here, did you meet Thomas's driver? Did he tell you I was here?"

"I knew you were here."

He kept his eyes on her face. She wanted so much to rush into his arms and beg him to hold her, but she forced down that feeling and said, "I—I have something for you." She walked over to her satchel and pulled out his shaving mug and brush. "You forgot these when you left the Triple R." She held them out to him. "I brought them to you."

He walked forward and took the items from her. "Thank you. Did you come all the way over here to bring me these?"

"Ah—I remembered that your father gave them to you when you were fifteen. I knew they were special to you," she said, avoiding a true answer to his question. "They are, aren't they?" Her voice trailed off. She closed her eyes for a second, and she took a deep breath. Why was she putting herself through this? He was right not to believe she came all the way to his ranch to bring that shaving mug.

Dear mercy! She felt wound so tight she labored for every breath. This was killing her. She had to say what she came to tell him, get it over with, and get out of his life before she did something stupid like beg him to love her.

"No, of course not. I didn't come just because of that mug." She hesitated as she looked into his eyes. Had they always been that deep shade of grayish brown? "In fact, I didn't know about it until after I told Mr. Rakefield I was coming to see you."

He put the cup and brush on a table and took another step closer to her. "Then why did you come?"

She willed her courage not to fail her as she lifted her chin and her shoulders and said, "Would you believe I missed you?"

He nodded.

"Would you believe I love you?"

"Yes."

Why was she telling him these things? Her only responsibility was to tell him he would be a father. He'd never offered her any kind of commitment. She wasn't supposed to tell him she loved him, but her heart wouldn't let her leave without saying the words just once.

He was close enough that she could have reached out and touched him. She wanted to, but something held her back.

"What about Cass?" he asked.

Juliana remained rigid and moistened her lips again. She could still feel Cassandra's arms locked around her neck, holding tight as she begged Juliana not to leave her. "She's had a hard time adjusting to her new life in some ways. It will take time but I think she's going to forget all that happened in Kansas City and what brought her here. Mr. Rakefield gave her a new pony the day before I left. That made her very happy."

"I'm sure it did. Does she ask about Cabot?"

"Not recently. Cass has had too much to deal with for her age. Whenever she asked questions about Ward being shot, we were always honest with her about that. Even though she still wakes up crying that she can't breathe, she's never remembered that Ward tried to smother her. Mr. Rakefield and I decided not to tell her that."

"What about your duty to her?"

It was a legitimate question—one that had always been important to her. "I'm satisfied I fulfilled that. It was difficult to leave her, but I knew it was time for me to go."

"Are you looking for work?"

She willed her excitement over his words to stay under control. "Ah—no. I—I—not right now."

"That's too bad." He looked deeply into her eyes and gave her a smile filled with promises. "I need a wife, and you're the only one I want."

Tension knotted her chest until her breath came thickly. "What?"

"That's right. I just returned from the Triple R. I didn't want to spend another day without you. Thomas told me you were on your way to see me."

His words snatched the breath from her lungs. She wouldn't, couldn't get her hopes up. He hadn't mentioned love. He didn't know about the baby. That would be a big responsibility. He might need a wife, but how did he feel about her, about being a father?

She chose her words carefully, breathlessly. "Did you go all the way to the Triple R just because you needed a wife?"

"No."

"Then why did you?"

He stepped closer. She felt his heat, his breath. "Would you believe I missed you?"

Her heart leapt for joy. She wanted to throw her arms around him and kiss him all night long, but she waited and only nodded.

"Would you believe I love you?"

"Yes!" she murmured huskily. Tears of joy filled her eyes and spilled down her cheeks.

Rill caught her up in his arms and held her tight for a long, long time. He kissed her thoroughly before looking into her eyes and saying, "I love you, Juliana. It's been hell living here without you."

She squeezed him closer to her. "Rill, if you loved

me, why didn't you ask me to come with you to your ranch?"

He looked down into her eyes. "I couldn't do that to you or Cass. I knew you wouldn't leave her until you thought she was ready. I didn't ask because I didn't want to put you in the position of having to make a choice between us. I left my shaving mug on purpose. I always intended to go back for it and you after—"

"After what?"

"You had some time to realize you loved me and that you deserved to have your own family."

She smiled. "I've known that for a long time."

"What about all those things your aunt taught you?"

"When I moved from Chicago to Kansas City, my world changed from the one I had known. She had lived in another time and a different place. She said I was to give up my own dreams of love and a family, and that my employer and his children would be my life. I admit I wanted to be just like her. I thought that was the best way I could repay her for all she'd done for me. I've finally come to terms with the fact that I can't do things the way she did. I'm not Victoria."

"No. You're the woman I love."

She reached up and kissed him again. He held her close. She loved the feel of his strong arms around her, but she still had to tell him about the baby. She pushed away from him and, reluctantly, he let her go.

"There's something else I need to say."

His eyes held a bit of worry. "What's that?"

A knot formed in her chest, and her legs felt trembly. "I'm going to have a baby. I'm going to have your child."

A gleam of wonder and happiness danced in his eyes. He laid gentle hands on her shoulders. "Juliana, are you sure?"

"Yes. It's all right if you don't want to marry me. I know how you feel about responsibility and—"

Rill's lips came down on hers, sucking the rest of the words from her mouth. She was breathless when he ended the kiss and stared into her eyes.

He let go of her shoulders and circled her with his arms. "You and my child are a responsibility I want. I love you, and I'll love our baby. I'll always take care of both of you, Juliana. Make no mistake about that."

Juliana smiled. "Rill, I love you, too, but I don't want to trap you into a marriage or a child you're not ready for."

"The truth is I never wanted either of those things until I met you and Cass. I couldn't understand why you had me thinking about love and homefires. Cass had me thinking about being a father and having children. For the first time in my life, I was thinking about something other than a ranch and cattle."

His expression was the gentlest she'd ever seen. Relief, happiness, overflowed inside her. "Rill, I love you."

"I love you, Juliana, and our child."

Rill's lips met hers in a passionate kiss. He lifted her in his arms and started toward his bedroom.

"I cooked for you," she said, pointing toward the kitchen.

"Good." He smiled. "I'm sure we'll be hungry after I get through showing you how much I've missed you."

❧ Epilogue ❧

A Year Later

"Rill," Juliana called. "Come into the kitchen and taste this soup. I want to make sure everything is perfect when Cass and Mr. Rakefield arrive."

"You've never prepared a meal that wasn't delicious." Rill strode over to the woodstove, holding a kicking little baby wrapped in a white blanket.

Juliana bent down and placed a kiss on her baby daughter's forehead, then looked back to Rill. "Do you think Cass will mind that we named her Cassie?"

"Of course not. She'll love it."

"I don't know. I'm sure her grandfather has spoiled her as much as her mother did. She might not like anyone else having her name. If you remember, she wasn't happy when we went to see her for her birthday and told her we were expecting a baby."

"I think she'll be delighted once she actually sees Cassie." Rill kissed the tip of Juliana's nose, then opened wide for the spoon of soup she fed him. "Mmm—it's just right." He smacked his lips. "You need to stop worrying about every little thing, or you're not going to enjoy their visit."

Juliana pushed the kettle to the back of the stove, where it would stay warm. "I know," she said.

"Come on, sweetheart. Relax." She untied her apron, and Rill took it and hung it on a hook near the window.

"It's just that I want them to enjoy their visit and to like our home. I want to look my best, I want them to think Cassie is pretty, I want them to—"

"Be happy for you," he interrupted. "Juliana, isn't that really all you want from Cass and Thomas?"

She laughed. "Yes. I'm being foolish, I know. What I'm really thinking is, this visit is just a trial run for when your family comes for a visit next month."

He held Cassie in one arm and wrapped the other around Juliana and pulled her close. "I've told you. We'll tell them not to come if you don't think you're ready for them. They can wait a month and still have time to visit before winter sets in."

Juliana smiled up at her husband. He was so loving, gentle, and understanding. "No, I want them to come now and see you and your beautiful daughter. I know they will be so proud of you, and we'll have a good visit."

"Stop worrying, and it will be. Now, is that a carriage I hear coming?"

She listened, then smiled. "Yes. Let's go wait for them on the porch."

Rill held Cassie close as they watched the enclosed carriage pull up to the front steps of their home. Juliana couldn't contain her happiness.

The carriage door opened and Thomas Rakefield stepped out, a broad smile on his face. "Juliana, Rill, so good to see you," he said.

He reached back into the coach, lifted Cassandra from inside, and stood her on the ground beside him.

"Juliana! Rill!" She waved to both of them, then looked back to the carriage.

Juliana felt as if her heart had fallen to her feet. Her smile faded into sorrow. Her eyes met Rill's, and she saw the hurt and disappointment in his eyes, too. Then Juliana noticed. Clutched tightly to Cassandra's chest was her doll, Miss Watkins.

Goose bumps pebbled Juliana's skin. Her eyes filled with tears. She and Rill had never given up hope that one day Cropper would ride back into their lives.

Cass held her hand out as another figure emerged and grabbed her fingers.

"Cropper!" Juliana cried. She rushed to him and threw her arms around him, giving him a big hug.

"I want a hug, too." Cass pushed Cropper and Juliana apart.

Juliana reached down and wrapped her arms around Cassandra. Feeling the little girl close to her again, she realized how much she'd missed her.

"I can't believe it," Rill said as he clapped his friend on the shoulder, then reached for his hand. "Why didn't you send us a telegram to let us know you pulled through? When we didn't hear from you, we assumed the worst."

"Most of the time, I didn't know from one day to the next if I was going to wake up. I didn't want you to think I was going to make it, then not be well enough to make the long journey out here."

"I want to see Juliana's baby," Cass said, pulling on Rill's arm. "Let me see her."

Rill knelt down on one knee and lifted the blanket from Cassie's tiny face.

Cass looked at him with a curious expression on her face. "She's so little and pink and wrinkled."

"That's the way all babies look," Thomas said.

Juliana hugged Cropper again and said, "The doctor gave us no hope you'd make it. I'm so glad you did."

"Didn't have much hope, myself. I saw the pearly gates more than once. Reached out and touched them a time or two, but whenever I started to go inside something would stick me in my side, right there in my ribs, and cause me this awful pain."

"That was your wound bothering you," she said.

"No, it was the foot of that dad-dern doll gouging into me, night and day. I told the doc to pack it up and send it on to Cass, but he wouldn't. I finally decided the only way I was going to get rid of that doll was to get better and bring the darn thing back to Cass where she belonged."

Cass looked up at Juliana and Rill with her big brown eyes shining and said, "You didn't tell us her name when you sent the telegram. What is it?"

Rill looked at Juliana, then to Cass. "We named her after you."

Cassandra's eyes widened in surprise, and she smiled. "You did? Which name? Cassandra or Cass."

"Well," Juliana said, "we named her Cassie."

Cassandra folded her arms across her chest and pouted. "No one ever calls me Cassie. That's not my name."

"It's close enough," Thomas said. "Let's go in. I want to hold Cassie."

"Me too," Cropper agreed.

"I'm first," Cass said as she ran ahead of the two men.

Juliana looked over at Rill with tears gleaming in

her eyes. "I can't believe he's alive. I'm so happy he's going to be here with us."

"So am I." He smiled at her and whispered, "I love you, Juliana."

She threw her arms around Rill and Cassie. "And I love you."

Stef Ann Holm

Nominated by Romantic Times for a Best Historical Romantic Adventure Award, Stef Ann Holm is renowned for her vivid depictions of love and adventure, with a gift for storytelling that allows her to summon the images and textures of a bygone era.

Crossings   51047-9/$5.99

Weeping Angel   51045-2/$5.99

Snowbird   79734-4/$5.50

King of the Pirates   79733-6/$5.50

Liberty Rose   74125-X/$5.50

Seasons of Gold   74126-8/$5.50

Portraits   51044-4/$5.99

Forget Me Not   00204-X/$5.99

Available from Pocket Books